PENGUIN BOOKS

THE CAS~~...~~

HÉLÈNE GRÉMILLON was born in France in ~~...~~ obtaining degrees in literature and history, she worked as ~~...~~ alist at the French newspaper *Le Figaro* before becoming a full-time writer. Her first novel, *The Confidant*, was awarded Monaco's Prince Pierre Literary Prize. She lives in Paris with her partner, singer and songwriter Julien Clerc, and their child.

ALISON ANDERSON is an American writer and translator based in Switzerland. Her translations include Amélie Nothomb's *Hygiene and the Assassin*, J. M. G. Le Clézio's *Onitsha*, Muriel Barbery's *The Elegance of the Hedgehog*, and Hélène Grémillon's first novel, *The Confidant*.

THE CASE OF LISANDRA P.

HÉLÈNE GRÉMILLON

Translated from the French by
ALISON ANDERSON

PENGUIN BOOKS

PENGUIN BOOKS
An imprint of Penguin Random House LLC
375 Hudson Street
New York, New York 10014
penguin.com

Originally published in French as *La garçonnière* by Flammarion, Paris.

LIBRARY OF CONGRESS CATALOGING-IN-PUBLICATION DATA
Grémillon, Hélène.
[Garçonnière. English]
The case of Lisandra P. / Hélène Grémillon ; translated from the French by Alison Anderson.
pages cm
ISBN 978-0-14-312658-4
I. Anderson, Alison, translator. II. Title.
PQ2707.R47G3713 2016
843'.92—dc23
2015018814

Printed in the United States of America
3 5 7 9 10 8 6 4 2

Set in Hoefler Text • Designed by Sabrina Bowers

This is a work of fiction. Names, characters, places, and incidents either are the product of
the author's imagination or are used fictitiously, and any resemblance to actual persons,
living or dead, businesses, companies, events, or locales is entirely coincidental.

For Julien, and for Léonard

But what does it matter, faint or loud, cry is cry, all that matters is that it should cease. For years I thought they would cease. Now I don't think so any more. I could have done with other loves perhaps. But there it is, either you love or you don't.

SAMUEL BECKETT, "FIRST LOVE"

This novel is based on a true story. The events unfold in Buenos Aires, Argentina. It is August 1987—winter. Seasons are not the same everywhere. But human beings are.

THE CASE OF LISANDRA P.

Lisandra came into the room, her eyes red, puffy with tears. She walked unsteadily, and all she said was, "He doesn't love me anymore." She said it over and over, relentlessly, as if her brain had stopped working, as if her mouth could not utter anything else—"He doesn't love me anymore." "Lisandra, I don't love you anymore," she said suddenly, as if his words were coming from her own mouth; and thus having learned her first name, I seized the opportunity to interrupt her outburst:

"Lisandra. Who doesn't love you anymore?"

Those were the first words I said to her, because "stop crying" and "tell me about it" were not commands she would have heard, and she stopped short, as if she had only just now seen me, and yet she didn't move. She stayed there with her back slumped in sorrow, her head sunk between her shoulders, her hands wedged between her crossed legs, but as my words had had the desired effect, I ventured to repeat them, more gently, looking into her eyes, and this time, her eyes were looking at me.

"Who doesn't love you anymore?"

I had been afraid that my words might have the opposite effect, plunging her back into the torpor of her tears, but this was not the case. Lisandra nodded her head and murmured, "Ignacio. Ignacio doesn't love me anymore." She had stopped crying. She didn't apologize, and generally everyone apologizes after they've been crying, or even while they're crying, a remnant of pride in spite of sorrow, but she had no such pride, or no longer had any. Now she was somewhat calmer, in her blue sweater. She spoke to me about him, this man who no longer loved her. That was how I met Lisandra; it was seven years ago.

Lisandra was beautiful, strangely beautiful, and her beauty had nothing to do with the color of her eyes or her hair, nothing to do with her skin. She had such a feminine shape but a childlike beauty, and I knew immediately through her gaze, her gestures, her expressions so hounded by sorrow, that the child in this woman was not dead. I was stunned that she could love like this. She loved to love. I listened to her. He seemed so wonderful, this man she loved so much.

"Stop talking about him, Lisandra. Tell me about yourself."

I knew my words might rush her. I had hesitated at first, but I couldn't help myself; already stupidly jealous, I could not stand to hear her talk about that man. She replied that she had nothing to say about herself, and before I could find any words to fill the silence and undo the damage I had just caused, she got to her feet, asked me where the restroom was, and didn't come back, either that day or in the days that followed.

Every evening I take a half hour break, half an hour of solitude to emerge from the tunnel of dissatisfaction, frustration, and despair into which everything I've heard during the day has plunged me. Forgive me for telling you this, Eva Maria, I shouldn't, but we've gotten this far, I may as well share what goes on behind the scenes. I pour myself a glass of brandy and I wait to feel a very slight numbing, which, paradoxically, restores me to my reality, the reality of my life. I've always done this, but on that particular day, that half hour lasted all evening. I couldn't stop thinking about her, about Lisandra, her eyes terrified by the reality of the love she had just lost. I've often seen people devastated by their sorrow in love, but I have never sensed such a degree of suffering in any of them, and it wasn't some sort of romantic or habitual despair, or posturing, but a despair that was truly part of her character, organic and visceral. There are individuals who will never know such despair, those feelings we all call by the same name, which we can all experience, and know. They vary in intensity with each individual, but because we want them to be universal, all too often we forget this, but my profession reminds me of it every day: suffering does not mean the same thing to everyone.

I tried to determine how old Lisandra was: twenty-five, perhaps, with her brown hair and her dark rosy skin—and her eyes? I hadn't even noticed the color of her eyes, because the only thing I had seen was her suffering, and her eyes, red and puffy. She had not even reached for the box of tissues I had placed between us, but nervously wiped her eyes and nose with the sleeve of her blue sweater; yes, I remembered the color of her sweater. The thought that I might never see her again made me pour a second glass of brandy, then a third, and then I went out to throw a different light on things, but the light was no different. All it takes is a thousandth of a second for an obsession to take hold. Time has nothing to do with it. I went down the street knowing full well that I hadn't a clue where I was headed, and not realizing that I had just set out to look for her . . .

There is a knock at the door. Eva Maria is sitting at her desk. She doesn't hear it. She is lost in reflection.

. . . Lisandra. I was overwhelmed by her sudden disappearance; I couldn't sleep; I cursed myself for causing her to flee. This had never happened before and yes, God knows how many individuals I've seen traipsing through my office, but no one has ever given me the slip like that. Of course there have been patients who don't come back to their second appointment, but to disappear like that, in the middle of a session, never; her resistance was immediate. I hunted for a clue in those few moments I had spent with her, a clue that might enable me to find her again; her first name, her blue sweater, that wouldn't get me far—I knew nothing about her. I mentally reviewed the image she had left behind, an image so precise it might have been etched with a painstaking scalpel: Lisandra, sprawled sideways on the sofa, drying first one eye then the other with the sleeve of her blue sweater. My selective, obsessive memory enabled me to recall the elements I had not grasped at the time, hanging as I was on her words and on her face. She was wearing slacks made of a light fabric, a sort of black cotton, and—how had I failed to notice at the time?—a fine pair of shoes, also black, astonishingly elegant in comparison to the rest of her outfit, high heels with a strap, and beneath her feet there were white spots on the carpet. I had to get to the bottom of it, and while I hesitated to congratulate myself too soon, I did not hesitate to go around to all the tango places and milongas in the vicinity—she must have just come from one of them, and it couldn't be far, otherwise the talcum powder would have had

time to disappear altogether. So she still had the courage to dance despite her sorrow. This reassured me, but what reassured me more than anything was that now I had a lead, and I could find her again.

Don't look at me like that, Eva Maria; I know what you're thinking, yes, yes, I can see it in your eyes, don't pretend otherwise. You're angry with me, I know you, but let me make one thing clear: the reason Lisandra's resistance was immediate was because I did everything I could to make it immediate, and when I want to reassure myself, I like to think that if I rushed her on the day we met I did it unconsciously, to make her leave, so I'd prevent us from starting to behave in that particular way that would have made any other form of intimacy impossible; you know there are ethical reasons. So let me make one thing clear, when I went looking for Lisandra, I was looking for a woman, not a patient, I insist on that fact, and I never felt guilty of any lapse with regard to my profession. I had found Lisandra weeping outside the door to my office, she had seen the sign as she walked down the street, she had no appointment, we didn't finish the session, no money changed hands, but it was the most shattering moment of my life. Don't you believe in that instant of immediate recognition between two individuals, Eva Maria? That's strange, I would have sworn that you did.

I wondered what Lisandra would look like as a dancer, with her long brown hair pulled up into a chignon. Would I recognize her from behind? No, I wouldn't recognize her. I had not yet acquired the familiarity that enables one to recognize someone from behind, so I waited for the dancing figures to turn around, or let me see their profiles, and then I asked, "Do you know a certain Lisandra?" "Is Lisandra here?" "Does Lisandra come here to dance?"

I might not have recognized her, the young woman who had sat across from me three days earlier, her head scrunched down between her shoulders—that young woman had disappeared behind this arched, vivid body, moving freely, with authority, and above all liberated. This was no longer the same young woman moving there before me: she had the fine neck of a dancer, all her wariness and hesitancy had disappeared, and even her sorrow—she was so sure of herself when she danced, the extreme freedom she radiated was striking in comparison to the brutal, lovesick self-abasement she had shown me, the servitude I had seen her struggling with a few days earlier. She wasn't dancing for the others, she was dancing only for herself. She was the "soul of the tango." I know that's a cheesy thing to say, but that's what I thought about Lisandra the moment she turned to face me.

"What are you doing here?"

Lisandra always believed it was "chance" that caused us to meet again, and she found this so "meaningful" that I never put her right; she wouldn't have found it so "marvelous" if she had known it was the product of my own eagerness. That's the way she was, Lisandra, she preferred the surreal to reality, and every time she remarked on how marvelous it was that we had met again, I let her say it. She never questioned what fortune had sent her way; fortune acted as a guide, as a guarantee, the sad emblem of those who lack self-confidence. We had dinner together and then we saw each other again and then we decided to be together, and very quickly, on December 8, 1980, we got married. I loved that woman, I would never have thought anyone could wish to harm her; she was not cut out to be involved in anything sordid. Tragic, perhaps, but not sordid. She was so fragile, Lisandra. I could never have imagined I might speak of her one day in the past tense . . .

Again someone knocks on the door. Eva Maria doesn't react. The door opens. Estéban is standing on the threshold.

"I'm sorry to bother you, Mama, are you having supper?"

Eva Maria doesn't turn around.

"I'm not hungry."

"What are you doing?"

"Nothing. I'm working."

"You're bringing work home now?"

Eva Maria doesn't answer. Estéban doesn't move.

"Well, okay then, shall I have dinner?"

"Yes, go ahead."

Estéban runs his fingers through his hair. He leaves the room. He closes the door behind him. Eva Maria takes a sip of wine.

... When I came home the door to the apartment was unlocked. I imme-diately noticed a terrible draft; very loud music was coming from the liv-ing room; everything was in a mess as if there had been a fight; chairs were overturned; the lamp was on the floor; it was so cold; the window was wide open. I knew at once something had happened. Lisandra easily got cold; even on terribly hot nights she would always sleep with a sheet over her, she said that only the weight of the material enabled her to fall asleep, as did my body, pressed up against her; she couldn't bear to feel the air on her skin, even when there was no breeze. I closed the window and looked for her everywhere. I ran into the kitchen, into the bedroom, the bathroom, and it was only then, when I saw she was nowhere to be found, that I retraced my steps and understood, was afraid that I had under-stood. I stepped over the shattered vase on the floor, with a puddle of water all around it, and at that moment I heard a shrill cry in the street, and I opened the window again. I didn't dare lean out. Lisandra, her body down there, she was lying on the ground, on her back, her head to one side. I couldn't see whether she was still breathing. Two young lovers were leaning over her, they were holding hands; I screamed to them not to touch her, not to move her, and I ran down the stairs. The two young lovers had stepped back, they weren't holding hands anymore—had they touched her? Her forehead was icy; a trickle of blood was coming from her mouth; her eyes were open, her eyelids swollen. I didn't kill Lisandra, I could never have killed her, you have to believe me, Eva Maria.

9

Eva Maria is curled up in her chair. She pours another glass of wine. Vittorio told her everything. Down to the smallest detail. He'd had no time to react. The police had come very quickly—someone must have called them, surely a neighbor; every light in the building was on. He'd gone back up into the apartment with the policemen and they'd asked him to go with them to the station while others stayed behind to seal off the crime scene and begin their investigation. They wanted to get his deposition; they had to act quickly because it was often the speed of an investigation that enabled them to find the murderer; it wouldn't take long: that's what they told him. He should have had the presence of mind to ask for a lawyer, but you don't go from a state of terrible shock to extreme vigilance just like that, or at least he doesn't, and besides he had nothing to reproach himself with, so it never occurred to him to imagine what lay in store. At the police station they took his ID papers and led him into a little room to take his deposition, and then they made him wait in another room that was even smaller, for him to sign the document before leaving. They brought him a cup of coffee to keep him happy, but he had time to drink three cups, he was exhausted, and the bright white light in the room was dazzling; but the clock had stopped, he had no idea what time it was, and had such a terrible headache, it seemed to him that it was taking a long time, but then, he wasn't used to this sort of thing, and anyway he couldn't think straight so he didn't even try. Finally they came back, but there were more of them this time, they had a few more questions to ask him. That's when everything really took a turn for the worse.

"Where did you spend the evening, Dr. Puig?"

"At the movies, I already told you."

"Alone?"

"But I already told you. I don't understand. What is the point of this new interrogation?"

"Dr. Puig, we ask the questions here. We're not in your office, do you understand? So, to sum up: your wife didn't feel like going to the movies, and when you came home, she was dead, is that correct?"

"Yes, the door to the apartment was unlocked, there were signs of a struggle in the living room, the window was—"

"Yes, yes, we know all that, you already told us all that."

"But I already told you everything."

"No, you didn't tell us whether the movie was any good."

"Whether the film was any good? Is this some sort of joke? My wife has just been killed and you want me to tell you about a movie?"

"Don't take it like that, we just wanted to know; we like going to the movies, too. The lady at the box office is a pretty nice-looking girl, don't you think? She has lovely big lips, and when I see big lips like that on a white woman, it always gives me ideas. I can't help it. I think it's what you call a 'fantasy,' right?"

"I don't give a damn about your fantasies."

"You're wrong not to give a damn, because in your case those beautiful big lips are important, even decisive. In addition to performing miracles in bed—I'm sorry, I can't help thinking about it—well, those beautiful big lips speak, and we're not too happy about what they had to say about you."

"What did they have to say about me?"

"That she didn't see you there this evening. And that's unfortunate, because she wasn't the only one. The usher didn't see you, either, but I may as well tell you, her lips were of no interest."

"That photograph is at least ten years old—you can hardly recognize me. What can they tell from a scrap of paper? That's ridiculous."

"You are right, it would be—how did you put it?—oh, yes, 'ridiculous' to rely solely on this ID photo. What's more, it's true you look quite a bit older now. But rest assured, we do our job properly. Do you see that mirror over there? Well, they have had plenty of time to look at you, from every angle, and they have confirmed that neither one of them remembers seeing you this evening."

"They don't remember seeing me, but do they remember not seeing me? Did you ask them that? It's not the same, to not remember seeing someone, and to remember not seeing someone."

"Spare us your doublespeak, Dr. Puig, we're not your patients, once is enough for us to understand things; but it's true we didn't put the question to them from that angle. We don't have your acute sense of questions, of nuances—we could learn a lot from you—but sometimes, you know, things are simpler than that."

"Simpler than what? Say what you have to say. Stop insinuating things."

"We're not insinuating anything."

"Well then, let me sign my deposition so I can go home. I'm exhausted."

"That's going to be difficult."

"What do you mean, 'that's going to be difficult'? Because two women who spend their evenings watching a slew of faces go by don't remember me?"

"No, not because of that."

"Why then?"

"Because these two women are two *men*, Dr. Puig, and we're very surprised you didn't point that out to us, and yet in your case you were not subjected to watching 'a slew of faces go by.'"

"Right from the start you have been talking to me about women, so all I did was repeat what you said."

"So if right from the start we had told you that you killed your wife, would you confirm that you killed your wife?"

"I don't remember who sold me my ticket, or who tore it in half. Was it a woman? Or a man? I don't have a clue, I don't remember."

"It would seem that everyone's memory is poor this evening. But we have to start our investigation somehow or other, and at the moment, people's memories are the only tangible elements we have at our disposal. It's the same as for you, you have to start your psychoanalysis somewhere, and a few memories, even vague ones, are enough, and in your case you don't even have to verify whether people's testimonies are real—you only get one side of the story, and with you the guilty parties are always the same. It's straightforward: the parents, the father and mother. But rest assured, as far as we're concerned it's the truth we're after, and that's why we're not going to stop there. And even if unfortunately these few memories don't speak in your favor, we do not doubt for a single moment that the ongoing investigation will prove your innocence, so don't you worry, it's surely only a matter of hours. Tomorrow night you'll be sleeping in your own bed."

"I refuse to stay here another second. I'm going home."

"Calm down, Dr. Puig. You mustn't get upset like this. Not at the police station."

"What are you doing? What is the meaning of this? Remove these handcuffs!"

"It doesn't mean a thing, but if you get agitated, we have to put handcuffs on you, that's normal. Not everything always has to mean something in life."

"You're overstepping the bounds of your remit."

"We're not overstepping anything. By law any suspect can be taken into custody. Let's just say that for the time being, unfortunately, you are a suspect."

"You're making a grave mistake! I want to see a lawyer. I demand to see a lawyer."

"Once again—calm down. On the other hand, you have every right to demand the one thing you are now entitled to, so you see, it's not so hard to come to an agreement. But first of all, let's get the night over with. Apparently it's best to sleep on things. Oh, yes! I nearly forgot, what size are you?"

"What size what?"

"What size jacket do you wear?"

"Why are you asking me this?"

"I'll say it again: we ask the questions here, you'll just have to get used to it. What size jacket are you?"

"Fifty-two."

"As I thought. Well, good night, then. And maybe tomorrow morning you'll remember something. With dreams you never know, since apparently you analyze them."

Eva Maria lights a cigarette. Vittorio told her everything. With the precision of someone who was used to words tripping over each other. She listened to him for nearly an hour. As a rule, he was the one who listened to her for nearly an hour. Eva Maria thinks, It's odd how our roles in life get turned around sometimes. She hears the sound of the bandoneon.* Estéban has finished dinner. He'll be going out soon. Eva Maria places her cigarette in the notch in the ashtray. She rummages in the pocket of her slacks. Pulls out a set of keys. Three keys hanging from a key ring. Which is itself in the shape of a key. Eva Maria looks at these four keys. One of which is a fake. She smiles. Vittorio could not believe his eyes when he saw them on the other side of the table. On the right side of the table in that fucking visiting room. It was too good to be true. Good God, how had she gotten hold of the keys to his house? What an expression on his face, when she told him the whole story. Eva Maria thinks back.

---

* A type of accordion typical to Argentina.

"Morning, Mama. Did you sleep well?"

Eva Maria didn't answer. She was stunned. She muttered to herself.

"It can't be. It must be a mistake."

Eva Maria couldn't take her eyes off the newspaper. Just a few lines. Estéban walked over to the fridge.

"It was a really nice evening yesterday . . . you know, you should come one day . . . people dancing, they're like sleeping volcanoes, except now they're awake . . . just tell yourself that."

Eva Maria folded the paper. Abruptly. So, from one day to the next, a man could find himself in the paper. Eva Maria stood up. She went out into the hall. She put on her coat. Tied her scarf. Picked up her handbag. Estéban went up to her.

"Are you all right, Mama?"

"Yes, yes . . ."

"What time will you be home tonight?"

"At five o'clock."

"Okay, I'll be here."

Estéban leaned over Eva Maria. He kissed her. Her mind was elsewhere. The door slammed. Estéban ran his fingers through his hair. He parted the curtain at the window. He watched Eva

Maria running down the street, her bag in one hand, the newspaper in the other. She was holding it tight. The pages crumpled in her fist. The bus was about to leave. Eva Maria pounded on the window. The door opened; she climbed on board. The bus pulled away. Estéban let go of the curtain. He went to sit at the table. In Eva Maria's place. His face went blank.

Eva Maria got off the bus. Her bag in one hand, the newspaper in the other. She had relaxed her grip. Her hair was loose. The day was over. Eva Maria was walking quickly; she had to check something. She walked past a small café. El Pichuco. The waiter called out to her. Eva Maria waved to him without stopping. She had to check something. She walked up to a building. Went in. Climbed up five floors. Rang the bell on the right. Vittorio would open for her. No one answered. She rang again. No one. It couldn't be. She pounded on the fake wooden panels. Stood there for a long while. Motionless. In front of the locked door, which didn't open. Her hand tightened around the newspaper. She went back down the stairs. Crossed the square. Went into the small café. The waiter came over. He put a glass of wine down on the table for her. He was very agitated.

"You're not the only one who found no one at home. Haven't you heard? He killed her. She's dead. Can you imagine, dead? But he won't get away with it, I can tell you that—he's in a real pickle. You can't imagine the chaos all day long, cops everywhere . . . A shrink who's a murderer, that will get people talking, I can tell you."

Eva Maria put her glass down. Abruptly.

"No, you can't tell me; that's just it! Shut up, Francisco, for once, just shut up, stop talking about things you know nothing about."

"But I do know—"

"No, you don't know anything."

Eva Maria stood up. She tossed a few coins on the table. Her tone was sharp.

"Just because you're dying to tell the entire planet you've been serving a murderer doesn't mean that the man is a murderer."

Customers at neighboring tables turned around. Eva Maria left the café. She tossed the newspaper into the garbage can. She walked across the square and sat on a bench. It was cold. Eva Maria lit a cigarette. She looked up at the window. She looked down at the ground. It must be roughly there that they found the body. The sidewalk was as smooth as if nothing had happened. There was no blood. Nothing. Places keep no trace of the corpses that were once there. Places don't like memories. Not the slightest dent on the asphalt. Not the slightest little alteration in the concrete. A falling body never causes the earth to move. Eva Maria looked up at the window. She looked down at the ground. From the sixth floor, it would have been a miracle if the girl had survived. Did her face hit first, or her body? Were her limbs dislocated, in a position that would have been impossible when she was alive? Did her hair form a screen? Or did it all mass together on one side, revealing a pallor that in and of itself was enough to place her already among the dead? Was she disfigured? Or was she as beautiful dead as she had been alive? Eva Maria had seen her in their apartment several times, a graceful figure who eluded her gaze, the way she must surely have eluded other patients' gazes. What was their arrangement? The premises belonged to her as much as to him, of course, except when a patient was coming in, except when a patient was going out. Doctor-patient confidentiality, it was called. Eva Maria thought about the newspaper in the garbage can. It was a pity the same confidentiality didn't hold true for journalists; it was a pity that anybody could appear as a suspect to the rest of the planet. Only a culprit should be allowed to appear in newspapers. Eva

Maria stiffened. A young man, an adolescent, was standing a few feet away, his eyes glued to the ground. He looked up at the window, one hand in his pocket, the other dangling by his side. Eva Maria observed him. Intrigued. If he'd had a different attitude, she might have been suspicious, but his gaze went no farther than this unfortunate back and forth between the window and the ground. After a while, the young man headed over to the building and went in. Eva Maria stood up. Just because you look unhappy doesn't mean you're not guilty. Eva Maria followed the young man. She heard his steps in the stairway. He was going up. She went up. He stopped. Sixth floor—she'd suspected as much. A patient. Eva Maria pretended to go by him. The young man was pounding on the fake wooden paneling. How many of them had there already been that day, making this incredulous pilgrimage? Eva Maria turned back.

"Are you looking for someone, young man?"

"I came to see the man who lives here."

"He's not here."

The young boy stood there without moving, at a loss. Eva Maria went back down one step. She would like to comfort him. Even if it meant lying.

"Can I help you? I live just above."

The young man took his hand out of his pocket. He didn't seem to know what to do with it. There was something shiny in his palm.

"I came to give him back his keys. He lost them yesterday, in the street, next to . . . next to . . ."

The young man couldn't finish his sentence. Eva Maria prompted him.

"Next to the corpse?"

The young man nodded. Eva Maria tried to stay calm.

"Were you there?"

The young man looked down.

"My girlfriend and I found her—it was our first dinner together, just the two of us, I mean; it was strange, but it went well. We were on our way home. I was happy because she took my hand—it was the first time, we weren't saying much and I thought I was kind of useless. What's crazy is that I was praying that something would happen, I swear, anything that would slow us up. I was kind of scared to see her to her front door. We've never kissed. I mean, there"—he gestured toward his lips—"you see . . . so I wasn't walking very fast. It was my girlfriend who saw her first. 'Look, over there, on the sidewalk, it looks like a body.' At first we thought it must be a tramp, but it's not really that kind of neighborhood, and when we got closer we saw it was a woman, wearing a nice dress, and we saw the open window. We ran closer. Just then her husband appeared in the window and he shouted something. We didn't dare go near the body; we didn't even dare look at it too closely, or at least I didn't. Her husband got there very quickly—he was screaming. He's the one who actually saw that she was dead. Did she commit suicide?"

The young man's expression was distraught. Eva Maria could sense his distress. He needed to move beyond this horrible scene that life had thrust upon him without warning: death, there before his eyes. Eva Maria did not hesitate for a second. Even if it meant lying.

"Yes, you're right. She committed suicide."

Eva Maria moved down the few steps between herself and the young man. She knew. In these conditions, concrete decisions were better than any emotional convolutions.

"You can leave the keys with me, if you like. I'll give them back to Vittorio."

The young man did not hesitate for a second. He handed the

set of keys to Eva Maria. And as if the fact of being free of them enabled him to relax at last, he sat with all his weight on one of the steps. He sighed. His body was relieved; his soul, not quite altogether.

"I had never seen a dead body before."

Eva Maria would have liked to take his hand, but thought better of it.

"Me neither. I've never seen a dead body."

"You're lucky."

"I wish I had."

The young man turned to her.

"That's a really weird thing to say."

Eva Maria squeezed her hands together.

"I had a daughter, her name was Stella. She was roughly your age. One morning I kissed her good-bye; she was on her way to class. I never saw her again. That was five years ago last week. So you see, I wish I could have seen her dead rather than just knowing she was dead."

The young man lowered his head.

"I'm so sorry. They killed so many people."*

They both fell silent, staring into space. Eva Maria tried to laugh. She decided to change the subject.

"Just between you and me, it could have been a very successful kiss . . ."

The young man smiled, a smile of adolescence, but he was still thinking.

"Did you know this woman?"

---

* On March 24, 1976, a military coup d'état imposed a dictatorship on Argentina. The junta, led by General Rafael Videla, was responsible for the torture and murder of thirty thousand people during its years in power. On October 30, 1983, democracy was restored with the election of Raúl Alfonsín.

"No, but I know her husband."

The young man's smile faded.

"The poor guy, he was circling around her like a crazy man, pounding against the wall with his fists and screaming. He was devastated."

"Did you tell that to the police?"

The young man went tense.

"The police? What do the police have to do with this business? I don't have anything to tell the police."

The young man panicked. He got to his feet. Rushed down the stairs. Eva Maria couldn't stop him. She didn't try to stop him. The young man fled the way any adolescent would flee from the word "police," not as a murderer. If a murderer always returns to the scene of the crime, this boy was no murderer; he didn't have what it takes. Eva Maria was convinced of that. Maybe he simply hadn't told his parents that he was having dinner with his girlfriend—he would have had to explain everything to them, and at his age, confessing to his parents that he'd had dinner with a girl was unthinkable. "Like parents confessing to their children that they made love the night before," as Vittorio might have said. Eva Maria shook her head. She could hear the young man disappearing down the stairway. In any case, the police would have brushed aside his testimony about Vittorio's sorrow and distress. "Pretending, acting," they would have said. "Every wife killer starts off acting devastated, circling around the victim like a crazy man, pounding against the wall with his fists and screaming. Then he confesses." Eva Maria stood there alone on the step. She looked at the keys lying in her palm, lying like a corpse on the ground. From the sixth floor. That poor girl's body must have been broken in several places, like any victim of a terrible fall from a great height. They also found such fractures on the bodies of the *desaparecidos** that the sea washed back up after a time, fractures that would be impossible for someone to cause with their bare hands or even with a weapon. Even if they really went to town. Eva Maria imagined Neptune surrendering the bodies, to prove the guilt of the arrogant, hitherto untouchable torturers. Neptune the Stern, Neptune the Just, bringing proof of the junta's abuse of power. Nature helping man to judge his fellow man. A part of Eva Maria was convinced that Neptune would have given Stella's body back to her, out of pity for a mother's heart that was dying from not knowing. But another part of Eva Maria knew that Neptune did not exist, and she wondered whether Stella's body still lay in the depths of the river. Stella, her beloved child: did they get rid of her the way they did the others? One Wednesday evening, with an injection of Pentothal and an airplane and an open door, and her living body hurled from up there into the Rio de la Plata, was she conscious? Was she in tears? Imploring them? Did she scream as she fell through the void? Did she feel her clothing undressing her? Or was she already naked? Did she know that her body was going to hit the surface of the water, that same water that up to now she had only known as gentle and penetrable? She, who loved the water so. How can a mother not sense it when her child dies? Stella cannot be dead, it's not possible. Eva Maria shook her head to banish the unbearable vision of her daughter's body lying on the bed of the river. The tears started down her cheeks. Eva Maria looked at the steps plunging downward. If the stairway could talk it would tell her who killed Vittorio's wife. She would give anything to

---

* The *desaparecidos*—the "disappeared"—were the victims of forced disappearance, secretly arrested and killed in Argentina during the "dirty war." The military, wanting to conceal its acts of violence, claimed that these people had simply left Argentina.

know the murderer's identity. Eva Maria got to her feet. She hoped that some light would be shed on the murder in the coming days and that Vittorio would be exonerated. She hoped above all that she would soon be alone with him, like before; she needed it so badly. She would never be able to go on without him, to go on living. Eva Maria left the building. Then the days passed. She decided to visit Vittorio in prison. She was afraid they might not allow her to visit. They didn't cause any problems. The only procedure was a mandatory search. It was too good to be true.

Eva Maria opens her eyes once again. She looks at the four keys. One of which is a fake. Vittorio couldn't believe his eyes when he saw them on the other side of the table. On the right side of the table in this fucking visiting room. The keys to his apartment in Eva Maria's fingers. At last a flicker of hope. "All this because a kid was afraid of a kiss." Vittorio had laughed. Too nervously. "You will help me, won't you? I didn't kill Lisandra, I could never have killed her, you have to believe me, Eva Maria, you're my only hope—what can I do locked up in this fucking cell? The cops have it in for me, they're convinced I killed Lisandra. At the crime scene they found a little porcelain cat, broken, just an innocuous little figurine, they noticed the collection on the shelf in the library, but they also found—evidence more compromising for me—a bottle of wine and two broken glasses on the floor: a tête-à-tête with my wife that turned ugly, it happens a lot, the evening starts out fine but ends badly, but no matter how I told them that those glasses could have been there for several days, that it didn't mean a thing, no matter how I tried to explain to them that we were not very tidy, they just said I wouldn't be the first man to get rid of his wife. Coming from them it's stating the obvious, a husband who kills his wife; it's routine, they lap it up, they laugh and say it's human nature, it's an impulse, which, it's true, affects every man at least once in his life, but I let my emotions get the better of me, and yet I should know so well how to control them, hold them back, reason with them, I was a shame to my profession, they weren't very proud of me. I could hear them asking each other out loud what my motive was, why did I do it; there isn't a hint of uncertainty in their reasoning, there's nothing I can say, they don't believe me, they're not looking for Lisandra's murderer, they're looking to accuse me, *let's have a shrink for a change*, what a stroke of luck, it's too rare not to seize the opportunity, for once they're getting talked about in the papers, that's a change. Those cops are crazy but they are patient. I'm alone against the world; the distrustful way my lawyer looks at me is hardly reassuring, only this afternoon he told me that things weren't looking good; even he doesn't seem to believe I'm innocent—yet another unbelievable thing about this whole business anyway. Since my arrest, I've had the feeling that everything I'm struggling against is unbelievable. You're my only hope, along with the keys to my apartment, it's just what I needed. We have to find Lisandra's murderer, the cops won't look for him, but you, you can look, you'll help me, won't you? Do you agree?"

Eva Maria can no longer hear the sound of the bandoneon. Estéban must have gone out to his party. Eva Maria puts the keys on her desk. She looks at the cigarette wedged in its notch in the ashtray, a long straight gray tube of ash balancing in the air, frail with its vulnerability to change. Eva Maria thinks about the frailty of vulnerability to change. She wonders how much longer those particles will stay compacted together. She is careful not to move the desk. A sip of wine. Two sips. Eva Maria is thinking. Those investigators are absolute idiots—of course you can't recall that the person who sold you your ticket to the movie was a man—but in their book, the arbitrary nature of memory is incriminating evidence; that's their point of view, their strategy, and all the rest is simply solitude on trial, which just means that you can never be alone, that you have to spend every single hour, every single moment in someone's company, if you want to be sure you have an alibi, just in case someday you are wrongfully accused, the way Vittorio is now. It's absurd, and impossible. Those investigators aren't looking any further than the ends of their noses; they reduce everything to the lowest common denominator. With them it's not reality that feeds statistics, it's statistics that make reality comply—but that's natural: since their profession brings them no reassurance from men, from human beings, they try to find reassurance in numbers. Some would call it professional conditioning, but Eva Maria thinks it's a sure path to judicial error. No, not every husband kills his wife. Eva Maria takes a sip of wine. It is as if the police are projecting their own fantasies, their own desire for murder, onto this type of drama. In any case, if she were the wife of one of those policemen, she'd be wary. Suspect Vittorio, granted, that was part of their job, but to condemn him before the fact was unacceptable. Numbers are there to be studied, not to serve as generalizations. It was as if, at the Center, she were to take specific data for definitive values: every volcano, every eruption has its own figures, but it stops there. Why can't we do the same with individuals? Simply because we identify with individuals; investigators, judges and jurors, and Sunday commentators do nothing more than project who they are onto the accused; from that point on, error is completely free to interfere. One should not identify with another man any more than one identifies with a volcano. And yet it's not hard to see that this man loved his wife. Eva Maria puts her glass down. The cigarette breaks in two; the long tube of ash has fallen. Eva Maria sighs. She has to get him out of there. She'll have to struggle on her own, in a place where there is no room for numbers, where only intuition can hold sway, because before we are logical we are pure instinct, and she can tell Vittorio couldn't have killed his wife. It's like with volcanoes: every day you have to conduct a new investigation; every day when you have some new elements you have to make them speak, and you have to trust them, you have to try to interpret them. A man is like a volcano: you wait for him to reveal a bit more of himself each day. Eva Maria reaches for her eyeglasses. She opens a little black leather notebook. Hardbound. She looks for a blank page. She writes quickly.

door to the apartment open
loud music in the living room
window open in living room
chairs on the floor
lamp overturned
vase on the floor, broken
water spilled
figurine broken (porcelain cat)
wine bottle
two broken glasses
lying on her back
head to one side
icy forehead, trickle of blood
eyes open, puffy

Eva Maria closes her little black notebook. She stands up. Puts the keys in the pocket of her slacks. She's made up her mind. She will do what Vittorio asked. She shivers. With a touch of fear.

"Estéban? Estéban?"

Eva Maria opens the door to the bedroom. Estéban has already left. The hook where he hangs his bicycle is empty. He has taken his bandoneon. In the corridor, she calls out again. No one. Eva Maria shrugs. Out again, until the crack of dawn. She puts on her black coat. Wraps her scarf around her neck. The white stands out against the black. Her gaze lands on the kitchen table. Her dinner is waiting for her. She adjusts her gloves. Black, too. Estéban prepared a plate for her. He covered it, to keep it from getting cold. Even covered, the plate must be cold by now. Everything eventually goes cold, even volcanoes. Eva Maria goes into the kitchen. She opens the cupboard. Pours herself a glass of wine. She drinks it down in one go. Switches the lights off behind her. It's cold out. Eva Maria lifts her white scarf to cover her hair. She hasn't been out at night for months. She takes the bus. She watches the lights go by through the window; it's pretty in its way, the lights at night, so quiet. She feels the keys in the pocket of her pants. She thinks about the young man, pictures him again gesturing briefly, there, to his adolescent lips. She wonders if he finally found the resolve to kiss his girlfriend, she wonders if it went well. Her gaze lingers on each passing lamppost. She remembers her first kiss. It did not go well. She smiles all the same. You always smile when you remember your first kiss—when it was granted willingly. The movement of her lips creases a few wrinkles around her eyes. Her white scarf brushes against her cheeks. A neon light flashes. What a shock it must have been for those two, after all, seeing that body, when they were still children, thinking about nothing more than the possibility of a kiss. "And when we got closer we saw it was a woman, wearing a nice dress." Vittorio hadn't mentioned it. Eva Maria takes out her little notebook. To her previous notes she adds,

Wearing a nice dress

The bus stops. Eva Maria is startled. Two more stops. She draws nearer to the door. She thinks about Vittorio. It must be completely dark in his cell, and there is no way to break that darkness, no switch to press, no door to open. He had immediately been surprised that the door to their apartment was unlocked. Lisandra always locked it when she was alone and she bolted it, too, even during the day; she was afraid, she always had been, even of the impossible—that someone would come in, and hide in a wardrobe or a closet and when night fell they would hurt her. Lisandra was so fearful, she was terrified of the night, as if suddenly it brought together all the conditions necessary for tragedy; if she was lost in thought and he came into the room to speak to her, she would look up with a start, she would stifle a cry. The first time he saw her, he was immediately struck by this vulnerability. It was true that she was crying but you don't assume someone is fragile just because they are crying; you can be sad without being fragile. Lisandra would never have opened the door to a stranger, Vittorio was sure of that; she never opened the door when it rang, he always had to go—he teased her about it sometimes, they were so different in that respect, she would lock the door for any reason, and he dreamed of a world without doors. He never should have made fun of her; in the end Lisandra had been right to be afraid. Did she know instinctively how, one day, she would die? And what if we all knew instinctively, deep down, how, one day, death would come for us, and what if our neuroses were nothing to do with our past, the way we always think they are, but with our future, cries of alarm? The bus stops. There were no traces of breaking and entering, so Lisandra had opened the door, and Vittorio could not rid himself of a terrible thought, an intuition, the one lead he could envision: a patient. A patient—Lisandra was used to some of them coming and ringing late at night; it was rare but it did happen. Lisandra never opened the door when he wasn't there, but that night perhaps the patient had insisted, he'd kept ringing, or *she*—after all, it isn't only men who kill—and Lisandra had opened the door in the end, driven perhaps by the inevitability of Vittorio's teasing; when he came home he would surely reproach her if she hadn't opened the door. Vittorio found it hard to believe that it could be one of his patients, but he saw no other explanation. The junta's violence was over, and he didn't believe in the concept of a stranger coming to ring their door to kill Lisandra. At least the cops were right about that: murderers don't appear out of nowhere to come and kill you for no reason, or only rarely, and nothing had been taken, he had to admit. He had gone all around the apartment with the policemen and apart from the mess in the living room everything looked normal, Vittorio had seen for himself, nothing had been stolen; the only undeniable thing was that there had been a struggle, and that must be why the music was so loud, to cover the noise, and the shouts, but what had caused the argument? And the nagging question, what if Lisandra had been raped; he was waiting anxiously for the results of the autopsy. The thought that someone might wish to harm her to the point of killing her seemed unthinkable, but perhaps she had served as a scapegoat; it was possible, after all—you can't stop people venting their frustration and bitterness and hatred on others. In any case they must have really hated her to want to kill her, because it was no accident; you don't open a window in the middle of winter for no good reason. What if it were transference, yes, a transference of emotions onto him, then onto her? If Lisandra had died because of him, he would never forgive himself. The bus stops. Eva Maria gets off.

one two three four five six seven eight nine ten eleven twelve
she has counted them so many times, these steps, since she has

thirteen fourteen fifteen sixteen seventeen eighteen nineteen twenty
been coming here every Tuesday for over four years it must be

twenty-one   twenty-two   twenty-three   twenty-four   twenty-five
the equivalent of climbing the Copahue volcano or even the

twenty-six twenty-seven twenty-eight twenty-nine thirty thirty-one
Payun Matru she hopes she's not doing something stupid Estéban

thirty-two thirty-three thirty-four thirty-five thirty-six thirty-seven
kept saying you have to get help Mama you have to get help I've

thirty-eight   thirty-nine   forty   forty-one   forty-two   forty-three
heard about someone who's supposed to be good go and see him

forty-four   forty-five   forty-six   forty-seven   forty-eight   forty-nine
Mama go and see him please do it for me she hopes she's not doing

fifty fifty-one fifty-two
something stupid

Eva Maria stumbles.

fifty-three fifty-four fifty-five fifty-six fifty-seven fifty-eight fifty-nine
Vittorio was the right one she could tell straightaway his questions

sixty sixty-one sixty-two sixty-three sixty-four sixty-five sixty-six
his answers and even their silences their disagreements she always

sixty-seven sixty-eight sixty-nine seventy seventy-one seventy-two
felt at ease with him he was never inane or arrogant and never

seventy-three seventy-four seventy-five seventy-six seventy-seven
insidious when she felt like laughing it was a desire to laugh along

seventy-eight seventy-nine eighty eighty-one eighty-two eighty-three
with him not a petty desire to make fun of him or his interpretations

eighty-four eighty-five eighty-six eighty-seven eighty-eight eighty-nine
the way she had with others that flash that said deep down you

ninety ninety-one ninety-two ninety-three ninety-four ninety-five
really don't get it do you man you're way off the mark and you

ninety-six ninety-seven ninety-eight ninety-nine one hundred
won't see me again Vittorio always knew exactly and he taught her

hundred-and-one   hundred-and-two   hundred-and-three
to see things from another angle a good angle it's strange she

hundred-and-four hundred-and-five hundred-and-six hundred-and-seven
always counts the steps going up but never going down she hopes

hundred-and-eight hundred-and-nine
she's not doing something stupid

Eva Maria stops to catch her breath. One hundred and nine steps. Still just as many. Not a single step has packed up and moved to a more illustrious staircase. Places are indifferent. Quick now, no one must see her. Eva Maria follows Vittorio's instructions. She puts the smallest key into the lock, pulling the door toward her. The handle yields beneath her fingers. Eva Maria slips into the apartment. Quickly. She locks the door behind her. Fear makes her breathing short, irregular. She leans against the door. Her eyes adjust to the darkness. She stifles a cry. Someone is standing against the wall. Eva Maria swallows. It's a coatrack. It looks just like a man. Wearing a gray jacket. Eva Maria brushes against the jacket as she goes by. "You! You gave me a real fright." She opens the door to the study. It's the first time she's touched it. As a rule, Vittorio was sole keeper of the door; it was his way of marking a parentheses, opening and closing the door as his patients came and went. She sits down on the sofa. To collect her wits. She knows it so well, this plush seat. Eva Maria looks at the huge peacock opposite her. She could never have imagined Vittorio sitting anywhere but in front of that huge painting. Eva Maria recalls the dirty beige walls in the prison. She closes her eyes. Opens them. She would have liked to see Vittorio sitting opposite her, wearing his reassuring smile. Instead, it is the smile of a seventeen-day-old crescent moon that is reflected in the peacock's feathers. Eva Maria stands up. She follows Vittorio's instructions. The little cupboard next to the heater. Behind his desk. Eva Maria gets down on her knees. She opens the door. She moves back to allow the moonlight to enter. Eva Maria can no longer follow Vittorio's instructions. She can no longer hurry. She can't tear her gaze away from these two shelves of cassettes. Hypnotic. Lined up in a row next to each other. Vertically. A white label on each spine. With a first name on each one. Eva Maria reaches for one of them. "Bianca." Another. "Carlos." Twenty-three cassettes in all. In alphabetical order. She sees hers. It makes her uncomfortable. To listen to the most recent session, to listen to them again, alone, going back over each one with a clear mind, hunting through the cassettes for the sentence or the word he might have missed during a session and which would shed new light on the psyche of those people he had been trying to understand, week after week, month after month, trying to understand what made them tick, their neuroses. That was what Vittorio had explained to her when she visited him in prison. One cassette per patient. Only the most recent session, as each new session erased the previous one. He did not listen to them again systematically, but he wanted to be able to; if a thought or some words came back to him, he wanted to listen to them again in context. He called it his "delayed awakening," because in all honesty, he didn't always pay attention; no human being can maintain that level of extreme awareness, of maximum receptiveness, for hours on end. There were moments when his mind wandered off, moments of distraction; it would be hypocritical to claim he was always attentive, bad faith on the part of the analyst. No man can claim to possess uninterrupted attention, so the tape recorder enabled him to remedy this weakness. Eva Maria gives a start. She hears voices. She turns to the door. It's the neighbors' television. Quick. She puts all the cassettes in her backpack. "Eva Maria." She looks at her own cassette. She can't really recall what they talked about during her last session, it was already so long ago. She could not bear to hear it, how awful! To hear herself commenting on her state of mind, gushing with feeling, circling around herself, and herself alone; for three-quarters of an hour never leaving herself behind—for a start the very principle had always embarrassed her, so fortunately she won't have to listen to this one. She hates the sound of her own voice. Eva Maria looks at her cassette. She makes a face. She has to hurry. She has to follow Vittorio's instructions. Get all the cassettes. Maybe they will yield a clue? A lead? Something that might have eluded him—he could no longer remember everything his patients had told him over recent weeks, thousands of words, meaningful silences, slips of the tongue, perhaps even innuendos, and what if one of them had warned him? Threatened him? Without him realizing—jealousy, revenge, after all, it was possible; in any case, it was what seemed the most probable among all the theories he was constantly rehashing in that fucking cell where soon there would be nothing left to do but count the bricks. Eva Maria closes the cupboard. She looks at her backpack. Vittorio's treasure. And most importantly, the cops must not get hold of these cassettes; those men are far too hostile. They are perfectly capable of destroying evidence. Visibly they would rather *have a shrink for a change* than lock up the true culprit. He was already paying the price for their shortcuts, their arguments for the prosecution, their way of coming to grotesque conclusions so they wouldn't have to fear them. Vittorio is surely right. Eva Maria frowns. She almost forgot. One more thing. She takes the box of tissues from the little table between the sofa and the leather armchair where Vittorio always sat and turns it upside down. The recorder is there, hidden in a recess where it just fits. There are no cassettes in the recorder. Eva Maria also takes the box of tissues, just to be on the safe side, for her peace of mind. Vittorio insisted on this. If the cops found the box, they were bound to question him about the empty recess and, at the same time, it would mean they were investigating—none too soon, but Vittorio would have to explain all his recordings, and above all justify them, and he could already tell where that would lead: the trial of the husband who kills his wife would become the trial of the psychoanalyst who records his patients. It's true, it wasn't *ethical*, but he was sure it was a good thing, and useful professionally; he'd had ample opportunity to verify that the practice helped him, and that was the main thing. Like some ideal archivist, it kept something close to an inalterable memory of his patients' altered memory and of his own. It meant that he left nothing up to chance—since when has the principle of keeping things been seen as detrimental? But of course he didn't tell his patients; if they had known they were being recorded it would surely have hindered them, embarrassed and intimidated them, and any- way no psychoanalyst tells his patients what he writes in their file during the session, but no one finds fault with that secrecy, it's true, because that's the Method with a capital "M." Well, his method with a lowercase "m" was to resort to these recordings; he had stopped taking notes during sessions long ago—it had been com- pletely counterproductive, because the note taking immediately introduced a distance, and his patients withdrew when they saw him writing, or they lost the thread of what they were saying, wondering if what they had just said was so important that he had to make a note of it, and then the session no longer flowed, was not as useful, something that never happened with a tape recorder. A profession is defined by its purpose, not by its method, and the police have differ- ent ways of extracting information from their witnesses and their suspects. It was the same thing for analysts—he himself had paid the cost every day. No science should ever be enclosed in a methodology.

Besides, if in Freud's era there had been tape recorders, discreet ones, the great pioneer would surely not have failed to use such a valuable tool. But as Vittorio knew, all the justifications on the planet would serve no purpose. A psychoanalyst recording his patients, how disgraceful! What a scandal! A professional Watergate. He would infuriate everyone—he could already hear them, all of his colleagues, expressing their outrage and disowning him. He had already been removed from his role as a husband; a few depositions would suffice to dismiss him from his role as a psychoanalyst. He would be the scourge of the profession, and almost certainly, at the same time, through a sinister game of one thing leading to another, the scourge of his wife: her murderer.

"Morning, Mama. Did you sleep well?"

The unread newspaper is on the table. Eva Maria looks up at Estéban.

"Can you lend me your headphones, please?"

Estéban heads over to the fridge.

"Which headphones?"

"To listen to music."

"But what are you going to use to listen to music?"

Eva Maria blows on her maté.* Her gaze wanders through the liquid.

"Oh, yes, you're right . . . Can you lend me your tape recorder as well?"

She puts down her maté cup. She gets up.

"Can I have them, then?"

"Now?"

"Yes."

"You're not going to work?"

"I'm working from home."

* A traditional caffeinated infusion drunk in South America, made from the leaves of the yerba maté shrub.

"What do you mean?"

"I have things to do . . . some documents to go over. It will be quieter here."

"Oh, okay . . . Is this new?"

"Yes, it's new."

Estéban runs his fingers through his hair. Eva Maria is getting impatient. From the table to the door. From the door to the table.

"So can I have them?"

"I'll go get them for you."

Eva Maria follows him out of the kitchen. A few minutes later, Estéban reappears. Alone. He sits down at the table. Pours himself a glass of orange juice. Opens the newspaper. He listens. He can't hear anything. Just the faint clacking of the typewriter keys. Estéban turns to the window. The shadow of the bus passes over the curtains. Estéban smiles. His expression is calm. His hands, too. He can imagine Eva Maria's face encircled by his headphones. He wonders what kind of music she might be listening to. She hasn't listened to music for such a long time.

ALICIA

VITTORIO

Good morning, Alicia.

ALICIA

Good morning.

VITTORIO

So, how are you feeling today?

ALICIA

I'm all right. It's just this boredom. It's always there. I'm sorry I have nothing new, I just can't get over this boredom.

VITTORIO

You needn't apologize.

ALICIA

You know that to get here I go past the Plaza de Mayo; it's on my way. And of course they were all there, like every Thursday afternoon; I slowed down and you know what I thought as I watched them walk past? There they were, so plain and unpretentious, wearing their horrible white head scarves—you have to admit that white head scarf is horrible, it being for a good cause doesn't make it any better—and I began to feel sorry that I hadn't lost a child, too. To wish I were a mother who had lost a child—do you realize how far gone I must be? I feel like I'm going crazy.

VITTORIO

You're not going crazy, I assure you, but why did you have a thought like that? Can you be more precise?

ALICIA

Why? So that I could put all my remaining energy into loss, into mourning. I tell myself that if I could walk around the Plaza de Mayo every Thursday afternoon along with those women, and demand in the eyes of the entire world the return of the child the junta took from me, my mourning and my desire for justice would be so extreme that I would no longer be aware of all the rest.

VITTORIO

What do you mean by "all the rest"?

ALICIA

How alone I am. You see, those women, when they look in the mirror, they search their features for what reminds them of their lost child, but me, every morning I just look for yet another wrinkle, yet another sign that my flesh is sagging, another obvious and chilling sign of age, and I figure maybe I wouldn't be so bored if I were in mourning. In any case I wouldn't be looking at myself so much and maybe even—this is my dream—I wouldn't see myself at all. The loss of a child—like that, tragically—is greater than any other tragedy. You must find me vile to be thinking this way, don't you? And you must be telling yourself that it would teach me a lesson if it did happen to me.

VITTORIO

No, I'm not telling myself that at all. I wonder if you aren't simply experiencing the feeling of having "lost a child" since your son got married? He's your only son and it's very recent, so it's only normal for you to be upset. When a child leaves home, it changes a mother's life. Perhaps that's why you have made this unconscious connection with the mothers on the Plaza de Mayo. It's your way of dealing with the fact that your boy has left home. To me personally, this seems the most likely explanation. What do you think?

ALICIA

When a child leaves home, it doesn't "change a mother's life," it destroys it. Ever since Juan left, everything has been ten times worse. Before, it still felt as if there was some life in the house; he wasn't always there, but it was enough to know he was coming and going. It hid the worst. Excuse me, may I use your telephone? I have to call him.

VITTORIO

Actually, my phone isn't working; the repairman has come three times and it's still out of order.

ALICIA

Don't you have another line? In the house? I'm sorry but I really have to call him.

VITTORIO

Wait here for a moment. [*Long silence.*] Go ahead, I asked my wife to let you use the living room so you can call. [*Long silence.*] Is your son all right? Do you feel better now?

ALICIA

I still can't understand how in one life he can have gone from a state of complete dependency, where as a baby he couldn't live one second without me, to this independence where even speaking to me on the telephone for two minutes seems to involve a major effort.

VITTORIO

So, Juan is fine. You see, just because you project yourself into an upsetting event doesn't mean it necessarily happens, or that you create it. Rest assured, we all have thoughts from time to time that seem terrible. You mustn't take them literally, you must just try and understand what they mean deep down where you yourself are concerned.

ALICIA

How old are you?

VITTORIO

Fifty-one.

ALICIA

And your wife? I just saw her, she's so young—what do you know, I didn't think you were that type.

VITTORIO

Alicia . . . let's get back to our discussion, please.

ALICIA

Why don't we play a guessing game? Apparently games alleviate boredom—do you still want to know why I wear these gloves?

VITTORIO

I've often wondered, but I have to admit I don't know.

ALICIA

Go on, try and guess.

VITTORIO
Honestly, I don't know.

ALICIA
Well, hey, you're not very playful, yet when you have a wife as young as yours, you should know how to play a little. You really don't know? Watch out, today's the big day! Drumroll . . . Ta-da! See?

VITTORIO
See what?

ALICIA
My hands are perfectly normal, that's what you're thinking, right? Hands that are perfectly normal for my age, well, that's the whole problem: *for my age*. Look at them, all those wrinkles, all those spots, I watch them accumulating in real time. Hands are the part of the body you see the most, and that's why they're there, those wrinkles, those liver spots, so that you'll never forget that you're getting old. It's like with giraffes, the color of our spots helps guess our age.

VITTORIO
You're exaggerating, you have beautiful hands.

ALICIA
That's very kind of you. But they're not as beautiful as your wife's hands.

VITTORIO
Don't be silly . . .

ALICIA
I'm not being silly. I may be old, but not silly, so don't accuse me of all the evils. Do you know where the word "menopause" comes from?

VITTORIO

I don't know . . . surely from Latin.

ALICIA

From Greek. You lose. You had a fifty-fifty chance. To be born a woman, like me, that is. "Menopause"—it sounds like the name of a muse, don't you think? Except that this muse doesn't inspire anyone—there's not a single poet who will sing its praises—but then, the names of diseases have never inspired anyone.

VITTORIO

Come now, Alicia, it's not a disease.

ALICIA

You're right, it's not a disease, it's worse, it's an incurable condition. *Meno*: month, *pause*: cessation. *The cessation of months*, that's clear, isn't it? But not expeditious enough. You know what I think? Women shouldn't live past menopause.

VITTORIO

Aren't you being overly dramatic?

ALICIA

I'm not being dramatic at all, I am coming up with theories. When you can't make poetry, you make theories. Might as well do something; you have to talk about it, right? And it does me good to talk about it. But maybe it embarrasses you? Or disgusts you?

VITTORIO

Why should it disgust me? On the other hand, I have thought of something: the "Plaza de Mayo" and "menopause"—there's an obvious link, don't you see?

ALICIA

I don't see any link whatsoever. But I'm eager to hear
what you have to say.

VITTORIO

You just said that "menopause" meant the "cessation of
months," right? "Plaza de Mayo." In both cases, there's a
reference to months: does this association of ideas
suggest anything to you?

ALICIA

Only that you want to bring this conversation to an end,
right? You want to impress me with your own secret
interpretation, so that I won't go any further with my
dreary assessment; but old age can't be psychoanalyzed—
you can't do anything about it; you can describe old age
and that's it. Aren't you disgusted?

VITTORIO

I'll say it again, no, it doesn't disgust me. Just stop with
your questions and answers.

ALICIA

May I continue?

VITTORIO

Please go ahead.

ALICIA

Yesterday morning, I measured my height, and guess
what? I have shrunk, already three-quarters of an inch.
That's it, it's the beginning of the end. To start with, you
get shorter—nature has gotten some things right after
all, so now you start off by taking up a bit less space in
other people's visual fields; it may be imperceptible to

the naked eye but it helps you convey to others that you are becoming less interesting and you are beginning to disappear. Everything starts shrinking now. I can see it with my breasts. People say that old women's breasts sag, but that's not right; they empty out, they become pockets of soft skin, hanging, dead. Death starts with the skin. Before, I had nice breasts, you know, full and perky, so full, even after Juan's birth, my breasts filled my hands. I loved to hold them, both at the same time, I loved that feeling, but now it's as if there's nothing beneath my fingers. I can pull on the skin and it stretches, like the deflated rubber of a child's balloon, which would have floated up into the sky when it was intact, but now it's stuck on the ground, for good. If a man touched me, he could wrap himself up in my skin. Not to mention the weight I put on even if I don't eat—it's as if menopause was eating away inside us, eating what used to be our shape to make us shapeless; it devours us from inside. It says, I'll take your breasts and put them on your hips, I'll take what used to be your pretty butt and spread it over your stomach and your back and your waist. Why do you keep looking at the clock? You can't wait for this session to be over, right? Men revel in the beauty of a woman's body, but they can't stand it if she's past it, any more in words than in pictures, and that's why you, too, have chosen a younger woman, to shield yourself from that vision of horror. You disappoint me. A person always wants their shrink to be different from everyone else, to be better, to be above the worst failings of humanity. But in fact, everybody is just the same. Does your wife shave, too? Apparently girls shave now; even at the age of twenty, they're already nostalgic for their youth. And it's not over, poor things, if they only knew. I hate them. Water still flows through their bodies, the running water of a stream, whereas only stagnant pond water fills our limbs, and distorts them.

But go ahead and laugh, young ladies, you cannot imagine what's in store, you'll have to go through it someday, too, so go right ahead, show them off, your little legs, show off your breasts and your firm arms, you'll have to hide them soon enough, you'll have to bury them beneath the long flowing garments that will fill your wardrobes one day, summer and winter alike, and the end will come for your pretty décolletés, your sexy negligees, your stockings, and your little skirts, and before you're buried in the ground your body will be buried under ever thicker layers of material, and soon your pouting lips will have no power over anyone. I hate them. I have to stop going out because just the sight of them all shiny and new drives me crazy. Yesterday I was walking behind this young girl who was swaying her hips and a bus was coming from the opposite direction at full speed, and all I felt like doing was pushing her under the wheels, and that's not the first time that has happened. What about your wife, does she do that, too? Does she shave, your wife?

VITTORIO

Stop talking about my wife, Alicia.

ALICIA

I shaved last night, too—I mean my privates, of course, that's what I'm talking about, well, what's left of it. I'd give anything to have a thick bush again, coarse and round, but there were only a few grayish hairs that fell into the tub. Even the evening light can no longer fool me, even a little candle doesn't give any erotic charge to my body anymore, or to my pussy—it, too, seems to be drooping, it just hangs there; my lips are all soft, they're like two earlobes flopping onto my pussy; and my clitoris, oh my God, you should have seen it . . . I took a photo . . . do you want to see?

[Sound of someone rummaging in a handbag.]

VITTORIO
Stop that, Alicia, no, I don't want to see a photograph.

ALICIA
I was just joking, I didn't take a photo . . . I scared you, didn't I? You should see your face—I finally disgusted you—but I had to speak to someone. Everything is shrinking, except my lucidity, which gets sharper by the day. It's so unfair. Does your wife like to tango? I didn't recognize the song in the living room—it was a nice piece; does she dance, too? I used to manage pretty well myself, but now when I dance I feel like I'm in disguise. I can hear my body begging me to stop: "Stop, I tell you, you can see I'm not graceful anymore, don't you get it, old girl? Your place—my place—is in this corner now, on this chair; from now on only chairs will want anything to do with our butts. Dancing, old girl, it's like with men—it's for young women." Oh, I should have let myself be loved by every man who ever desired me; at least that way I would have a wealth of memories to comfort me, all that fucking, and then some—my mind would be full of fucking. And then so what if now my sex is full of nothing. Maybe memories would have been enough to fill the void.

VITTORIO
You are not old, Alicia, stop going on about it. You still have many beautiful years ahead.

ALICIA
That's the whole problem. To do what?

VITTORIO
There are plenty of things to do on earth.

ALICIA

"There are plenty of things to do on earth"— I'm used to better advice from you. No, there are not "plenty of things to do on earth." Making children is all there is to do on earth. Longevity is the worst thing there is for women. We get a reprieve only to see that everything has been taken away from us, a reprieve that serves no purpose other than to reduce us to a pulp; scientific progress is the best instrument there is to torture women. At least in the old days we died before we had to go through all that: how many women made it to menopause? Who was the first one to have to pay the price? Women had to learn to live without procreating, which is absurd. Women as eunuchs. An emasculation of nature. And since the point of sexuality is procreation, the decline of sexual desire—because you can say all you like that sexuality has nothing to do with childbearing, it's not true, no more period no more sex, the door's been bricked up, it's all dry in there anyway, there's no room for anything. So you're supposed to put up with yourself for years on end as a member of the living dead? Is that it? Whereas men go through their whole life with their ability to procreate. How can you demand equality between men and women under such conditions, when we're fighting a losing battle? How can we reproach men for going after women who are still fertile, where their sperm will serve some purpose; it's atavistic, it's not even really their fault, it's their reproductive instinct. There is nothing to reproach them with; they are not to blame; it's just another example of nature leading us around by the nose, only God is nature. Life has it in for us; it can't be any other way and no feminist will ever be able to change that. The world belongs to men, and to young women.

VITTORIO

Men are forced to deal with other problems, Alicia; they know other forms of withering.

ALICIA

Ah! At last you're using the right words; you were beginning to disappoint me. "Withering," you mean "droopy dick," is that it? You see, there isn't even a scientific word when reality is not as pressing. And so what, what does that change—droopy dick or not, you can still do it. Why can men have children until the day they die, but that right is taken away from us years earlier? Why doesn't it stop for everyone at the same time? Isn't it the worst form of punishment for a woman to see her role in life taken away from her? You have nothing to say, do you? I think it would be a good idea to have euthanasia for women once they're barren. For their own good. One year without their period, and then off you go, straight to the abattoir. And if they need convincing, have them watch a film documenting the erectile potency of their husband, boyfriend, or partner as measured when in the presence of two categories of women: young and old. And fill their glass with a deadly poison—how eagerly they'd drink it down; they're dehydrated from watching that penis they hadn't seen that stiff in so long. Without anyone knowing why, women would disappear, and that would kill two birds with one stone, putting an end to their misery and reducing the rate of aging in the population, which, as we all know, will become the scourge of the planet. Wolves, you know, kill pack members that get sick—we should be like them, we should copy the behavior of animals; they're the ones that have got it right. So, how do you intend to comfort me now? A little erection? I don't think you could, could you? I do understand. If I find my body repulsive, shouldn't it be repulsive to others, too? Forgive me.

VITTORIO

Don't worry about it; sometimes it's good to let it out.

ALICIA

I haven't cried here in so long.

VITTORIO

That's true.

ALICIA

You know that women have four times as many tears as
men? It's biological—it just goes to show which sex was
designated by nature for sorrow.

VITTORIO

Sorrow is not the sole lot of women, you know that
very well.

ALICIA

That's not what I'm saying. I'm simply saying that our
suffering is inscribed in the quantity of tears that nature
has placed at our disposal: four times more than for men.

VITTORIO

That is absolute nonsense.

ALICIA

No, you can read it in a book. If you only knew how
much I read these days. A book, you can keep hold of;
not a man. So, tell me how I am to replace love if I can
no longer inspire it—not with children, they leave home,
too—look at Juan, he's gone. It seems like everyone
leaves us at the same time, men and children, and I still
don't know why Luis left me—"You've done nothing
wrong, that's just the way it is." He didn't even have the
courage to admit, "Because you're too old. Because you
don't look like the young woman in our wedding photo
anymore," but he doesn't look like the young man in
the photo, either, it's just that women still find him

attractive. Apparently a woman seems old to a man once she reaches the age his mother was when he was an adolescent; I'll bet you didn't know that, either. My ex-husband was careful not to tell me that he moved in with a thirty-year-old woman, but I found out, because Juan told me. Juan thinks I have *the right to know*, my dear boy who doesn't even come to see me once a month, and when he does it's to bring me news like this on top of it. His father met a woman who is thirty years old and I have the right to know, he rages. He didn't ask me whether I wanted to know, but he's not being cruel, just naïve. Is it really only young women who can have such an impact on men? Tell me. But you're not exactly in a position to tell me otherwise. With your young wife.

VITTORIO

What I am hearing, above all, is that you have not yet finished mourning the separation from your ex-husband. That's what we're really talking about—your ex-husband is with another woman, is that it? And she's thirty years old. Answer me, Alicia: did your ex-husband meet another woman?

ALICIA

The only way I could have an impact on Luis would be to commit some monstrous deed, for example, if I hurt his new fiancée, and yesterday I threatened him, and he said, "If you so much as touch a hair on her head I will blow your brains out." "One day," I said, "you pathetic old man, that blonde or brown or red hair you caress with so much passion and surprise will turn gray, too. She can't escape; no matter how much you caress her hair it won't prevent the gray from taking hold, at the root, and while you're at it take a closer look next time—the evil process may already be under way. Spread her hair instead of spreading her legs and take a close look." And you know what he replied? Something monstrously egotistical: "I won't be there to see it." Just like with the baby, he won't be there to see it grow up, but he doesn't care about that, either, he—

VITTORIO

Hold on a minute, Alicia, what baby are you talking about? What baby won't your husband see grow up?

ALICIA

The one he's having with his whore, of course. Just like that, as if it were some Christmas present. Juan is going to have a little brother or a little sister, and I had nothing to do with it, can you imagine?

VITTORIO

I'm so sorry, Alicia, truly I am. It's true that this is unfair. But that's the way life is; we can change a great many things, but certain circumstances are rigid, imposed. We can't change them; all we can do is try to see things from a positive point of view. Your son will surely have a child with his wife and then you'll see how happy you'll be, you'll be able to look after the baby, you'll—

ALICIA

You really don't get it, do you? I don't want to be a grandmother, I still want to be a mother! It seems like you don't understand how important motherhood is to a woman.

VITTORIO

No, I do understand.

ALICIA

No, you don't. You have shown no empathy, from the very start of this conversation. I can tell, you feel nothing, you're distant. You're going to have children with your wife, aren't you? She's pregnant, too? That's why you're so embarrassed . . .

VITTORIO

My wife is not pregnant. She doesn't want children.

ALICIA

That can't be, it's like the poet's "darkness visible"— there's no such thing as women who don't want children, they don't exist, they—

VITTORIO

You are wrong, Alicia. They do exist.

ALICIA

No, they don't, and if I were you, I'd be worried. Your wife is hiding something from you; you should—

VITTORIO

My wife is fine, Alicia, thank you very much, but you are not a benchmark for all women, and you should stop saying "we" when you speak, you should say "I." It might not come as easy to you, but it will be more accurate. At the moment, you are under the impression that you are weeping for all women, that you're defending a cause, "women," as if you were part of a relief organization. But just let me remind you that your tears are yours alone; they belong to you and are not a symbol for anyone else. There are many women your age who are happy. They don't all think the way you do, and you shouldn't go on believing they do. I'll tell you what's at stake here, it's your anger, your sorrow alone. At the risk of repeating myself, there are many women your age who are happy. You'll start making great progress if you understand this. Life doesn't stop, Alicia, and those who want to stop the flow of life are bound to lose. I'm sorry, but this is just a bad period to get through. You may be under the impression that your ex-husband can do everything and you can do nothing, but things will get better; you must simply be a bit more patient. You seem to enjoy being bitter and despondent. But if you face reality, you will see that not all women are bored the way you are. Forgive me, Alicia, but it's not a child you need to lose to feel less bored, it's your money.

ALICIA
You're right, it's time to pay for my session, but you might have pointed it out more courteously.

VITTORIO
That was not what I wanted to point out.

ALICIA
Of course it was.

VITTORIO
You're wrong, Alicia.

ALICIA
Of course I'm wrong. I should never have had this conversation with you, with a man. I should have thought of this before. One should always choose a psychoanalyst of the same sex.

Eva Maria looks at herself in the mirror. Moves closer. Runs her hands over her face. Her daughter had her nose, the shape of her eyes, but not the same color, just the shape. Stella also had a dimple in her chin. Like the bed of a cherry stone. Eva Maria didn't like it on herself, but on Stella she always thought it was pretty—adorable when she was a child, lovely when she had grown up. The paradox of motherhood was that now that dimple was what Eva Maria liked best of all about her face. Eva Maria moves closer to the mirror. Her fingers slide across her face. Her cheeks. Her neck. Her skin is fading, it's true. And it's true she never looks at herself. And it's true she no longer sees herself. Eva Maria places both hands on the edge of the sink. Does not take her eyes off herself. She opens the mirror of the small bathroom cabinet. She takes out a little white makeup bag that has yellowed slightly over time. She takes out her mascara. Tries to paint her eyelashes. She has shed so many tears that she is no longer used to putting on makeup. The mascara has dried out. Eva Maria gives up. Not altogether. She puts a little bit of lipstick on her lips. She looks in the mirror. For once she doesn't look at her dimple. Or her nose. Or the shape of her eyes. But she doesn't judge the result for all that; she doesn't pout or even smile. You can't do everything the first time. Eva Maria closes the little white makeup bag. Yellowed with age. She listens to the sound of the zipper. Her eyes without mascara are shining. Eva Maria has an appointment with Vittorio. He is going to be pleased with what she has found.

"'I should have thought of it sooner. One should always choose a psychoanalyst of the same sex.'"

Eva Maria stresses the last two sentences. Emphatically. Like a bad actress laying it on thick when the text alone would be enough. Her mouth is dry from reading so much. The lipstick has faded. Eaten away by words. Eva Maria gathers up the typed pages. She looks at Vittorio sitting opposite her. She is like a child waiting to be congratulated. Vittorio smiles, in spite of himself. Surely a nervous smile.

"Alicia is a desperate woman. Not a murderer."

"And yet killing seems to be the most extreme expression of despair."

Vittorio shakes his head.

"Not always. And above all, not in Alicia's case."

Eva Maria sits up straight.

"But she goes on and on about how much she hates young women, and about your wife. This last session clearly indicates what she was capable of."

"On the day we had that session, Alicia used Lisandra as a pretext to tell me everything she had to say. But as for Lisandra herself, Alicia couldn't have cared less about her, believe me. But I can see why this cassette would upset you. In a way she's talking about you, the mothers of the Plaza de Mayo, the loss of a child . . ."

Eva Maria moves closer.

"And what if her motives were not as precise as you would like to think they were? What if this woman had decided to take revenge on you for everything she thought she had ever been a victim of? In a fit of madness. What if she decided to attack the symbol of everything tragic in her life by attacking your wife, who was so young, or younger than you, in any case. She says herself that she could kill."

Vittorio smiles. Quite openly this time.

"Not all people who say they could kill actually do kill."

"Stop laughing, Vittorio, this woman is violent. Don't you remember the sound of her voice? It gave me the shivers, just transcribing the cassette."

"A voice can be deceptive—if you knew Alicia, you wouldn't say that. She's a tiny little woman."

"So? Even tiny little women can kill—even 'little old women'— she was that furious with you when she left. It seems you don't realize the state you had gotten her in. You didn't say even one word to comfort her, to defuse the situation."

Vittorio drums his fingers on the edge of the table.

"I didn't get her into any state, she left in that state, and the way a session ends is never just by chance. The patient reaches a point they were bound to reach. If there is one place where chance does not exist, it is in the psychoanalyst's office. Everything there is a matter of will or, if you prefer, of the unconscious, and that's fine, even if a patient is angry when she leaves. If you knew how many times that has happened to me."

Vittorio stops drumming on the edge of the table.

"Even with you, for example."

Eva Maria sits back.

"With me?"

"Yes, if you'll recall . . . the day we disagreed about your son, when I told you that you weren't looking after him properly, that you were leaving him too much on his own. It was a session that was absolutely comparable to this one, don't you remember?"

Eva Maria looks down. A shadow passes over her eyes. Vittorio continues.

"You see, Alicia would have come back—she would have let some time go by, I'll grant you that—but she would have come back. Believe me, intervals like that are often beneficial during analysis."

"Because it was a long time ago, that session?"

"I can't remember . . . roughly two months ago."

"You see, I was right! I'm sure of it, there's something weird going on, I tell you, that woman was prepared to do anything. Maybe she was in love with you?"

"Of course she wasn't; how many times do I have to say it? That session was simply very immodest, and now Alicia must be extremely embarrassed for having said all that, but it won't go any further. Alicia has nothing to do with Lisandra's murder. Is that all you found? Have you listened to all the cassettes?"

Eva Maria goes through the motions of gathering up her papers again. She looks at the wrinkles on her hands. She sees them as if for the first time. She thinks she can even see two brown spots.

"And you didn't even call her when you saw she didn't come back the following week?"

"It's against the code of professional ethics."

"But I thought you had to know how to bend the code when necessary? When it's your recordings, it doesn't bother you. However, it doesn't even occur to you to transgress the code for a poor woman who's having trouble dealing with her runaway old age, no, in that case, not even a little phone call. And what if she's committed suicide, have you thought of that? You disappoint me."

Vittorio remains silent. He looks at Eva Maria.

"I disappoint you. Have you heard yourself? You sound like Alicia now. The point is not to identify with a patient's unhappiness or distress, and that's precisely what you are doing. And yet how hard is it to see that this woman's grudge is not against me, but against life in its most basic form, nature. She says as much, over and over, doesn't she? There is nothing that could comfort her or reconcile her with herself other than to wake up one morning with her twenty-year-old face and body. But that is not in the realm of my power, so I'm sorry if I 'disappoint' you. What did you want me to do for her? Go on, give me the solution! It interests me. What would you have wanted me to do for Alicia?"

Eva Maria looks down. She remains silent. Vittorio places both hands on the table. He leans closer.

"Sleep with her, maybe? To give her back a bit of her femininity, do my utmost, session after session, to fuck her so she'll keep her self-confidence, and while we're at it, should I even stop making her pay for her sessions, just so she won't think I'm sleeping with her for the money, but simply from pure desire—*basta*! I'm not in the mood for barroom psychoanalyzing; we're in a prison here, or more precisely, *I* am in prison, and at the risk of sounding snide I'll say that as prisons go it's not quite as natural as old age. This conversation is absolutely meaningless, and besides, you're not even defending Alicia, you're attacking me. You're attacking me because of what I just reminded you of."

"You didn't remind me of anything!"

"I did. I spoke to you about your son. And you can't stand that. But today wasn't the first time. I was wrong to drag you into this business—you're too fragile, you can't help me; no one can help me. I'm up against the wall."

Vittorio raises his hands to gesture to the guard. Eva Maria grabs his wrist.

"Excuse me, Vittorio, I'm sorry, stay here—you're right, it's not Alicia who killed your wife, if you say so; you know her better than I do. I don't know what came over me, forgive me. But I haven't found anything else, nothing at all, and I've already listened to over half of the cassettes. So when I heard this session, I got carried away, I thought this was it, I thought I'd found a lead to get you out of here. Forgive me, Vittorio."

"Over half of the cassettes." Vittorio shrivels on his chair. Slumps over.

"I'm the one who has to apologize," he says. "I should never have blown up at you like that, but I've had too much in the way of bad news today. I'm at the end of my rope. Believe me, Alicia has nothing to do with Lisandra's death, but I can understand how you might have thought she did; if I'd been in your shoes, I would surely have had the same reaction."

"So tell the police. If I could believe it, they'll believe it, too—there's so much incriminating evidence against her: the argument between you began about your wife, and the way she kept harping on about her, and attacking you where she was concerned. They'll go and question her, and even if she's not the one, even if as soon as they start questioning her it becomes obvious she's innocent, it will teach them to look elsewhere, it will teach them that you are innocent, Vittorio, by suggesting the possibility of someone else's guilt. Even if you don't believe in it, I beg you; otherwise they'll never look elsewhere, they'll stubbornly keep after you. And besides, they might be mistaken and lock up the wrong innocent person in your place."

"Now you are talking nonsense."

"I'm exaggerating... but at least if she were in prison, that woman would no longer have a mirror to look in—she might even be happier. But what did you find out? What is the bad news you mentioned just now?"

"The final results of the autopsy have come through: Lisandra died from her fall. Instantly. Her feet struck the ground first. Incredibly violently. Her high heels pierced her ankles. Her thigh bones were broken. Her body bounced. The back of her skull hit the ground. The back of her head was smashed. Internal bleeding. The autopsy shows no sign of a fight. No sign of strangling. No scratches or bruises. No sign of any blows. At least, not any blows that left a trace. The blood tests show nothing out of the ordinary. There was no trace of alcohol, drugs, or medication. But above all, and here the autopsy is categorical: Lisandra was not raped. I was so relieved when my lawyer told me. I had been thinking about it all the time; just the thought of it terrified me; I couldn't stand the thought she might have suffered like that. But just as I was feeling calmer, at least where that was concerned, my lawyer whispered to me that this was not a good thing. Didn't I realize what this would mean where I was concerned?"

"Come back down to earth, Vittorio! I'm your lawyer, aren't I? You have to trust me. Stop thinking as if you were a free man, and try to think the way the investigators do. The question now is very simple— 'their' question is very simple: 'Who might have killed her without raping her?' A lot of people, obviously. But who else? Who more than anyone? 'The husband,' of course. It's logical, the husband would not take by force something he could have whenever he wanted. And then, a husband who kills his wife, in principle, doesn't really desire her anymore. The results of the autopsy perfectly corroborate their suspicions. The noose is tightening around you. They have no proof, but according to their reasoning, everything is proof. The minute anything changes in their assumptions it points to you. Get a grip, Vittorio; again, come back down to earth."

"I'll never get out of it. If they'd found my sperm on Lisandra, they would have concluded that just because someone just made love to his wife doesn't mean he didn't kill her. I can hear them already, coming out with a new version of the facts, which, once again, will incriminate me, because it's the only story they want to write, a story where I'm the guilty one, I'm the murderer. They've almost managed to make me sorry Lisandra wasn't raped, that there was no trace of someone else's sperm on her; that at least would have put my mind at rest; no, that's not what I mean, but I would have been exonerated, automatically ex-on-er-ated. I've even reached a point where I imagine wanting to kill Lisandra and wanting to tell them how I would have gone about it—I would never have pushed my wife out the window . . . I might have poisoned her . . . or God knows what, I would have rigged some car accident . . . In any case, I would have fixed it so that my alibi was rock solid . . . I would never have been found at the crime scene, acting silly and stupid like that . . . I'm more clever than that, I would have made things disappear so it would look like a burglary . . . but in any case, I wouldn't have let myself be caught red-handed . . ."

"Stop right there, Vittorio, you are talking about murder with malice aforethought, and they're talking about an unpremeditated murder. Which leaves the door wide open to madness, clumsiness, a lack of caution, and which in turn often leads to obvious and indefensible guilt, and that's what they're accusing you of: unpremeditated murder. Nothing more, nothing less. An argument that turned ugly. Why didn't you tell me you'd had an argument with your wife that evening?"

"What are you talking about?"

"Unless your neighbor's deposition was a pack of lies? This is the last time I'll ask you: why didn't you tell me you'd had an argument with your wife that night?"

"I didn't think it was important."

"You didn't think it was important? That you had an argument with your wife the night she died? You have two options: either you tell me what really happened that evening between you and your wife, or else I'll tell you the way I see it—you'll have to get a new lawyer, you'd be better off. Personally, I don't like wasting my time."

"Can't you imagine the way I feel? My life with Lisandra

ended in an argument. My guilt at having walked out like that. It's unbearable, so yes, the less I think about the argument, the better I feel."

"Except that now you are going to have to think about it. You don't choose your next-door neighbors."

"That bitch . . . It's no surprise, coming from her. It must have been her hour of glory, with real policemen, and a real dead body, what a nice change from ordinary little crimes, like who let their garbage cans leak in the stairway, or whose stroller is always in the way in the hall on the third floor, so this time, a dead body, she must have put all her energy into it; she's a nasty piece of work, with spiteful anger to spare, a witness who can only be for the prosecution—all she knows is how to stir up shit, and she invents that shit so it will correspond to her own twisted view of life. So what did she say? What could she have heard, that harpy, with her ear glued to the wall?"

"Don't turn the question around; it's your version of the facts I want: one more time, Vittorio, why did you argue with your wife?"

"Over some trifle."

"If you want my opinion, the investigators will not be satisfied with that answer."

"I hadn't noticed that she was wearing a new dress, I didn't notice anything anymore, I didn't look at her anymore, I didn't love her anymore—that's why we argued, will that do you?"

"Is it true?"

"That I hadn't noticed she was wearing a new dress, yes, but the rest, no, of course not."

"And is that why you went to the movies? To get away from the argument?"

"No, I was already about to leave when Lisandra began criticizing me."

"The neighbor said you argued a lot."

"But my neighbor does nothing all day but look for signs that other people's lives are as miserable as her own. What do you want me to say? That woman is poison. I always used to laugh at her malicious gossip. I would never have imagined that one day it would be turned against me. She's hysterical, and there are millions of gossips like her on the planet. Every time Lisandra and I made love, that crazy bitch would start banging on the wall; it was as if she were following us around the apartment, moving around her place according to how we moved around ours; she would bang and bang again; it was as if she wanted to kill us for loving each other, but she didn't tell them that, of course she didn't, because it would have proven that we loved each other—although the investigators would have rushed to point out that plenty of people make love even when they don't love each other."

"Actually, you're wrong there; she did talk about it, but that was not exactly her version of the facts."

"Oh, no?"

"No. She said that at least your constant arguing spared her from—and I'm quoting here—'your inappropriate cries of love,' your 'shouting like rutting animals,' and that all things considered she actually preferred your arguments—they weren't as obscene. She said that over the last few months your shouting had been nothing less than cries of hatred, and that there were no other cries of any kind that might have pointed to some sort of reconciliation, but of course she could never have imagined it might all lead to a crime. She thought you were just the umpteenth couple who, having exhausted the pleasure they could find in each other's bodies, had ended up hating each other, and were tearing each other apart with their mutual lack of desire. 'After the cries of the body, the cries of the weary soul,' that is exactly what she said, and I can tell you that her deposition had an impact on the investigators."

"Vicious tongues can be quite poetic."

"The problem arises when they are convincing."

"But just because you have an argument with your wife doesn't mean you go and kill her. It's true that we had been arguing quite a lot lately; she was irritable and I was preoccupied, or the other way around; you never know who's at fault at times like that, you just hope that this argument will be the last one and that the happy days will return—but you must know about all that; I hear about arguments like this every day in my office, and even nastier ones; believe me, every couple goes through them."

"I know. But when one member of the couple is found dead, the argument no longer belongs to the basic nature of a love story. It becomes incriminating evidence."

"Except that I did not kill Lisandra, the way those maniacs are insinuating—but what else did my dear neighbor hear that night? I hope that they asked her, at least?"

"Of course."

"Well?"

"Nothing. Her deposition is categorical. She says she didn't hear a thing after your argument, other than the loud music. She says that's all she heard, loud music."

"I don't believe it."

Eva Maria looks at Vittorio. Vittorio takes his head between his hands.

"That's the bad news for the day. You can see why I'm a nervous wreck. Don't look at me like that, Eva Maria."

"And what if it was your neighbor who killed Lisandra? That would explain why she wasn't raped; one woman can't rape another."

A sad smile crosses Vittorio's face.

"You, at least, are on my side. Unfortunately, we can't go jumping on everyone as if they were all potential murderers, and the investigators did do their job: she had an alibi, she was with her daughter. And, no, don't tell me it could be her and her daughter. You have to face facts; my lawyer was right, everything is conspiring against me, one thing after another, irrefutably: the circumstances, the timing, and now the results of the autopsy, and the testimonies. At night I wake up in a sweat, I feel as if I'm caught in a storm forever raging; everything is in disarray . . . And the worst thing of all is Lisandra's funeral . . ."

"What do you mean, Lisandra's funeral?"

"It's tomorrow. And they don't want me to attend. 'Legally, you do not have the right to be present.' Do you realize how far they're prepared to go? How can this be, not allowed to attend my own wife's funeral? She didn't make a will. She will be given the 'ordinary treatment' applied in these cases, a 'standard' mass, and I have no say in the matter, no right to ask for anything, not a song, not a text, not a prayer; there's nothing I can do—they are treating me like a dangerous criminal who will use Lisandra's funeral as an opportunity to escape. And the only thing they'll allow is a bouquet of flowers. They have agreed to leave a bouquet of lilies for me; those were her favorite flowers—I always gave her some on the anniversary of the day we met."

"What's wrong, Vittorio? Are you all right?"

"Yes, yes, I'm fine. I'm just exhausted, that's all. The chief of police hates me; he took an instant dislike to me; it's as if he were making a personal matter out of it—do you know what he said? That the day my name was cleared all I had to do was dig up my wife and have a new funeral more to my liking, but now for the time being, as things stood I'd do better to concentrate on my defense. No matter how I pleaded with him, and told him I would agree to go under escort, he just laughed and said, 'Be reasonable, we're not going to let a suspect attend the funeral of the woman he is supposed to have killed,' and he told me that for a psychoanalyst I was singularly lacking in common sense, although that didn't surprise him—all psychoanalysts lacked common sense."

Eva Maria got there first. Now she looks at the lilies on the steps. She chose the color herself. White. That is how she sees Lisandra, or perhaps Death. There are not many people. People must not have known; they would have had to read the newspaper. There is another bouquet of lilies. Red ones. Vittorio's bouquet. Or so Eva Maria supposes. That is his idea of Lisandra, or perhaps of their love. The color he gave her every year on the anniversary of the day they met. Vittorio does not know that Eva Maria is here. One adjective springs to mind. *Unusual*. A court-appointed church. A court-appointed priest. Police standing guard at the entrance, in their car with tinted windows. Eva Maria got there first. She sat at the back. She watched each of the mourners as they came in. People don't enjoy funerals the way they enjoy weddings. There is no talk of outfits, or hats, or how beautiful some of the women look, or how others have such bad taste. There is no commenting on the guests, other than deep inside. And anyway, there are no guests, just those who want to be here, those who know about it. Eva Maria tries, from their attitude, to determine what ties might have connected each of them to the dead woman. Some faces are openly sad, others impenetrable. She can tell which ones are Lisandra's parents, all the way at the front, weeping. But the others? Friends?

Other patients, like herself? The neighbor? Here the neighbor must not be bothered much by shouts, maybe just the odd rumor. Vicious tongues always find a way to wag. Eva Maria looks at all these bodies gathered here, all these bodies that have finished growing up. She thinks, Childhood is sorely missing at funerals. Eva Maria feels like an outsider. Anyone is allowed to join a funeral procession, and that is precisely why she is there. Perhaps the murderer is there, too, hiding among friends and family, come to attend the ultimate consequence of his act. A madman. An invisible deus ex machina. Eva Maria watches as they all file past the coffin. She wishes a red light would come on above the murderer's head. An elderly couple lingers for a long while, holding hands. They are beautiful. Might they be Vittorio's parents? Eva Maria wonders if she would have grown old at her husband's side if Stella had not died. Their daughter's disappearance brought with it the disappearance of their love, with terrible simultaneity, where her love was concerned, in any case. Eva Maria looks at the "court-appointed" coffin. How comfortable it seems to her, reassuring, compared to the nowhere to which her daughter was consigned. Stella. The bodies of the dead are subdued, made orderly, made-up, a part of humanity restored to them before they are removed from it forever. Her daughter, on the other hand, had remained behind, in the inhuman posture in which death had captured her. As always, Eva Maria's thoughts turn to those who were caught by lava, the men and women and children, the dog pulling on its leash after its masters had fled. All trapped in midgesture, living statues, with lava for a sarcophagus. Water was Stella's sarcophagus. A liquid sarcophagus, gently rocking her, perhaps, but not bringing her back. Eva Maria closes her eyes at the thought that her daughter's eyes are still open, somewhere at the bottom of the Rio de la Plata. And the image becomes even more vivid with her eyes closed—she opens them again, quickly. Her tears fall. Eva Maria is one of those who usurp sorrow at funerals. Who do not weep for the dead body there in front of them, but for the death it reminds them of, or the death it makes them fear. She wanted so badly to bury her daughter. She wonders what Vittorio is picturing at this moment, locked away in his cell. Lisandra lying there between four wooden boards. He can't picture anything. He doesn't even know how she is dressed. Who chose her clothes? Surely her parents. Eva Maria is not the only one who is thinking about Vittorio. Everyone is thinking about him. There is even an empty place in the first row, close to the coffin. As if everyone were waiting for him show up. The awkwardness in the church is palpable, perhaps even more palpable than sorrow. As if the person most entitled to mourn were missing, Vittorio, the tearful husband, the presumed killer. Everything is backward. The funeral of a dead woman is one thing, but of a murdered woman, that's something else entirely. The sorrow of not knowing how she died, this woman they are burying: it impedes mourning, and nothing should ever impede mourning, or there can be no healing. Can anyone here imagine Vittorio pushing his wife out the window? Is anyone here absolutely convinced he did? Eva Maria got there first, and she will be the first to leave. The policemen are waiting. Talking. Laughing. Eva Maria hides behind a tree. She watches as people leave the church. You don't take photos at funerals. Her camera sounds like the song of a sick bird. She doesn't want to miss anyone. Eva Maria is beginning to have a taste for suspicion, the stifling sensation that anyone could have killed Stella. She meant to say Lisandra. She's confusing them. Mixing things up. In her mind now the two dead women are overlapping. The one who makes her suffer so much that she cannot bear to think of her, and the one who did not suffer, who occupies her thoughts for hours on end. And the beggar at the entrance asking for money, the beggar to whom she gave a few coins in exchange for a promise to tell all the women wearing gloves that they are beautiful. You never know, if Alicia is there, she will go away happy, comforted, perhaps reconciled. And what if it was him? That beggar, the madman, the invisible deus ex machina, come to mingle with the procession. Eva Maria wants a red light to go on above his head. The camera hanging from her neck oppresses her. With her hand she squeezes the bark of the tree, tight. Too tight. A few drops fall on her shoes. Red. Her blood dripping. Pain cannot be eased as long as anger reigns.

Eva Maria takes a sip of maté. The newspaper lies on the table, unread. Estéban comes into the kitchen to make his breakfast.

"Morning, Mama. Not too tired?"

Estéban heads over to the fridge.

"I'm sorry about last night . . . for coming into your room like that. But since I saw a light, I thought that—"

Estéban stops. Embarrassed. He runs his fingers through his hair. Eva Maria looks up at him.

"What did you think?"

"Nothing."

Eva Maria takes a sip of maté.

"I was working."

"I saw that. You have a lot of work at the moment."

"Yes."

Estéban busies himself by the toaster. Eva Maria gets to her feet.

"I'm off."

Estéban turns around.

"But it's Saturday."

"So?"

"You don't work on Saturday."

"I've got errands."

"Errands?"

"Yes, I feel like going out."

"Oh, good idea . . . I'll come with you! I feel like going out, too."

"I'd rather go on my own, forgive me . . . I—I'm going shopping for clothes. You'll get bored waiting for me."

"Clothes? But you haven't bought anything in ages."

"Well, you see, anything can happen."

Eva Maria leaves the kitchen. The door slams. Estéban turns around. He parts the curtain at the window. He watches Eva Maria walking down the street. A backpack on one shoulder. He's never seen that backpack. No, wait a minute. It looks like Stella's backpack. Estéban watches as Eva Maria boards the bus. He can't get over it. For the first time in years, it's not to go to work. "You see, anything can happen." Estéban smiles. The shadow of the bus passes over his face. Estéban's eyes are gleaming.

Eva Maria puts the backpack on the table. Vittorio is sitting opposite her.

"I'm so glad to see you," he says.

"You're going to be disappointed. I haven't found anything."

Eva Maria takes out a thick folder.

"I listened to all the cassettes, even the most neutral ones, even the most friendly ones, but I didn't find anything. I'm so sorry, maybe I missed something; it's not crystal clear, you can interpret things so many ways, and above all I don't know your patients well enough—we already made one mistake with Alicia. I brought you all the transcriptions—you're the only one who might be able to see clearly into all these sessions, maybe you'll find something. I'll leave them with the guard so that you can read them again at your leisure."

"No, don't do that, they would read them and they'd be bound to ask me questions. Give them to my lawyer instead—but did you say that you have them all?"

Eva Maria hesitates. Ever so briefly. For a split second.

"Yes."

Vittorio joins his hands. In a gesture of answered prayer.

"So you have Felipe's, then?"

"Felipe?"

Eva Maria thinks, then says, "The guy who was having problems with his wife."

"You could put it that way. So you have it, right? I have to check something. I thought about it two nights ago and it's been bugging me ever since. I have to see if I'm right."

Eva Maria opens the folder. She hunts among the many typed pages. She does indeed remember that session, a rather tense one, but nothing particularly unpleasant. Vittorio, however, seems sure of what he has said.

"Do you mind reading it to me? I'm always better at listening than reading. Read me everything; I want to hear it all, from the first to the last word."

Eva Maria begins reading. Vittorio closes his eyes. Felipe's face comes to him. His body, too. His gestures. It's like when he used to listen to the cassettes again in the evening alone in his office. Without thinking, Vittorio's hand closes around the shape of a glass, a brandy glass. His attention focused on Eva Maria's voice.

FELIPE

VITTORIO
Good morning.

FELIPE
Morning.

VITTORIO
Am I mistaken, or is something bothering you?

FELIPE
As Borges used to say, "A gentleman can only be interested in lost causes." We had another argument.

VITTORIO
With your wife?

FELIPE
Who else would it be?

VITTORIO
What about?

FELIPE
About everything; she never stops, she finds fault with me over everything.

VITTORIO

But what exactly was it, during this most recent
argument?

FELIPE

I'll tell you, I don't even know how it started. All I do
know is that it always ends in the same way.

VITTORIO

Meaning?

FELIPE

She begins to cry and scream and hurl insults at me.

VITTORIO

And what do you do?

FELIPE

Nothing. I go into my study and wait for it to blow over.
There's nothing I can do.

VITTORIO

Perhaps you should talk, stick up for yourself, if you
think she's attacking you unfairly.

FELIPE

Of course she's attacking me unfairly! But there's
nothing I can say. Have you ever tried to talk to a woman
who's in the middle of screaming?

VITTORIO

Haven't you?

FELIPE

What do you mean by that?

VITTORIO

Was your argument about your little boy again?

FELIPE

I don't know; it might've been.

VITTORIO

Yes or no?

FELIPE

She didn't want to take him to the park. I told her that a little boy can't stay shut inside all day long. A boy needs physical exercise. *Mens sana in corpore sano.*

VITTORIO

And she didn't appreciate your remark.

FELIPE

Apparently not.

VITTORIO

How did she react?

FELIPE

I told you. The way she always does. She went into a state, began crying, screaming at me, and calling me every name in the book. In front of the boy, on top of it.

VITTORIO

So you went into your study.

FELIPE

Well, I asked her to be quiet. Because of the boy. But she shouted even louder. I gave her fair warning. She should have shut up.

VITTORIO

Fair warning about what?

FELIPE

That I would slap her.

VITTORIO

You slapped your wife?

FELIPE

She was asking for it.

VITTORIO

That's your opinion. We'll get back to that. Tell me what happened next.

FELIPE

There's nothing to tell. She went out.

VITTORIO

You didn't go after her to apologize?

FELIPE

The boy was really frightened when I stood up, but I apologized. I explained that these are things that happen when grown-ups get into big arguments.

VITTORIO

And did you apologize to your wife?

FELIPE

She acts as if I don't exist. She took her things. She's sleeping in the other bedroom. If she thinks I'm going to give in . . .

VITTORIO

Is this the first time?

FELIPE

Yes. We've always slept together.

VITTORIO

What I meant is, is this the first time you've slapped her?

FELIPE

What do you think? That I beat my wife?

VITTORIO

I don't think anything, I simply wanted to know whether it was the first time you had come to blows. Perhaps I'm mistaken, but I do get the impression that things have not been going well between you and your wife since your son was born.

FELIPE

Indeed, you are mistaken.

VITTORIO

How was your wife's pregnancy? You've never told me about that period.

FELIPE

Her pregnancy went very well, thank you, Doctor! After all, as St. Jerome says, "Pregnancy is no more than a swelling of the uterus."

VITTORIO

Spare me, please stop talking through quotations. I've already told you a hundred times, it's *your* words I want to hear.

FELIPE

What do you want me to say? You accused me of not talking about my wife's pregnancy. I'm talking about it as best I can.

VITTORIO

I'm not accusing you of anything. I'm simply taking the liberty of pointing out that you often argue about your child.

FELIPE

And I tell you you're barking up the wrong tree.

VITTORIO

I'm not barking up the wrong tree, I'm trying to find an explanation.

FELIPE

There is no explanation; we argue—we argue, that's all.

VITTORIO

Why don't you want it to be about your child? It happens a lot with couples.

FELIPE

She wanted that child; there is no reason for us to argue over him.

VITTORIO

"She wanted that child." Why? And you didn't?

FELIPE

Of course I did.

VITTORIO

For a split second there, I might have believed the opposite.

FELIPE

You should never trust a split second.

VITTORIO

Here, I do. You didn't want a child?

FELIPE

Stop asking me that! I told you I did.

VITTORIO

You see, it's not very pleasant when someone has to worm it out of you.

FELIPE

I don't like your tone, Doctor.

VITTORIO

It's not my tone that you don't like, it's my question; you didn't want a child, is that it? You reluctantly agreed to have a child, maybe to please your wife. And now your wife has realized that she forced you into having a child with her and she cannot stand the thought. She's making you pay the price of your reluctance and her remorse.

FELIPE

Of course I wanted a child, perhaps not as much as she did, but of course I wanted a child—who doesn't want a child?

VITTORIO

Then why didn't you take him to the park yourself? Don't you look after your son?

FELIPE

But of course I look after my brother.

VITTORIO

Your brother?

FELIPE

What do you mean, my brother?

"Slow down, Eva Maria."

VITTORIO

You just said, "But of course I look after my brother."

FELIPE

I said "my son."

VITTORIO

No, you said "my brother."

FELIPE

Well, I meant to say "my son"—I made a mistake;
everyone makes them.

VITTORIO

No, not everyone. You see, session after session, no
matter where we start, we always end up back with your
brother.

FELIPE

No, we don't always end up back with my brother.
I made a mistake; let's not make a big deal about it.

VITTORIO

Do you miss him?

FELIPE

Who?

VITTORIO

Your brother.

FELIPE

Not at all.

VITTORIO

How long has it been now, since he died?

FELIPE

I don't keep track.

VITTORIO

Does your son remind you of your brother?

FELIPE

Not at all; why do you say that?

VITTORIO

How old is your son now? Around four years old, isn't he?
When your brother was four, you were six, which is
when memories begin. Maybe subconsciously your little
boy reminds you of your brother.

FELIPE

No, he doesn't remind me of my brother. Not at all.

VITTORIO

You reproached your mother for loving your brother
more than she loved you. Maybe you think your wife
loves your child more than she loves you?

FELIPE

If it pleases you to think so.

VITTORIO

It doesn't please me, Felipe. How am I supposed to help you if you don't tell me everything? I get the impression you are hiding things from me.

FELIPE

I'm not hiding anything.

VITTORIO

You're not hiding anything?

FELIPE

No.

VITTORIO

Then if you're not hiding anything, I'll tell you what I think. I think your wife wants to leave you and she doesn't dare tell you. These repeated arguments are her way of trying to get through to you. She doesn't dare take responsibility for causing the breakup, and she is waiting for it to come from you, so she's trying to drive you over the edge.

FELIPE

Do you really think she wants to leave? What about the boy?

VITTORIO

I think it's not easy for a woman to abandon her child. Maybe she can't get used to being a mother; maybe she can't find her place. It happens; there are women who don't accept their children. At least, not if it means sacrificing their own life. Maybe she's not happy with you anymore. Maybe she has a lover.

FELIPE

She doesn't have a lover.

VITTORIO

How do you know?

FELIPE

I would know.

VITTORIO

The very principle of a lover is that the husband doesn't know he exists.

FELIPE

It's not possible. I did everything I could so she could get this child. She can't leave because of him.

VITTORIO

And when you say "so she could *get* this child," what am I supposed to make of that?

FELIPE

Nothing. You're not supposed to make anything of it.

VITTORIO

Forgive me for belaboring this, but for her to *get* a child, that is a rather strange expression to use to refer to pregnancy.

FELIPE

What do you want me to say? That we adopted our child, well then, so be it: we adopted our child. It's not a crime.

VITTORIO

But you told me your wife was pregnant.

FELIPE
She wasn't pregnant. We tried for two years and finally adopted.

VITTORIO
Why did you never tell me about this?

FELIPE
I tell you about my problems and it wasn't a problem.

VITTORIO
Maybe the adoption was not such an easy thing for her.

FELIPE
She was overjoyed when she saw the little baby. She wanted a child so badly. It was afterward that she changed. Later. After a few months had gone by.

VITTORIO
You really should talk to her about it. Having a child of your own or someone else's child is not the same thing, no matter what people say. To make it become the same thing, you have to want it. It requires acceptance on a psychological level. Great serenity. Your wife still doesn't know that you come to see me.

FELIPE
No.

VITTORIO
Why don't you tell her?

FELIPE
It's none of her business.

VITTORIO

You should tell her. You could even come with her.

FELIPE

Are you kidding? There's nothing for her here.

VITTORIO

You know, I do consult with couples. You should come with her. At least once. Maybe in my presence you could get some things out into the open, clarify them.

FELIPE

All she'll do is ask you questions about me.

VITTORIO

What sort of questions?

FELIPE

I don't know, she'll try to find things out. But there's nothing to find out. I love her, I've never cheated on her, I've never hurt her.

VITTORIO

Apart from that slap.

FELIPE

She was asking for it, she was screaming in my face—I couldn't get her to shut up—and then the boy was there; it was as if that was just what she was waiting for.

VITTORIO

Maybe.

FELIPE

What do you mean, "maybe"?

VITTORIO
Maybe she was waiting for precisely that. Maybe she wanted to prove to herself that you could be violent.

FELIPE
What do you mean?

VITTORIO
You really should talk to her.

FELIPE
You think she wants to leave me.

VITTORIO
I don't know; I said that mainly to get you up against the wall.

FELIPE
You, too.

VITTORIO
Me, too. You should ask her, quite simply. Things can only get better through dialogue.

FELIPE
She doesn't talk to me anymore.

VITTORIO
You managed to get other people to talk.

FELIPE
What did you say?

VITTORIO
Nothing. Time is up, Felipe; I have another patient in five minutes. Think about everything we've just said;

we'll talk about it again next time. You know the
way out.

FELIPE

Yes, I do. I can trust you, can't I?

VITTORIO

Trust me?

FELIPE

You won't say anything.

VITTORIO

Say anything about what?

FELIPE

Well, about it.

VITTORIO

What "it"?

FELIPE

The adoption.

VITTORIO

Well then, just say so! Call things by their name.
Adoption, as you say, "is not a crime." No, I won't say
anything. It's my job, to know how to keep quiet.

"The door to your office closes, and you can be heard murmuring, 'Filthy bastard.'"

Eva Maria's voice is lifeless. She creases the pages. She can't turn them anymore. Her finger is dry. Eva Maria has no more saliva. She needs a drink. But in this visiting room, she can't drink. The sentences are echoing in her head. In her dry throat.

Have you ever tried to talk to a woman who's in the middle of screaming?

Haven't you?

You see, it's not very pleasant when someone has to worm it out of you.

Maybe she was waiting for precisely that. Maybe she wanted to prove to herself that you could be violent.

You managed to get other people to talk. Filthy bastard.

Eva Maria's gaze is unsteady. Vittorio's eyes are glued to the table. His head between his hands. She is afraid of understanding. She asks him a question. Vittorio doesn't answer. Lost in thought, he says repeatedly, "I was right. I was right." So Eva Maria asks her question again. Louder, her voice even more toneless.

"That man belonged to the junta, didn't he?"

Vittorio raises his head. He nods. Eva Maria recoils.

"And you have been seeing him?"

"Yes."

"But how could you agree to see a bastard like that?"

"Because he came to me."

"Because he came to you? But you should have spat in his face, you should have kicked him out of your office, literally, smashed his face in, that's all he deserves. And then you saw me, after that? As if it were no big deal. And you tried to comfort me for Stella's disappearance, even though only a few minutes earlier, you might have been comforting her murderer."

"Every patient is a unique human being, independent of my other patients. They come to me with their problems and I try to help them; it's my job. He worked for the ESMA,* that's all I know. No sooner did we bring it up than the subject was closed."

"The Navy School of Mechanics—they were the worst."

Vittorio waves his hand in space.

"The worst was everywhere in those days, and you know that very well. In any case, Felipe didn't tell me any more about his work back then than he does now."

Eva Maria seems even more upset.

"'His work back then'—I don't understand. How long have you been seeing him?"

"There's no point counting the years, but yes, I was already seeing him . . . back then . . . if that's what you want to know."

Eva Maria leaps to her feet. She shouts.

"You're just like them!"

The guard moves closer to her.

"If you don't calm down, señora, I will have to interrupt your visit."

Eva Maria sits back down. The guard moves away. Eva Maria collapses.

"By helping that butcher, you were part of their murderous system! And how many others did you see?"

Vittorio leans closer.

"What did you think? That Felipe came to see me to ask me to help him kill? Don't be grotesque. His only problems were always his childhood, his brother, and his wife. Let me repeat, he never spoke to me about his work."

---

* ESMA: Escuela Superior de Mecánica de la Armada (Navy Petty-Officers School of Mechanics). This military school was the largest of the 340 detention centers used by the Videla dictatorship; over five thousand people were tortured and murdered there.

"This man doesn't come to see you because he has a bad conscience about torturing and killing but because things are not going well with his wife—and that butcher, that piece of shit, has found someone he can talk to, and that someone is you! My daughter was killed by a guy like him—he may even be the one who killed her—and you want me to accept the fact that you are his shrink?"

"Who knows whether Felipe might not have done even more harm if I hadn't been seeing him? I've always hoped to change him, but not by attacking him head-on about the things that seem as unacceptable to me as they do to you. One time I did try to open his eyes, but the conversation quickly turned ugly. He went into an icy rage; his rationale was as solid as a rock; his convictions were unshakable; he said he was acting for 'national security,' that the communists and all the *subversive elements* were dangerous—he had to prevent them from causing harm, he had to neutralize them. Felipe believes that it is thanks to these methods that he got the job done. He has no remorse. He gives orders and takes them, no qualms; all that matters is success. After all these years, I have figured out what makes him tick. I told myself that if I managed to help him deal with his childhood trauma, I would help the man he had become. I was under the impression that I had some sort of control over him, but I was wrong, completely wrong. I could never have imagined he would do such a thing. Why didn't I see the connection earlier? It seems so obvious to me now. But I didn't see a thing, I didn't suspect a thing. I had to be in prison to understand."

Eva Maria sits up straight.

"Understand what?"

"I can't say for sure, but everything points in that direction. It's a known fact that they were reserved for officers."

"What are you talking about?"

"The child. His little boy. He wasn't adopted. He's a stolen child."

Eva Maria stifles a cry. Vittorio stares into space.

"And if what I have imagined is correct, it doesn't stop there."

Eva Maria looks at Vittorio. Vittorio looks at Eva Maria. He no longer sees her. He is using her. As a visual support for his thoughts. His reasoning is not in place. He needs to speak in order to reason. To voice his thoughts. Vittorio is not speaking to Eva Maria. He is thinking out loud.

"Felipe had always despised his brother, a latent jealousy that went back to childhood. It happens a lot, the older child toward the younger, finding it hard to accept the new birth. According to Felipe, his parents preferred his brother—whether it was an imagined or a real preference, I have no idea. Felipe and his wife had already been trying to have a child for some time, without success. I remember it very well; he spoke about it a lot. One day, he came to my office very perturbed: he had just found out that his brother's wife was pregnant, yet again—his brother succeeding where all he did was fail. He probably couldn't stand it. A few months later, I can't remember exactly how much time had gone by, he told me they had died, his brother and sister-in-law. It was brutal. A car crash. 'Natural selection,' was how he put it, coldly, for sure, but given the lack of love he showed for his brother, it didn't surprise me. I could never have imagined he was involved. When shortly after the accident he informed me that his wife was pregnant, I didn't think there was anything amiss. How could I know? It was his brother's imminent fatherhood that must have blinded him and driven him to act. For the sake of his competition with him he was prepared to do anything. It's so sordid, and yet it makes sense. That's why he made the slip. 'But of course I look after my brother.' The child, the child he says he adopted. It's his brother's child. He took him. After killing the parents, or arranging for them to die, I have no idea. And his sister-in-law, like most of those so-called subversive elements, must have given birth in one of their special cells, the cells they set aside for pregnant women, and after that they got rid of her, too, like the other mothers of stolen babies. After he had helped himself to the child. It was too easy, too tempting to use the system that was already in place, the existing organization, to deal with his personal problems. Felipe was surely not the only one who had done something like that. Violence had become the answer to all his problems. He slapped his wife, and it wasn't a matter of ideological conviction, either, simply anger. He didn't want his brother to have a baby if he couldn't himself. Childhood jealousy with an adult's weapons."

Eva Maria is speechless. Her analytical mind is paralyzed. Vittorio's is going full steam.

"So this is what might have happened that night. When Felipe left my office, he was already sorry he had revealed his secret and, above all, he believed I had figured out what really lay behind this so-called adoption: the fact that his son is a stolen child—he may even have thought that I figured out it was his brother's child. When a person is afraid of being found out, they are afraid of being completely exposed; they don't realize that the whole truth rarely comes to light all at once. Maybe he also heard me calling him a 'filthy bastard' through the door—a torturer's ears are used to listening out for the slightest murmur—and the insult touched a sensitive nerve. And then there were all my insinuations—I couldn't help it, some thoughts just slipped out. He knew very well what I thought of him deep down."

Vittorio closes his eyes.

"So. Let's just suppose. Felipe now thinks I have become dangerous. His enemy; in any case the enemy of his secret. So he decides to get rid of me. But that evening, I'm not at home."

Vittorio opens his eyes.

"Here's what happened. Felipe came upon Lisandra. Maybe it was an accident? A botched attempt. No, Felipe is no amateur. Maybe he sent someone to do the dirty work for him? So he wouldn't get his hands dirty. Maybe things went wrong with that someone. No, Felipe wouldn't have involved anyone else in his crime, no accomplices; that would be taking the risk of being betrayed one day, and that's not a risk Felipe would have taken—he knows only too well how impulsive betrayal can be. He used to say, 'In every friend there sleeps half a traitor.'"

Vittorio formulates his questions and his answers. Like during a session. But today, it's not a patient's life that is at stake, but his own. His life. His freedom. Vittorio knows this. But he's never experienced it the way he does right now. All the difficulty of reasoning for himself. For the self that is in danger.

"And what if Felipe had it all set up so I would be accused? In prison, accused of the murder of my wife, I could no longer harm him.

"No. There's no proof that in prison I can no longer harm him. And besides, that's too complicated; yet again, it would be simpler just to kill me."

Vittorio has only one lead to find his way out of here. He cannot let it go. He crushes it. Pounds it. Vittorio is losing all lucidity. He is eager to find another culprit. His reasoning is leading him astray. He is no longer driven by a thirst for truth but by the fear of remaining in prison. His thoughts are getting carried away.

"And what if he spoke to his wife the way I advised him to? What if he told her he had confessed to me that the child was not theirs? Besides, how much did she know, exactly, about the child? Surely Felipe would not have told her anything. Surely she would have figured it out for herself a few weeks or a few months after the arrival of this *prodigal child*; she suspected the terrible truth. Because she must know, that alone would explain why she behaved the way she did toward Felipe, her permanent anger. She knows that her son is one of the five hundred children stolen under the junta, the five hundred children the state is looking for, to give them back to their biological families. So she asked him to eliminate me, out of a fear of losing her child. When you have learned to kill for ideology, you can kill for love. He is used to obeying orders. He goes home. He talks to his wife. Except that she asks him to kill both of us. Lisandra and me. I can hear her from here, using her female psychology, sharpened by the maternal paranoia of losing her child—so her thoughts were definitely criminal—to suggest that it wouldn't be enough to get rid of only me. I was bound to have spoken to my wife, for sure; this story was far too interesting for a husband who wanted to entertain his wife over the course of a meal, a meal which as a rule was too silent, to relieve her of boredom, a terrible story about a child—no one could resist telling such a story, whether they were a shrink or not, whether there was doctor-patient privilege or not. It wouldn't be enough to get rid of me; he would have to get rid of my wife as well. They couldn't let anyone else find out. So, let's just suppose. Felipe comes to our house, he rings the bell, he doesn't give up; Lisandra eventually opens the door; Felipe makes all those gestures he is specialized in, until he pushes Lisandra out the window; he thinks he'll find me in my study or somewhere in the house—I should have been there, as a rule Tuesday evening I am there, it's Thursday evening that I go out—and he is getting ready to deal with me as well, according to who knows what sort of gruesome scenario: the famous lovers' quarrel that has turned ugly, everyone seems to like that one, there's no reason for them not to have thought of it as well—'a man commits suicide after pushing his wife out the window.' Perfect. The perfect crime. As screenplays go, you can't beat it. Except that I'm not there. And we know what happened after that."

Eva Maria looks at his thick black hair as he shakes his head left to right. She stares at it so hard that it seems to her it is his hair that is speaking. Where else could such a dark voice come from?

"I don't know anymore . . . I don't know what I'm saying . . . just because Felipe deserves to end his life in prison doesn't mean that he killed Lisandra."

Vittorio falls silent. Not because he's finished, but to gather his thoughts. Then he continues.

"You're right: I have to show those bastard cops that I must be innocent. I can't give them the cassette, no—for sure that would backfire against me. But my memories can be very precise. I can imply that I have my doubts regarding Felipe; they'll conduct their investigation, and even if they don't go about it altogether whole-heartedly, at least they will check his alibi for that evening, the night of the murder—they will have to, my lawyer will make sure they do. After that, we'll see."

This time Vittorio falls silent for good. As if he had been making an intense physical effort. A thin layer of sweat is pearling on his forehead. Eva Maria says nothing. She, too, is drained. Without having said anything. Drained from having discovered such an unthinkable truth. *Vittorio, shrink to torturers.* Vittorio looks at her. He knows. Something has broken between them today. In her. He hears the guard coming up behind him. The visit is over. Vittorio stands up. He gives Eva Maria a small wave. To say good-bye. Eva Maria doesn't respond. She sits with her fists clenched on the table. Her body is as stiff as a robot. Her right hand opens then closes. She doesn't realize. Vittorio thinks about sign language. He remembers the day Lisandra cried out, unhappily, "Deaf people cannot dance. How sad for them. Why don't you learn sign language, my love? Deaf people, too, have the right to see a psychologist, and besides, it would be a change for you from always having to listen or speak, if you could look, simply look; it's so good sometimes, my love." Lisandra was like a child; when she thought she had a good idea, she always went on and on about it. "Tell me, will you do it, my love?" And just as he would have done with a child, he let her believe the dream was possible. "I'll think about it." "You promise?" "Promise." Vittorio thought of all the times he had promised; promises he made to Lisandra that he never kept. But Lisandra expected too much from human beings; it was her shortcoming to always want them to be better than they could ever be. Because human beings are bad, that's the way it is, and he should never have let her believe the contrary. Perhaps none of this would ever have happened. Behind Vittorio the door to the visiting room slams. Vittorio is wrong. Wanting human beings to be better than they are does not mean one does not know they are bad. If only Vittorio could have imagined just how profoundly Lisandra knew how evil human beings are.

Eva Maria comes to her senses. She doesn't remember leaving the visiting room. She doesn't remember how she got here. She looks at all the passengers around her. Felipe might be here among them. Torturers take the bus nowadays. Felipe. Maybe she has already seen him at Vittorio's office. She has sat right where he sat. On the sofa. Her clothes have touched his clothes. Unsurprisingly, Eva Maria feels nauseous. Unsurprisingly, the nausea does not go any further. All these years, Eva Maria's body has denied her even the relief of vomiting. A last sign of pride? She has no more pride, and it's not such a bad thing that it is confined to her body. Felipe. The guy goes on living, whereas her life has stopped, perhaps because of him. Felipe what, anyway? Vittorio refused to give her his last name. He was already sorry he had told her as much as he had; he didn't want to run the risk that she might go looking for Felipe; she was mistaken if she thought he hadn't understood what she had in mind. It was too dangerous. She wanted to take the law into her own hands? Did he have to remind her that the law had absolved Felipe, along with all the others? There was nothing she could do against him. Vittorio was right. Eva Maria looks at the passersby on the sidewalk. Nowadays torturers are free to roam the streets. Felipe might be there among them. All these torturers had to do to go on living was get lost in the crowd. It was impossible now to separate the wheat from the chaff. Eva Maria winces. No one will ever bother them again. Last Christmas, the worst one in her life. The fifth Christmas without Stella. And above all, that law. A national disgrace. Law 23,492, passed just like that, on the night of December 24, like all the worst laws, the ones they don't want anyone to oppose, the ones they want to push through quickly without anyone noticing. Criminal pursuit forbidden. Against all the crimes committed under the military dictatorship. Pardoned! The arbitrary arrests. The torture. The assassinations. *Punto final.* A new class of citizens in Argentina was born that Christmas night. Those who are granted impunity because they are military. And now *Due Obedience*, which absolves also the lower-ranking officers in the name of the hierarchical principle. Alfonsín!* What a bastard! To give the torturers the task of being their own judges. The decontamination of self by self. Hypocrisy. Sophism. The torturers decided on the amnesty: they colluded in the worst forms of inhumanity. In Argentina, we drink maté and we swallow impunity; in Argentina, we dance the tango, and so do torturers. But you won't find that in the tourist guides. Eva Maria looks at the woman sitting across from her. Whose side was she on? Impunity resolves nothing. Impunity imposes impossible cohabitation on murderers and their victims; it exacerbates suspicion and hatred. In the deepest recesses of the soul. In that secret place where bile gathers and accumulates. The heart of a volcano. In that hiding place where the most violent anger lurks, the anger that ravages everything when it erupts. Because it will not fail to erupt. In the light, perhaps, of another historical context, but it will erupt. And

---

* Raúl Alfonsín, the Argentinian president behind the two laws on impunity, the Full Stop Law (*Punto Final*) and the Law of Due Obedience.

if this generation doesn't demand justice, the next one will. Stella, my beloved child, the torturers really are roaming the streets today, and you are not, you are not having a happy life in Paris or London or New York, and no, you are not a "so-called" *desaparecida*, you truly are one.* Eva Maria feels like screaming. She remains silent. She is not the only one. Impunity, the straitjacket of the Argentine people. Eva Maria could make her accusation, but there is no one to arrest them. She lifts her fingers to her mouth. A warm liquid flows through her fingers; all her pride has just given way. The woman sitting across from her holds out a handkerchief. Eva Maria doesn't see it. She is looking at the stained floor at her feet. She is thinking about volcanic eruptions and she reminds herself that they make the soil more fertile. She wonders if tomorrow, on the floor of this bus, a vine stock will have grown.

---

* "Believe me, there are a lot of so-called *desaparecidos* living very well in Paris, London, New York, or Washington." These were General Videla's words to brush off the thousands of *desaparecidos* massacred by his regime.

Eva Maria slams the door. She thinks she is walking. She is running. She bangs into the furniture in the corridor. Without even thinking, she finds herself naked in the shower. She turns the faucet. The water is scorching. Eva Maria fills her mouth. She spits. To get rid of that vile taste. She spits. How could Vittorio have been treating that piece of shit? She will never forgive him. He could have told her anything—she would have understood anything—that he had been a coward, that he had been afraid of reprisals, that he had feared for his life—anything—if he had agreed not to continue sessions with Felipe. Everyone knew about it; the military could intervene wherever they liked, whenever they liked. But Vittorio had never thought about it. Eva Maria had read as much in his eyes: they accepted everything without flinching. She would have understood anything. Anything except to hear him tell her that it was his duty to help Felipe the way he helped her, that he must not make any distinction, it was his job. What a fine cover-up! He called it his job, but it was voyeurism, an unhealthy curiosity, an attraction to the dark side of humanity. In the end psychoanalysts have no interest in just looking after good people, it has to be said; the deeper they explore the nature of evil, the dregs of humanity, the more alive they feel. Didn't she "study only dormant volcanoes, leaving aside the extinct ones"? She knew what it meant, after all, to "study what was harmful and ignore anything tranquil"—she could understand him, right? Yes, she could understand. But she could not forgive him. It is not always enough to understand in order to forgive. Eva Maria scrubs her body with all her strength. How could she have let Vittorio sit there and tell her all that? The sound of the water on the tiles cannot stop her from hearing him, still. Clearly. "You set yourself up as the supreme judge, Eva Maria; you have told me what you think deep down, and I'm going to tell you what I think deep down. Because you think that with your nose stuck in your little diagrams, in your little notebooks, and your little curves you are useful? Don't make me laugh! If a volcano is going to become active, it will become active and you can't stop it, any more than I can stop my patients from being first and foremost autonomous, active human beings. Our two professions are very similar, in the end. Preventive, that's what we both are, preventive. And prevention has never stopped tragedies from happening. Even if you are there, you and all the analysts on the planet, when the planet wants to lose its temper, it loses its temper. So please, Eva Maria, don't talk to me about usefulness. I have failed, too, as surely as you have; we all fail in that little territory where the purpose of our work is set. Sometimes I go about it badly, to be sure, but I think I have helped more individuals on this planet than you have, so don't come here singing your refrain about humanity. Go back to your diagrams, study your photographs, without even being capable of looking after your son, who is far more alive than any of your volcanoes, just in case you hadn't noticed, and who has a far greater need of you." Eva Maria is sitting on the floor, under the shower. Her head between her knees. "Whether you like it or not, I will go on thinking that I did what was best where Felipe was concerned. Don't get me wrong, I find that whole period as repulsive as you do, but I've chosen my side, that of neutrality, that of wanting to help, without preconceived ideas, or by trying at least to have as few of them as possible, the only side that seems tenable to me with regard to my profession. I can appreciate the fact that you don't find it convincing, but that is my job and that is the way I intend to perform it, or at least intended to perform it, because now that I'm in this fucking prison, I can't really help anyone. But that must make you happy, no? You must be really pleased now?" Eva Maria turns off the water. She stands there with her heels firmly on the streaming floor. Yes, indeed, she is very happy, for if Felipe was the one who killed Lisandra, well then, for Vittorio it's like Frankenstein—the creature has turned against him. He's learned his lesson. You cannot play the sorcerer's apprentice. Not with bodies or with souls. Eva Maria wraps a towel around her damp hair. Anger cannot be cleansed. She takes the photographs out of her bag. She had completely forgotten to show them to Vittorio. Eva Maria is beside herself. Not for one second did Vittorio look at the stolen child as a drama in itself; not for one second was he moved. All that mattered to him was that the child represented a possible motive for Felipe in Lisandra's murder. Eva Maria no longer recognizes Vittorio. She had always felt so close to him, but now she hates him, despises him. She lets out a laugh. Vicious. Sarcastic. Maybe Vittorio didn't want to give her Felipe's last name, but the man will pay all the same. The case of "stolen babies" was not covered by the laws of impunity. Under the military dictatorship, they could torture and kill, but not steal babies. There were limits, after all. A fragment of justice in a swamp of injustice. All the forced, contrived adoptions—that's where they'll get Felipe. The moment Vittorio shares his doubts with the police, they will open a new investigation. Felipe may not pay for all his crimes, but he will lose the child. The boy will be taken away from him and restored to his biological parents, and if Vittorio's version is correct, if his biological parents are dead, then he will be given to his grandparents, who will know how to protect him against their Cain of a son. Eva Maria spreads the photographs of the funeral out on her desk. She starts looking. A couple with a child. A man with a child. A little boy. Education, for a torturer, surely begins by teaching children to confront death. Very young. As early as possible. To make death seem normal so that one day you can spread it around without having any qualms. *FELIPE: You see, my boy, there is a lady lying in that wooden box over there: her eyes are closed; she's dead; they're going to put her in the ground. THE CHILD: But Mommy told me you go to heaven when you die . . . FELIPE: That's just rubbish for girls that your mother has been making up; don't listen to her. When you die, you go in the ground, my boy, and you don't come out again, and that lady, it's even a good thing she died, believe me, good riddance— sometimes people have to die, that's the way it is.* But there is no little boy in the photographs. Eva Maria knows this. She remembers now. She had noticed. How there are never any children at funerals. And besides, she knows these photographs by heart. She has looked at them so many times. Without ever seeing a child. She even had them enlarged, hoping that the change in format might cause the murderer to emerge. Now as she looks at them, Eva Maria is still hoping. A red light. Her magical thinking does not abandon her. It's stubborn. Eva Maria is waiting for these photographs, like a horror film, to suddenly reveal the presence of an individual she had not seen at the time. A couple with a child. A man with a child. A little boy. Then she would take the incriminating photograph to the mothers on the Plaza de Mayo and it would be the first exhibit for the investigation. But life is not a horror film. Unfortunately. Eva Maria shoves the photographs away in a rage. There is a knock at the door. She jumps.

"Just a minute!"

Eva Maria hastily tidies the photographs into her desk drawer.

Eva Maria turns to look at the door to her room. Estéban is standing on the threshold. In high spirits.

"So, can I see them? The clothes?"

"What clothes?"

"You went shopping . . ."

Estéban steps closer to his mother. Eva Maria stiffens.

"I didn't find anything."

Estéban stands still. He runs his fingers through his hair.

"It doesn't matter; there's always next time."

"That's right. Next time."

"We won't be eating too late, will we?"

"I need another hour or so."

"Okay. I'll wait for you. I thought I'd make some empanadas, is that okay?"

"That's fine."

Estéban leaves the room. Eva Maria looks at the door. Closed. Silent. She stands up and walks across the room. Very quickly. She opens the door.

"Estéban?"

Estéban turns around. At the far end of the corridor.

"What?"

"Do you think she might have been pregnant?"

Estéban's face stands out against the darkness of the corridor. Just as everything ends up standing out against the darkness. His face looks like a mask.

"If who might have been pregnant? Who are you talking about?"

"Stella."

Estéban doesn't answer. He doesn't move. It's not the question that bothers him. He thinks he must have misheard. For five years Eva Maria has forbidden him from saying Stella's name in her presence. Her tone becomes more urgent. Insistent.

"Do you think she could have been pregnant?"

"Why do you ask?"

"I don't know ... all these stories about 'stolen babies,' I thought that maybe ..."

Estéban rushes to answer. In this faint suspension of her hesitant words. His tone is categorical. His voice is firm. He goes up to Eva Maria.

"No. Of course not. Stella wasn't pregnant. What are you thinking?"

Eva Maria gets annoyed.

"How can you be so sure?"

Estéban thinks.

"She . . . she didn't have a boyfriend."

"How do you know?"

"She would have told me."

"Do you really believe a sister tells her brother everything?"

Estéban doesn't answer. Eva Maria takes advantage of his silence.

"You know very well that there's an age where secrets ripen, when before, there was only a sort of sibling complicity, and the word 'secret' only existed when it was shared. Stella was two years older than you—that changes everything. She could have had secrets, secrets you never even suspected."

Estéban interrupts her, his voice suddenly sounding older.

"If she had secrets, it wasn't from me."

"What do you mean?"

"I mean that Stella wasn't pregnant, that's all."

"Well, I think she could perfectly well have been pregnant."

"No. Stop imagining things."

"I'm not imagining things."

"Yes, you are, and there is a very precise reason why Stella could not have been pregnant."

"And what's that?"

"A very simple reason."

"Which is?"

"Do you really want to know?"

"Yes."

"Stella liked women. That's it. You wanted to know."

Eva Maria greets this revelation as a revelation that changes nothing. There is a gentle smile on her face. Slight surprise. Stella liked women. It's funny, she would never have thought so. She wished she had known. Or guessed. But it doesn't matter, it really doesn't matter, it just proves how free her daughter was, and that she already knew. Eva Maria runs her thumb over her dimple. The dimple in her chin. The bed of a cherry stone. A bed for girls, she thinks. Suddenly learning something about Stella gives her the faint impression that Stella is still alive. Eva Maria closes the door behind her.

Estéban leans against the wall. Relieved. Eva Maria greeted this revelation as a revelation that changed nothing. But he knew, on the contrary, how much this revelation changed everything. It would prevent Eva Maria from doing what she otherwise would have surely done. She would have looked at every four-year-old child as if it was Stella's child. She would have sunk into conjectures. And she would have been lost. His mother could not spend the rest of her life running after a void. Or after the dead. Or the fruit of her imagination. Estéban runs his fingers through his hair. His body relaxes into a smile. Of relief. Of the sudden awareness of what he has just said. Of mischief, too. If Stella had heard him, she would have had a good laugh. He grabbed at the first thing that came to mind. When you're surrounded by madness, it's important to know how to lie. Estéban has just learned.

Eva Maria pours another glass of wine. She looks down at her desk. Her gaze wanders to her tape recorder. What sort of music did Stella like? She'll have to ask Estéban. Her gaze follows the black cable joining the tape recorder to the headphones. It's like an umbilical cord. A Playmobil umbilical cord. It looks like the Rio de la Plata, winding its way into the sea. Eva Maria scribbles on the page of her open notebook. She puts down her pen. She winds the black cable around her fingers. She removes the jack from the tape recorder. Puts it back in. Removes it. Puts it back in. Removes it. How long has it been since she made love? Eva Maria gets up. She goes over to her wardrobe. She opens it. She gets down on her knees. She rummages behind her shoes. She takes out her brown backpack. She hunts among the cassettes. She checks the spine. "Miguel." Yes, that's it. *Miguel.* She can't remember the names of all the patients, but she remembers that name. Even though she didn't listen right through to the end. The only cassette she has not transcribed. She didn't have the courage; it was more than she could do; she couldn't face it. Eva Maria shakes her head. She has to listen. To all of it. What will remain of the duty of memory if the torturers do not pay, if the victims stay silent, if she doesn't listen to Miguel? She has to build up her courage. One must always build up one's courage. Drinking will help. Eva Maria pours another glass of wine. She puts the headphones on her head. She takes a blank sheet of paper. Feeds it into the typewriter. She rewinds the cassette in the tape recorder. Presses *Play*. And yet this is not a game.

MIGUEL

VITTORIO

Miguel? What are you doing here? I'm sorry, Lisandra isn't at home. And I have a patient coming any minute.

MIGUEL

Is it Mr. Bach?

VITTORIO

How did you know?

MIGUEL

Because that's me!

VITTORIO

What do you mean, that's you?

MIGUEL

That's me as well—it was my name back then, and since I've come to talk to you about back then, I gave you my name from back then. Can I come in?

VITTORIO

Into my office?

MIGUEL

Yes. I have an appointment, may I remind you.

VITTORIO

Of course, come in, please. Your name from back then? I
don't understand.

MIGUEL

"Number 2137" was my real name back then, but if you
replace the figures with letters, you get "B-A-C-H."
Incredible, don't you think? Unless they did it on
purpose. But I think it was a wink from Providence, a
sign to hang in there, rather than proof of their
intelligence; unfortunately, they did not choose to put
their intelligence in the service of poetry. It's funny you
didn't recognize my voice on the telephone. I was sure
you would recognize me.

VITTORIO

You worry me, Miguel, I've never seen you so agitated.
What's going on? Why are you coming to see me, pretending
to be someone else? You should have told me it was you.

MIGUEL

I thought it would be easier if it was "Mr. Bach" who
came to tell you.

VITTORIO

Tell me what?

MIGUEL

About everything that happened there. Tell someone at
least once. Tell you. So that I would learn how. I've
already told myself—in my head, first, and then out
loud—I've already done all that, I've turned the terror
into a story, and given it the necessary narrative form;

I've found the right words, at least those that work best
to express the images; and I've even found a certain
chronology—that was what was hardest, to introduce
the order of time into fear, to join elements together,
and gestures, and events, which until then had been
superimposed in a sort of layer cake of fear; everything
had existed outside time, violently, and I had to reintro-
duce it, time that is, this notion that is peculiar to
humanity and which disappears as soon as inhumanity
comes on the scene. But I managed, I've done all that
already, all on my own. Now I have to tell someone the
story, with all its words, shaped by chronology; I have to
tell someone and then, at last, it will become more
natural, that's what I figure; it's like music in your head,
first you need the notes, you have to look for the ones
you hear, find them, and then in the end someone else
has to hear them, otherwise there's no point, except to
lock yourself away and listen over and over. Fear
remains, along with the inability to pour the story into
another ear, and for a long time I wondered who I could
tell, and suddenly I thought of you. You're my friend,
and besides it's your job. I'm sure you can help me,
Vittorio. I have to tell someone, don't you see? I want to
spend my life telling the story. Not to shut myself away,
but to free myself. Do you hear me? Answer me. Do you
agree that we can act as if I were a patient? For once. Just
this once. Do you agree?

VITTORIO

Of course, of course. I'll cancel my next appointments,
I'll take the afternoon off; we'll have more peace and
quiet that way.

MIGUEL

Oh, but don't do that! Our conversation mustn't change
anything, it mustn't be any more important than your

other patients' conversations; that would just make it worse. Do you understand? I've practiced—it won't take any longer than any of your other sessions, I promise.

VITTORIO

Fine. How do you want us to go about it? Do you want me to start with a question?

MIGUEL

Anything but that. I want to manage on my own. Without gathering momentum. Because if I expect someone to ask me questions, I won't tell the story to anyone. It's incredible, the number of people who never ask questions; it seems that curiosity is a talent that is restricted to childhood. Don't you think? No, it's true; how could you think that with your job—you ask the questions, you spend your life asking questions—but think about it, do people, other people, do you think they ask you questions? I don't. Honestly, this deliberate silence, this way of making everything around us official without any questions asked, astonishes me. Questions can even be a bother! It's like smiles; you say to yourself, What do they want from me? You take it the wrong way, you suspect a smiling person of some evil intention, you sigh at the intrusion. At least where you are concerned, your profession feeds on questions, and that's good. It's a good thing. Do you like your profession, Vittorio?

VITTORIO

Yes.

MIGUEL

And I like my profession, too; it's the thing I love best on earth. It's good when you love your job more than anything on earth, but at the same time it's a bad sign. Now I wish that I could love Melina more than anything on earth.

VITTORIO

I know.

MIGUEL

They started following me more and more often, in groups of four or five, young men no older than twenty-two, twenty-four; sometimes I would turn around in the street to show them they couldn't fool me; I would ask them the time or even come straight out and say didn't they have anything better to do. I wasn't afraid, I thought the fact that I was a public person would prevent them from acting, the political consequences would have been too serious to risk. But that evening, I noticed some people in civilian clothing up on my neighbor's roof busy doing something and I understood that something serious was about to happen. I called some friends to tell them that if the next morning at seven a.m. I gave no sign of life, they should be worried, and then my line was cut. I had to make all my other calls from the house of another neighbor who wanted to help me, so I urgently contacted the embassies—French, German, Canadian, American, and Brazilian. Not one of them would take the risk of getting involved. They all told me the only embassy that could intervene was the Argentine embassy. Might as well call my torturers directly. While I was making all these phone calls, two Fiats had parked outside my house with armed people. Finally there came the assault. I didn't put up any resistance; they dragged me into an army truck that was waiting down the street. Already during the transport they started torturing me. When we got there they took me into a room and on the door it said *Servicio de Informaciones del Estado*, the only words I would read all through those long months. They stripped and gagged me. They tied me to the table, sprayed me with water, then they used the *picana* to apply electricity, concentrating on my hands in particular; they kept on saying, "No more piano playing for you; you'll be a wreck by the time you get out of here. You're worse than a guerrillero because with your smile and your piano you have made the *negrada** think they have the right to listen to Beethoven. You're a traitor to your class. Beethoven is ours. And so we're going to make you pay a heavy price. We're going to destroy you, completely." When they'd finished, they untied me and left me on the floor; they wouldn't give me any water. I'd bitten myself so hard that the blood from my mouth was running down my throat, but blood doesn't quench your thirst. They left me in the basement in a cell without light or food. There were two of us to a bed. It was cold and damp. There were no blankets. There was a concrete bench. We had to urinate and do the other business on the floor. They tortured me every day. It was as if they made it a point of honor always to torture me differently, but they always used the same words: "No more piano playing for you, ever." They went on focusing on my hands and arms. When they hung others by their feet, they would hang me by my wrists. "You like listening to music, huh? You like music? So listen to this one." And they beat my ears so hard—they'd go about it a few of them at a time—I thought my ears would tear; I could hear the cartilage cracking; they threatened to pierce my eardrums. There was nothing I could do to make them stop. They weren't trying to get any information out of me—I had none to give them, I had nothing they wanted—they just wanted to hurt me as a punishment, they wanted to annihilate me. I never saw anyone. I had cotton over my eyes, a blindfold, and a hood. I never saw anything. I heard, I listened, and I counted roughly twenty-four different voices. By ear. I recognized their

---

* The underprivileged class in Argentina.

voices—the timbre of the tenors, baritones, sopranos . . .
There was quite a mixture, even girls. French accents,
and German. They told the torturers what questions
to ask; apparently they were experts in psychology,
specialized in the interrogation of political prisoners.
There were constant references to the Nazis. One day,
two young officers forced me to repeat maybe five
hundred times: "National Socialism is the most beautiful
doctrine ever invented by human beings." "Louder.
Louder. Sing the words. Go on! Put them to music."
Sometimes they tortured me as if I were a textbook case,
to teach others, the new recruits, how to torture,
because everyone was torturing, it was part of their
training. So in that case, it was cigarette burns, the hairs
on the genitals ripped out by the handful, and I heard
them say, "Go on, take the cigarette, press down on it,
for fuck's sake, press; you're not supposed to make him
come, you wet dishrag, look, go on, on his back." And
down came the cigarette on my cheek. They tore the
skin from my hands with tweezers. Every day the wound
got bigger, purulent; I would lick it like a dog, hoping to
disinfect it. "You're nothing but a pile of shit in our
country!" They wanted to destroy me, but I had figured
out that if I concentrated really hard, I didn't feel the
pain so bad, so I tried to think about technical problems
related to the piano, or to reconstruct a work, or listen
to Melina's voice singing that work—if you only knew
how thinking about my wife helped me to resist—and I
resisted throughout the torture sessions thanks to these
tricks you learn in this hell: when it didn't hurt so bad I
screamed like a crazy man, and when it really hurt, I kept
silent, so that they'd concentrate harder on those places
where I'd screamed louder when it came time to beat me
or electrocute me. But before long I lost all sensitivity
in both my hands and my arms. As a musician I was
afraid that I had lost it all forever. Day and night, I did

exercises. I couldn't feel my fingers, but I didn't want to lose my digital memory, the distance between notes, so I drew piano keys on the floor, in the dirt, and I looked at my hands, even though I couldn't feel them, I watched as they moved heavily, and I would erase my makeshift keyboard the moment I heard the door open. I had huge gaps in my memory. When I tried mentally to recover a score, I might recall, say, twenty-four bars really well and then suddenly there would be a gap, an ocean, and I could remember the score in a fragmentary way, but I couldn't remember all the development, for example. Digital memory helped me to fill those gaps. The worst thing was that it was my most developed sense that was subjected to all that torture, and I was filled with sounds, voices, those voices . . . I can't get rid of them, the cries of pain, the cries of hatred, the cries pleading for mercy, the cries of insults, the cries as they urged each other on. I have no images. The sensations are fading. But the voices, those voices won't leave me. Noise was the worst torture for me. Every night they would bang on the pipes and the sounds would echo inside me: I could hear notes, dissonant notes, always the same ones, brutal and soulless, notes made of metal; I'm sure it was something they'd planned, to stun me with noise, to kill me with noise, with this unbearable, appalling racket. It was calculated, with a shrink's logic. You have no idea, but there were shrinks everywhere. Embedded with the army. Our guards were shrinks, our censors were shrinks. Forgive me, I don't mean you, Vittorio, but your profession is not always spotless. But shrinks are human beings, after all, they don't always want to do good, either. They knew how to destroy us; they crammed us with medication. I learned how to pretend to take them; I even asked for some, to allay their suspicions. And then I gave them to my companions who wanted them— everyone had their own way of putting up with this ordeal; some of them needed medication just to survive in the hell we were in. For me to survive I had to stay in contact with reality more than anything—it was unbearable to feel I was losing the notion of time. They would deprive us of food for several days in a row; we would hear the cart go by in the corridor but it wouldn't stop for us, then one day it did stop—we didn't know why that day and not the day before or the following day. It was always the same moldy, half-cooked rice, with "meat" they told us was from the scalp of executed victims. From time to time they came to see me, they would remove the blindfold and give me cigarettes; but there were other times when they took out their guns and fired just next to me to frighten me. Another one of their shrinks' ideas. You couldn't make friends—divide and rule, they were really good at that game; we never really knew who was hiding behind a prisoner. A friend or an enemy. Certain prisoners they bought, tempting them with food, perks, or promises if they would denounce others. Sometimes you were denounced for things you hadn't done. Their prison methods were very sophisticated. It was a real laboratory; the procedures were incredible. There were individual or group policies for each floor. I still don't know how the system held together. That was the shrinks' job. Their aim was to destroy me via my passion, my profession. My hands, my hands, always my hands. I know they meted out roughly the same punishment to surgeons. To kill a man by killing the potential for his passion. There was a shrink behind each torture session. I counted five in all, in addition to the French and the Germans; their voices had become familiar—even beyond their voices, their breathing. If you listen carefully, Vittorio, there is a particular sound to every breath, you know. I can recognize a ton of people by their breathing alone. What about you, do you hear breathing? Block your ears, there, you can hear your breathing, can't you? Well, when I concentrate, I can hear every breath the way you hear yours when you block your ears. When they told me they had arrested Melina, that was worse than any torture. I tried to tell myself it was the ultimate bluff. To destroy me for good. They were threatening to torture her in front of me. Throughout that entire period I stopped practicing in secret—I was afraid they might carry out their threat—I even took the medication. I did everything to be an exemplary victim. And I tried to imagine Melina safe at home. But there was nothing I could have done to prevent them from going through with their sadistic fantasies. Nothing I could have done. "Two one three seven! On your feet!" They took me into the room. *Servicio de Informaciones del Estado*. They made me sit on a chair and they removed my blindfold. Suddenly I heard music. Playing very loudly. It was Ravel's Concerto for the Left Hand. They left me there the time of the entire concerto, and during that time I felt an immense happiness come over me, and then the concerto came to an end. They gave me a cigarette; they asked me if I had enjoyed it, Concerto for the Left Hand; they asked me if I smoked with my left hand or my right—they were all wearing hoods; and in any case they wanted to hear it again. They put the concerto on again even louder this time. They tied my right arm to the table, my body to the chair; they put up a black cloth between my arms and me—I could no longer see my hands—and then they turned on an electric saw—do you hear me, Vittorio, an electric saw. "We're going to cut your hand off, just like we did with Victor Jara,* and after that we will kill you." You cannot imagine the horror of that noise when it comes near your hands. I felt death go

---

* A famous Chilean guitarist who was abducted and assassinated under the Chilean dictatorship.

through me. One of the shrinks began to shout: "You will no longer be the pianist you once were, you will no longer be your children's father, or your wife's lover; you will be nothing but a wreck." I managed to contain myself a bit longer, but when I heard the sound of the electric saw coming closer I let out a scream the likes of which I have never heard: "No, dear Lord! Dear God, have mercy!" That's when everything stopped. Silence. Miraculous. They untied me; they were laughing. They asked me if I had enjoyed their joke. Okay, it wasn't exactly a joke, because they were right, never again will I be my wife's lover, but it was a lesser evil. They were laughing. They told me they were cool guys, decent, they could have cut my hand off, they'd decided it was better to kill my wife. A lesser evil, don't you think? You can always find another wife, but another hand, that's more complicated. And besides, it was her last wish, after all, "for him to stay alive, a pianist, for him to be able to go on playing," and they had respected it; they wouldn't go and burn in hell: they had asked her which she preferred, "either we kill you, or we cut your husband's hand off," and she's the one who wanted them to kill her—she even begged them—they couldn't go and refuse her now, could they? They were gallant around here; I was really lucky to have a wife like her. They were laughing. And they let me go. Back to my house. I thought Melina would still be there. I hoped with all my soul that they had been lying, that it was some nasty infantile prank their filthy shrinks had come up with. I was praying; I swore I would never complain about anything ever again, I would never again feel weary or tired, I would never ever forget to tell Melina how much I loved her. But when I got to the house, I could tell that no one had been living there for weeks. It's something you can feel, an immediate sensation, space telling you that Love has disappeared. It's searing. The food on the kitchen table, they must have come upon her while she was having supper. I looked at that layer of mold on the tomatoes and I knew Melina was dead. And then I collapsed, the way I had not collapsed all that time in prison. Everything had been thought out, scripted by their shrinks. They knew that this would be the worst thing for me. To lose my wife. There we are, Vittorio, as I promised, less than one hour, incredible, isn't it? The sum total of those eleven months fits into less than an hour. No matter what we say, words reduce everything; no matter how precise your words try to be, they can never express the real length of time. The only good thing about words is that they set the voice free; for the rest, they're not reliable. You cannot imagine what it's like to lose your wife, Vittorio, if you only knew how much I miss Melina. By the way, how is Lisandra? I found her distant, the last time we met.

VITTORIO

She's fine.

MIGUEL

I tell you, I found her really absent, preoccupied; is everything all right between you?

VITTORIO

Everything's fine.

MIGUEL

You're so lucky to have her, I hope you tell her that every day. Vittorio?

VITTORIO

Yes.

MIGUEL

I also came to tell you I'm leaving the country.

VITTORIO

What do you mean, you're leaving the country? What are you talking about?

MIGUEL

I'm moving to Paris.

VITTORIO

Paris?

MIGUEL

I'll be back, but for now I'm leaving; I have to, I need to get away, I can't stay here.

VITTORIO

But why? It's all over now, all that.

MIGUEL

One time I recognized a voice. At a party. I closed my eyes, and it was him, the same voice. I'd swear on my right hand, no pun intended. I couldn't speak all through dinner. I had my eyes glued to my hands. To hear that man's voice brought back all the suffering, these sharp stabbing pains in my hands, a burning sensation; it was awful. I wanted to say something, and I couldn't, not a word would come out, and it was then, at that moment, that I decided I had to learn to tell my story. But there was one thing I could do: I asked the pianist to let me sit in his place. I didn't wait until the end of the dinner. I couldn't stop myself, I had to do it. And I played. Ravel's Concerto for the Left Hand. I played. As if I were possessed. And at the end of the piece I went and sat back down at the table and started eating again. Now I was calm. Calmer. I couldn't look him in the eyes, but I wanted to show him that his efforts had been in vain. That he hadn't destroyed anything. But . . . don't you remember? You were at that party, you and Lisandra.

VITTORIO

Yes, indeed, I remember that party.

MIGUEL

Aren't you going to ask me who it was?

VITTORIO

If you want to tell me, you can tell me.

MIGUEL

I see. The aim of your profession is to ask questions. But not all questions.

VITTORIO

No, not all.

MIGUEL

And above all not those questions whose only motive is to satisfy personal curiosity.

VITTORIO

Exactly.

MIGUEL

A voice is a deceptive thing, all the same. It's incredible you didn't recognize me on the telephone. I was sure you would. I would recognize your voice anywhere. It must be a question of context, that's all I can see: you didn't expect to suddenly see me show up among your patients, so you didn't recognize me, and besides, your profession is words, not sounds. I would have recognized you at once, but then sounds are my job; to each his own trade, that's what it always boils down to. Oh, yes, that's it, I have one last thing to tell you. I almost forgot . . .

Eva Maria presses all the buttons. Nothing. The cassette has reached the end. This session had lasted longer than Vittorio's usual sessions, after all. And Miguel hadn't finished. Eva Maria drinks the rest of her wine.

"But what? What did he still have to tell Vittorio? What had he forgotten?"

Eva Maria turns the cassette over. She wants it to continue on the other side but that would be impossible; Vittorio would never have turned the box of tissues over. He would never have opened the tape recorder to change the side of the cassette before asking his friend to go on. Go on, my dear Miguel, please. Eva Maria turns the cassette every which way. As if she's gone mad. She starts over five times. Nothing. Not a sound. Not a voice. There is nothing on this other side. Nothing to indicate how the session really ended. Eva Maria presses all the buttons. She feels rage. Incompetence. She knows she has drunk too much. The bottle is empty. Eva Maria gets to her feet. She heads for the bathroom. She opens all the cupboards looking for another bottle. Why hadn't she figured it out on her own? She starts thinking out loud. Spitting out her words.

"These cassettes . . . of course they were a psychopath's idea . . . to want to record his patients . . . the persistence of a method they used at the time . . . vittorio puig in fact what do I know about him about his past his life a first name a last name all my trust how can you know the people you think you know . . . but miguel found it all out miguel the lifelong friend miguel the tortured miguel the widower he'd recognized his voice that famous evening he recognized your voice vittorio puig the baritone . . . the way you end your sentences with a mannered little drawl like some intellectual esthete watch out vittorio puig is going to speak may the silence stop may the reign of pure reason and understanding begin . . . now now eva maria think carefully eva maria now now eva maria you just don't get it vittorio puig oh no you just don't get a single thing . . . you thought your friend miguel was coming to give alms to you with all the details of his sad story but miguel had found out . . . he'd recognized your voice you were one of the psychiatrists there and miguel knew it he found out he was coming to warn you watch out vittorio puig you are in for it that was the first stage of his revenge to come and see you and warn you . . . but you didn't try to read between the lines not even for one teeny tiny minute and yet it was clear to anyone who cared to see but vittorio puig is not a person you warn he's a person you revere you venerate you listen to and keep quiet . . . mediocre vittorio puig so focused on your own words that you don't realize they're talking about you . . . a person doesn't choose to be a victim he becomes a victim and everybody is the victim of someone so for the second stage of his vengeance he rang at the door ding dong vittorio puig miguel is going to repay you in kind . . . he's going to do to you what you did to him or one of your acolytes did that's not the problem you're going to pay he's going to take your wife the way you or one of your acolytes took his . . . violence is arbitrary ding dong the hour of vengeance has come lisandra puig opened the door she's not afraid of your friend miguel hey miguel! what a nice surprise! what are you doing here? come in! no vittorio's not here . . . at the movies . . . would you like something to drink? a nice glass of white wine they would chat for a bit while they waited for vittorio puig . . . while they waited for you to come back from the cinema where you went to improve your exquisite general culture instead of making love to your wife to seek her forgiveness because you hadn't noticed her new dress to reassure her to make her laugh a little to show her that after all having an argument is no big deal . . . but you would rather leave instead arguments are vulgar especially when you can't kill isn't that right vittorio puig? . . . how are you dear lisandra? miguel asked her to put on some music what a pity if she'd had a piano he would have played her his latest piece . . . to get her opinion the evening went by sweetly her favorite tango? good idea louder he loved that tango too and then it wasn't hard to get her to go over to the window to open it maybe to see you coming look! there's vittorio puig coming back let's call out to him! ciao vittorio puig ciao ciao and they both leaned out ah no it wasn't him . . . so he whispered in her ear that he was sorry he had to do this because he liked her but the problem was that she was the wife of vittorio puig and that vittorio puig had killed his wife maybe it wasn't actually him but one of his colleagues violence is arbitrary vengeance is too so he was going to show him what it meant to lose his wife and she turned around because she couldn't believe that vittorio puig was the monster miguel was talking about or maybe she knew that vittorio puig was a monster but it disturbed her to hear miguel come straight out with it . . . as a rule no one dared to say it and anyway who cares what she thinks vittorio puig's wife wheee out the window vittorio puig's wife out the window hickory dickory dock the mouse whirling whirling whirling round the clock in the night and in the empty air the last air she'll ever breathe . . . the immortal air for millennia which hovering near her nostrils will watch her crash bang and splat then breathe out to go and be recycled in other nostrils other windpipes lungs bronchial tubes in the nostrils of the young man who was afraid of a kiss in the nostrils of the young woman who would have done better to give him his kiss not her hand . . . the air that keeps us alive and the air that watches us die and then goes off elsewhere the little mouse stella oh stella my beloved daughter how you loved that nursery rhyme . . . what did they do to you those bastards? how could anyone kill a beautiful young woman like you? how it hurts still where are your little feet that grew up so quickly . . . ah there they are give me your socks oh that's fine thank you let's do humpty dumpty—humpty dumpty sat on a wall humpty dumpty had a great fall all the king's horses and all the king's men couldn't put humpty together again stella come back let's sing it again let's begin again let's live again stella again again again something anything . . . but let's do it again don't leave me like this sing with me stella why can't I hear you stella sing sing louder . . ."

"Mama!"

Estéban opens the door to the bedroom. Eva Maria is lying on the floor. Her hair damp and matted. Estéban comes back from the bathroom with a wet towel. He revives Eva Maria. He takes her in his arms. He carries her to her bed. Raises her head on the pillow. He pulls off the socks she has put on her hands. Estéban is not surprised. He wipes her face. Her mouth. Nothing surprises Estéban anymore. He removes her sweater. Estéban bends over. He picks up the two bottles of wine. He cleans up. He wipes the headphone cable. It is soaking, too. The tape recorder is going round and round. He stops it. He leaves the bedroom. His tape recorder under his arm. Estéban doesn't question what he has just seen. Estéban is like everyone. The first time, you question. Not the hundredth. Everything becomes normal by dint of repetition. Even the most terrible things. Tomorrow, as always, Eva Maria won't remember a thing. She never remembers a thing. Estéban, too, prefers to forget. No, he won't feel guilty. No, he is in no way to blame. What he made up about Stella has nothing to do with all that. Eva Maria doesn't need anyone to get herself into that state. For years now, night after night, Eva Maria has gotten herself into just such a state.

Eva Maria takes a sip of maté. The newspaper is on the table, unread. Estéban comes into the kitchen to make his breakfast. He puts a cassette down next to her.

"Here, this is yours."

Eva Maria places her hand on Miguel's cassette. As if she wants to hide it. But it's too late. There's no point anymore. Eva Maria vaguely remembers spending last night listening to his story, picturing him as the murderer. And Vittorio as a shrink in the junta. Wrongful accusations imagined in her drunken delirium. She puts the cassette in her pocket. Estéban goes over to the fridge. Eva Maria looks up at him. Embarrassed. Defiant, too.

"Where did you find it?"

Estéban stops what he's doing.

"In the tape recorder."

"You've been going through my things?"

"I am using my things."

"Did you take the tape recorder back?"

"Yes."

"When?"

"Last night."

"I didn't hear you."

"That's not surprising."

Estéban points to the two bottles. In full view next to the sink.

"I found those in your room."

Eva Maria gets to her feet.

"So? I do as I please."

Eva Maria leaves the kitchen. She slams the bedroom door behind her. She opens her wardrobe. Gets down on her knees. She hunts around behind her shoes. She pulls out her backpack. Puts Miguel's cassette in with the other cassettes. She sighs. She stays there for a long while. On her knees. Then she gives a start. She gets back up. Abruptly. She didn't hear Estéban come into the room.

"Now what? What are you doing here?"

"Telephone. For you."

Eva Maria hangs up. It was Vittorio's lawyer. "Felipe has been cleared. My client asked me to call you to keep you informed." Eva Maria paces back and forth along the corridor. *Cleared.* That didn't take long. "Felipe was at a charity event the night of Lisandra's murder. With his wife. He has the entire navy and terrestrial army as an alibi." It just keeps getting better and better. Never mind what your alibi is, provided you have one. That's the way it goes. Felipe and his wife had shown up at the police station presenting a united front, thick as thieves. Then Eva Maria tried. One last time, hoping with him it might work.

"Felipe—what was his last name again?"

To no avail. The lawyers, the psychoanalysts, they are in it together, they chatter and spout their ideas, then suddenly, the minute there's someone genuine and intelligent, seeking the truth, they clam up, they frown and claim client privilege. "It is not in my remit to share that information with you." And yet the lawyer's voice continued on the other end of the line.

"Moreover . . ."

"Yes?"

"My client instructed me to inform you about . . . about the child."

"Yes?"

"He told them everything. Commissioner Perez has promised to launch an investigation, in spite of everything, independently of Lisandra's murder. He promised to get this matter out into the open, and although the matter doesn't come under the jurisdiction of his department, he will refer the case."

"And what if he doesn't refer anything at all? We can't trust him. Not completely. There's a much quicker, easier solution. Since you know Felipe's identity, go and see the grandparents and share Vittorio's suspicions about the child with them."

"That is not within my remit. I absolutely refuse to get involved in such a personal matter."

"Well then, go and inform the Mothers of the Plaza de Mayo. You have to hand the matter over to those who are prepared to fight, and they will get involved, they will start an investigation, of that you can be sure, and that way, if one day the child finds himself asking questions, there will be a file on him somewhere, and he'll be able to get at the truth."

"That is not within my remit. But my—"

"Then what is within your remit?"

"I will thank you to let me finish. It is not within my remit but my client was so insistent that I have just mailed a letter he wrote to them. To the Mothers of the Plaza de Mayo. So that has been done."

Eva Maria feels her heart soften. That is the Vittorio she knows. The Vittorio she likes, intelligent and thoughtful, altruistic. Eva Maria walks back and forth. She could have blackmailed him, threatened to tell the cops everything about the cassettes if he didn't give her Felipe's name. And he could have led her on, promised her he would go and find Felipe if he ever got out of jail. He could have waved a carrot under her dumb-ass nose, just so she would continue to help him. But they had done nothing of the sort. He hadn't; she hadn't. When you have been a victim of human baseness, you owe it to yourself to keep above what is vulgar, above the crowd, and that was what they had done. Both of them. Eva Maria feels comforted. Somewhere deep inside. But sad, truly sad. Before hanging up, the lawyer implied that Vittorio had clearly given up the fight. For the last few days he had been only the shadow of his former self. A reenactment was planned for the following day. Vittorio was terrified at the thought of taking part in such a sordid exercise. He was convinced that Commissioner Perez would use the opportunity to come out with the final elements that would convict him once and for all. Eva Maria shakes her head. With helplessness. Is there nothing more she can do for Vittorio?

Eva Maria goes into Estéban's room. She has been pacing restlessly around the house all day, and the day is over. Estéban is sitting on his bed. He is polishing his bandoneon. Eva Maria plants herself in front of him. She looks at the tape recorder next to him. Estéban intercepts her gaze.

"Do you need it again?"

"No. Can I borrow your bike?"

Estéban puts down his bandoneon.

"My bike? What for? Where do you want to go?"

Eva Maria tries to lift the bike from its hook on the wall. Estéban gets up off the bed. He goes over to help her. Eva Maria pushes him away.

"Leave me alone, I can manage on my own."

Estéban forces Eva Maria to one side.

"No, you cannot manage on your own."

Estéban unhooks the bike. He sets it down in front of Eva Maria.

"You can't always do everything on your own in life."

Eva Maria looks at him. She takes the bike. She bumps into the door as she leaves the room. She bumps into the furniture in the corridor. Estéban stops her.

"Go ahead. I'll take it out for you."

Eva Maria lets go of the bike. Estéban lifts it up over his head.

"Years of experience, not to wake you up at night. You've got to admire it."

Eva Maria opens the front door. Estéban puts the bike down next to her.

"Where are you going?"

"I'll be back."

"When?"

"I don't know."

Eva Maria sits on the bicycle. She is awkward. She puts her foot on the ground several times. Estéban shouts to her.

"The brake is on the left."

Eva Maria eventually finds her balance. Estéban watches her figure move away into the night. A neighbor goes by with his dog. Showing approval, the man raises his thumb in the air, pointing at the now-empty street. Estéban gives him the thumbs-up. What else can you do to transform a tragic situation into an ideal one? He goes back into the house. He looks at the coatrack. Shakes his head. Eva Maria didn't take her coat. Or her handbag. What is going on with her these days? "I need your bike," Estéban mutters. "I need you." Estéban thinks about the cassette. "Miguel." He didn't listen to it, out of respect. Estéban wonders if there's any point to respect. Who is this Miguel? What is it all about? Estéban wonders what Eva Maria is playing at. Then Estéban amends his thought. Eva Maria hasn't been playing at anything for a long time. Estéban remembers how they used to play Truco,* how it used to be so much fun. Why does life do this? Estéban heads toward Eva Maria's room. She's always accusing him of going through her things; at least now she won't accuse him wrongly anymore. He wants to know. Only by knowing can he protect her.

---

* Argentinian card game.

Eva Maria pedals. She hasn't ridden a bike in years. She had forgotten this sensation, how the wind plays in your hair. Over your face. Over your hands. She opens her mouth to take in the air. She doesn't know how she can help Vittorio anymore. Eva Maria has come here without thinking. Usually she makes a detour to avoid this place. Not today. Eva Maria imagines the mothers of the Plaza de Mayo, sadly making their way, each playing a bit part in the national tragedy. The photograph on a sign hanging around each woman's neck. Eva Maria will never come here to lose Stella among all these photographs. She will never reduce her daughter to a photograph. A photograph reveals a person's appearance, not their significance. She doesn't want to talk about her misfortune; she doesn't ever want to seek comfort in the sound of a "That's how it was for me." No! It's not how it was for you, dear! Only with Vittorio had she been able to talk about it. Eva Maria looks down, the wheels of the bike spinning quickly, spinning around the square, around the obelisk, the tires whirling like the moon around the earth, every year moving 3.8 centimeters farther apart. A single step on the moon, hundreds of feet pounding the square, every Thursday. Eva Maria rides over their footsteps. The very idea she might lose her balance and have to put a foot on the ground causes her toes to curl, like claws, causes her entire being to cling to the pedals. She mustn't get involved in any of that, must never be part of it. Eva Maria swerves to one side. Abruptly. She pedals faster than ever, to get away from the plaza. To flee. Eva Maria had forgotten this sensation. The wind playing in her hair, over her face, over her hands. She had forgotten that the wind can make your tears so cold. One should always stay away from squares. Eva Maria thinks about the Capacocha. The main plaza at the heart of the city of Cuzco, in Peru: the symbolic center of the Incan world. Summer solstice, winter solstice. Eva Maria thinks about the feast days that are beginning, the luxurious holy days sacrificing children. A young girl with long braided hair. A little boy. And a very little girl. The most beautiful children, chosen from among the elite. The most beautiful children of their age group. The very little girl is six, the little boy is nine, and the young girl with long braided hair is fourteen. You can see them in detail. Not a single imperfection. The slightest blemish or physical anomaly would have disqualified them from the start. Supreme beauty, supreme responsibility. The children are received by the Incan emperor. On the morning of the eleventh holy day, the little boy, the very little girl, and the young girl with the long braided hair depart. They are followed by a procession of close relatives and sun priests. They travel a thousand miles along roads through the Cordillera of the Andes, several months of pilgrimage until they reach the Puna. A place where the convulsions of the earth's crust caused some of the highest summits of the planet to emerge. The volcano is there. The highest of all. A sacred mountain joining the earthly and the divine. Its gray rocky mass culminates at 6,739 meters. The children chew and chew coca leaves they have been given to withstand the high altitude and lack of oxygen. Between 5,800 and 6,500 meters, the slope becomes very steep and the terrain more unstable. Once they reach the summit, the three children are each clothed in an *unku*, an official tunic which is too big for them, but which will allow them to continue to grow through all eternity. They are given chicha to drink. To make them drunk. To make them drunk to help them fall asleep. The young girl with the long braided hair allows herself to be lowered into the pit that has been dug for her in the dark volcanic earth; she sits cross-legged and waits, a noble vestal, drugged; she is wearing a headdress of white feathers, feathers to resist the demons; the young virgin is wrapped up in a man's tunic, the one her father had placed on her shoulders during the feast days; she falls asleep; the pit is covered with stones; she dies. The scientists who find her five hundred years later will call her "the Maiden." The little boy does not want to go into his pit. He wants to stay with his mother. He puts his head in the lap of the woman who nursed him at her breast and he curls up like a fetus. Wrapped in several lengths of fabric, he is wearing moccasins and short socks of white fur. His mother makes him drink the chicha. His mother strokes his hair. The sun priests place the offerings in the pit dug for him in the dark volcanic earth: a necklace of shells, more valuable than gold, because water is beyond price in these arid lands; two little male figurines; and three figurines of llamas. The sun priests are cautious. These items have magic powers. The little boy no longer feels the biting cold. "He is asleep," murmurs his mother. "What do we do now?" ask the men around her. One of them has an idea: he unwinds a long rope that was holding a bag, and winds it around the boy's knees to hold them together. Thus they lower the little boy into the pit, in a posture worthy of his rank, now that of a deity; he has a large silver bracelet around his right wrist, and in his left hand he holds a slingshot. Something drops to the ground beside him; it's a pair of sandals, for his journey into the Other World; the pit is covered with stones; he dies. The scientists who find him five hundred years later will call him "the Little Boy." The very little girl, six years of age, squeezes her knees in her arms, and by her side there are statues, pottery, sacks filled with food, and a bag of coca made with the feathers of an Amazonian bird; she turns her head to the sky, to the faces and voices of her parents, who are comforting her from up above, encouraging her, telling her how proud they are; she doesn't understand; she is trusting, her face turned to the voices of those who brought her into the world and who are now dismissing her from the world; she falls asleep; she is covered with stones; she dies. After thousands of days go by a storm will erupt, the sky will be streaked with lightning, the lightning will strike her. More than a meter beneath the ground, a face turned toward the sky, a face that had failed to stop her parents, will draw down the crazed bolt of lightning. Five hundred years later the scientists will choke on the smell of burning when they move the stones aside. They will call her "the Thunderstruck Little Girl." "The Capacocha rite is finished. The children did not die, they became gods, intercessorial gods, protective gods who watch over their people from the highest summit of the highest volcanoes. Now everything will be all right: famine, epidemics, military defeats; the life of the Incas will be better." The archaeologist takes the liberty to add, "We do not discuss their customs. Nowadays these practices seem cruel, but for the Incas, these children were entering into a divine world." Eva Maria raises her hand. She begins to speak. "Monstrosity never thinks it is monstrous; it always finds reasons within itself to behave as it does—acts of torture become acts of justice, or even honor—but one must never excuse monsters, ever, unless one is oneself an unrepentant bastard." Eva Maria loses her balance. A car blows its horn. Another car blows its horn. She had raised her hand, just like the day at that seminar. She may still know how to ride a bike after all these years, but only with both hands. Eva Maria remembers the day they removed the training wheels from Stella's bike. Stella would not have been chosen for the Capacocha: she was not noble and she was not perfect, she had a little dimple in the middle of her chin. But she was chosen by other monsters, for something else. To each monster his own prey, and all criteria are valid when you're a monster. And Lisandra? What other sort of monster had killed her, and why? And that, too, was on a square . . . Eva Maria says to herself, Stay away from plazas—she has said it before, "Stay away from plazas"—but it will be her duty to come back to this one.

Eva Maria climbs off the bike. She looks up at the window. She's back to square one. You always end up back at square one. Time to decide whether to stop. Or to go on. Eva Maria crosses the plaza. She leans the bike against the wall. She goes into the little café. Francisco turns around. He raises his arms to the sky. Eva Maria thinks about the Incan rites.

"Eva! What a nice surprise, we haven't seen you in a long time."

"That makes sense . . . I haven't been coming."

"You're not the only one."

"I can imagine."

"The usual?"

Eva Maria sits at the counter.

"No, a coffee, please."

"Oh, really? Right, then, one evening coffee coming up!"

Francisco looks at Eva Maria.

"Have you been crying?"

"It's the wind."

"Do you miss him?"

"Who?"

"Vittorio."

"I haven't thought about it."

"It must be tough to stop like that overnight."

"I haven't thought about it."

Francisco puts the coffee on the counter.

"It must make a strange impression all the same, to find out that the guy who's been explaining life to you is a murderer; it's as if I were poisoning my wife—that would send a chill down my customers' spine . . ."

"What, you have a wife now?"

"Just a manner of speaking."

"Go on, then, *Poisoner*, make me another coffee instead of talking nonsense."

Francisco sets the cup down in front of Eva Maria.

"Two espressos in the evening; you're in for a sleepless night."

Eva Maria drops a sugar lump into the steaming liquid.

"Coffee only prevents happy people from sleeping. With others, it's not the coffee that keeps them from sleeping."

"I'll quote you on that one."

Silence falls. Eva Maria drinks her coffee. Francisco plays with a little spoon next to the saucer.

"Still, you have to wonder, a shrink who turns murderer . . ."

"Haven't you heard of 'presumption of innocence'?"

"In case you hadn't noticed, your innocent man is still in prison."

"You really have it in for him."

Francisco strikes the zinc counter with the little spoon.

"I don't have it in for him; I just know."

"Do you hear what you're saying?"

"I have proof."

"Oh, really?"

"Yes."

"What sort of proof?"

"I have proof that Lisandra had a lover."

Eva Maria shoves her coffee cup to one side.

"That's the first I've heard."

"And it's because Lisandra had a lover that Vittorio killed her."

"That's pretty simplistic."

"If truth has to be complicated, well then, there's nothing I can do for you."

"I'm not expecting anything from you."

"If you weren't expecting anything from me, you would have sat in the room, the way you usually do, and not at the counter."

Eva Maria touches his temple. Twice.

"You've certainly got your share in there."

"Yeah, well, see, a waiter is like a shrink, only not as expensive."

"I would've said more like a private detective, given everything you seem to know."

Francisco busies himself folding the dish towel in front of him.

"A madwoman who drives you crazy—it wouldn't be the first time."

"Stop making these mysterious pronouncements. If you have something to say, say it."

Francisco starts wiping glasses.

"If she did it with me, she surely did it with others."

"If she did what with you?"

"Carried out her weird plan."

"What weird plan?"

"You'll never believe me."

"Of course I will."

"I tell you, you'll never believe me."

"Try me."

"One morning she came to see me and she asked me if I would sleep with her."

"What?"

"It's the truth; she was even sitting right where you are. She told me to meet her that evening at the hotel at nine thirty; she was wearing a very short skirt, to give me something to fantasize about. Well, it's true she often wore these risqué kinds of outfits, but this skirt was *really* short, it really was to get me fantasizing."

"In the end, did you go?"

"No, not 'in the end'; why are you saying 'in the end' when you know I'm giving you important elements? If you want to go to your grave with your own idea about the matter, we may as well stop talking about it, it's pointless."

"All right, then, I didn't say 'in the end.' So she often wore these risqué outfits and it's important. So . . . you went to the hotel."

"For a start, you have to know, that girl always did something to me, I don't know . . . whenever I saw her, and it wasn't just because of the way she dressed, if it came to that, in my profession . . . In fact, it was as if I had always known something would happen between the two of us."

"So you went."

"She had me say my name twice before she opened the door. When I came in, she told me she didn't want to hear the sound of my voice, I would have to murmur. She gave me a flask made of transparent glass—there was no label—and she asked me to put some on, this cologne and no other, she insisted on it. She said would I leave as soon as we had finished—she would go into the bathroom to do what she had to do and when she came back into the room she wanted me to be gone. She gave me the key so that I could come in without her having to open for me and then she made me go back out. I didn't understand what was going on. I put some cologne on and I came back in using the key. She had her back to me; she had pulled up her skirt; she wasn't wearing anything underneath. I came closer and I took her from behind, well, not from behind, but from behind . . ."

"Yes, yes, it doesn't matter, go on."

"No, don't say, 'it doesn't matter'—it's important: she wanted everything her way. She took my hands and did everything she wanted, she told me the words I had to murmur to her, and she saw to me, to what I had to do. We did everything she wanted to do and then she went into the bathroom; that was the signal, so I left. And that was the first time."

"Because there were other times?"

"Yes. The following week, same hotel, same thing: she had me repeat my name when I arrived, she slid the key under the door, she was standing in exactly the same place as the first time, in the same position, her skirt up, her ass out to me. Same thing. She asked me to say the same words and make the same gestures as the first time. It was crazy, she wanted exactly the same scene all over again. I saw Lisandra four Tuesdays in a row—it was all I was waiting for, all I could think about; I went over it again and again in my head, I knew exactly what I had to do, I knew exactly how I would find her: she was always dressed in the same way, take her from behind, get her clothes off, quick, hold her tight, say dirty words to her, and tender words, too. She always had her eyes closed, and she said, 'Yes, that's it, like that, yes, like that.' She would adjust my hands when they weren't doing what she wanted. We drank white wine, no toasts, no looking at each other, ever; the bottle was already open when I got there and our glasses were filled. She wanted to do it everywhere: first on the chest, and on the floor, and then afterward in the bathroom, always in the same order, then we ended up on the bed, her legs around me, her cunt in my mouth; she sucked me, I sucked her, there was something so impatient about it, even if it was methodical, so strong; she'd get on top of me and jerk me off; I had to look inside her, I had to describe the shape of her cunt, with the words she whispered to me and which corresponded so exactly to what was before my eyes that afterward I knew them by heart and she didn't have to repeat them to me anymore; I had to fuck her, but it was always the same. And with each passing week it got better and better. There was nothing but pleasure in it for me. I've never been used in this way. I've never had so little freedom, and yet I felt so free, because she liked everything I was doing to her. I would get a hard-on as soon as I left her, and the closer the days got to Tuesday, the harder I got. But I wanted to keep myself for her; I was so impatient, I felt so alive when I took that girl. When she came. And she got off on it, too; that was the one thing that varied during the two hours we spent together: she never came at the same time, and that's how I know it was genuine."

Francisco had whispered everything he said. As if in one breath. Now Eva Maria watches him inhale deeply. His eyes are big.

"Then one day I fucked up."

"What did you do?"

"I stayed in the room after it was over. That girl had gotten under my skin; I'd fallen in love with her—it was driving me crazy and I had to tell her, and besides I believed she had fallen in love with me, too, what an idiot. She came out of the bathroom; at first, I saw she was a little bit afraid—she didn't expect to see me there—but very quickly she got hold of herself and looked at me so coldly. She wouldn't let me speak; she picked up her handbag and left the room—I can still hear the door slamming. The next day she came by the café. I apologized, I told her that next time I would leave. She told me there wouldn't be any next time. I asked her if it was all over between us— I should never have said that to her, what an asshole I was. She replied saying that for anything to be all over it had to have actually started. That's how it ended. No one has ever got me as hard or done such a good job putting me in my place as that girl did."

Eva Maria doesn't know what to say. Francisco continues his story. More about himself, this time. Quietly.

"I just didn't get it. Why? Why this? Why me? She could have any guy she wanted."

Eva Maria thinks it over. Francisco goes on. Louder this time. Emphatically.

"But I'm sure she replaced me after that. With someone else. Another more disciplined sexual object. She was sick, I can tell you that much, she couldn't have stopped from one day to the next; that girl had to fuck, she needed it. If Vittorio had been a good shrink he would have realized his wife was a complete wreck; before he went helping others he would have done better to pay attention to what was happening at home, and looked after his own wife."

"When was this?"

"Next Tuesday will make three months."

"Which hotel was it?"

Francisco doesn't answer.

"You'd rather not say?"

"No."

"Why not?"

"I don't know; I just don't want to, that's all."

"Have you been back to the hotel since then?"

"Every Tuesday. I went back there every Tuesday after she left me, and every time I was full of hope, and every time they told me they hadn't seen her again. I don't see why they would lie to me. She changed her lover so she must have changed her venue. I was probably not the first; she must have changed dicks the way she changed her underwear."

"Except that she didn't wear any. You see I've been listening to you."

Francisco suddenly stands up straight.

"You don't believe me, do you?"

"Yes, I do. I believe you."

"Then why are you looking at me like that?"

"I'm not looking at you 'like that.' Come closer."

Francisco moves his face closer to Eva Maria's. Eva Maria buries her face in Francisco's neck. She sniffs him. Francisco recoils.

"Stop it! What are you doing?"

"The bar stool must be giving me ideas."

"You're such a bitch."

"This is the cologne she asked you to wear, isn't it?"

"How do you know?"

"I recognize it. I know someone who wears it."

"Well, that's really helpful."

"Vittorio wears this cologne."

"Who?"

"Vittorio."

"No way; what the hell is going on?"

Francisco shakes his head. He opens the dishwasher. He takes the cups out one by one. All the glasses, one by one. He sets them onto a tray. Eva Maria watches him. She knows it's not these objects he's tidying away but his thoughts.

"I hope he'll get life."

"It must have been hard when it stopped. How did you deal with it?"

"What do you think? It's not every day that casual fucking of this caliber comes knocking on your door; already sex is addictive enough as it is, but like this . . . and besides, I fell in love with Lisandra, really."

"You were mad at her for stopping."

"How could I not be mad at her?"

"She died on a Tuesday, or hadn't you noticed, the day of your appointments."

Francisco turns around. Abruptly. His gesture dislodges the

tray. The cups and glasses go crashing to the floor. The white porcelain mixing with the transparency of the glass.

"Fuck, what the hell are you insinuating by that? Stop right now, Eva. I've got nothing to do with Lisandra's death."

"It doesn't take long to toss a woman out the window. The time it takes to smoke a cigarette."

"I don't smoke."

"So you never go to the toilet, either?"

"Just stop your nonsense right there. Anyone rather than him, is that it? You would rather I got locked up than to lose your precious shrink. You can replace a waiter, but not a shrink. Sorry to inform you, I've got an alibi from every customer I had that night."

"The cops might find all of this very interesting."

"Don't worry, they already know about it."

"What do you mean?"

"I already told them everything."

"You? You told them everything?"

"Yes. I want that fucker to end up in jail. I am sure he knew that Lisandra was cheating on him—he must have realized and he went berserk, that's what happened; it may be 'simplistic,' as you say, but murders are not exempt from clichés and I want to see justice done."

"You don't want to see justice done. What you want is to get your revenge."

"My revenge for what?"

"You're jealous, Francisco."

"Jealous of what? Tell me. Some guy whose wife cheated on him for nearly three months? Please, Eva, use your head."

"Jealous of the husband she cheated on yet didn't leave. May I remind you that you are the one she left. Not him. Some lovers have the distinctive gift of returning a wife to her husband more loving than ever. Moreover, he could make love to her whenever he wanted; that must be hard to bear, or am I wrong? Did you know that your relationship would go no further? That's why you allowed it to deteriorate. Or am I mistaken?"

"Yes, you're mistaken, across the board. That's absolute nonsense. I don't even know why I told you all that, maybe so you would drop the matter, but it seems it's a specialty with you, not to want to look truth in the face. Go ahead, think whatever you like, I don't give a shit. Fuck off!"

Eva Maria climbs down off the stool. She turns around to face Francisco.

"In fact, if I sat at the counter, it's only because I left the house in a hurry, without taking my bag, and I figured you might treat me to a little coffee at the counter. You see, you don't always guess right."

Eva Maria does not tell Francisco that she could see Lisandra's window from there, but not from her usual spot. Eva Maria doesn't tell him that she wanted to see if the cops were preparing the reenactment for the following day. She would have liked to have seen what that Commissioner Perez looked like. Eva Maria leaves the bar. She turns around. She looks one last time at Francisco as he sweeps up the broken glass. She shouldn't have given him such a hard time, she went too far, but he annoys her with his certainty, his conviction. She wanted to teach him a lesson, to prove to him that even the tiniest bit of bad faith can make anyone seem guilty. But she knows very well that he isn't guilty. She likes Francisco. She always has. She feels sorry for him, pities him more than anything. Life allowed him a glimpse of the sublime, only to snatch it away again. Eva Maria knows that Francisco is not Lisandra's murderer. His way is to dwell on things, rehash them, not to lash out. He will never get over that affair, but he would never have pushed Lisandra out the window. All he can do now is to transform his sorrow into hatred for Vittorio, into an absolute conviction. One absolute conviction pitted against another, that is the way of the world. Eva Maria climbs onto her bike. She looks up at the window. Darkness reigns. Back to square one, yet again. Time to decide whether to stop. Or to go on. Eva Maria cannot drop Vittorio, just like that.

Eva Maria lights a cigarette. You don't make it up, the sort of thing Francisco just told her. She now has a very important element for the investigation, and Vittorio didn't know about it, otherwise he would have told her. The police want to cover up this business about a lover, because they are firmly convinced of Vittorio's guilt, they don't want to be hampered by a testimony that might allow doubt to creep in, and besides, this so-called lover has an alibi, so it's nothing to make a fuss over. Or else—yes, maybe that's it—they're saving it for the trial, this business about a lover, it's their trump card; they'll take it out at the last minute so that Vittorio won't have time to prepare his defense. Lisandra had—or used to have—a lover; Dr. Puig knew about it and killed her out of jealousy. "Simplistic" it may be, but it happens too often not to be convincing. That Commissioner Perez. The neighbor. And now Francisco. All these people who want to make Vittorio pay for the wrong reasons: she finds it disgusting. Eva Maria suddenly pictures the offhand manner in which Commissioner Perez must have analyzed the crime scene; convinced as he was of Vittorio's guilt right from the start, he certainly didn't try to interpret the elements in any other light. She absolutely must inform Vittorio's lawyer about Francisco; she has to call him. What was his name again? She can't remember. She strikes her hand against the wall. It won't come to her. The sound of that unfamiliar, formal voice had destabilized her; she had not retained the lawyer's name—surprise had blocked her memory. And fear, too. Every time she heard an unfamiliar voice on the phone, she dreaded it was someone about to tell her they had found Stella's body. Eva Maria opens her desk drawer. A green file: "His lawyer . . ." "Vittorio Puig's lawyer . . ." "his lawyer . . ." The lawyer's name did not appear anywhere in the press clippings. Eva Maria closes the file, the drawer; she's going to have to wait until her next visit—five more days until she can find out more. Eva Maria is smoking. Francisco and Lisandra, Lisandra and Francisco—their affair is not the key to Lisandra's murder, she is sure of that; at most it is a symptom, but not the key. And Eva Maria is looking for the key. The murderer. Eva Maria reaches for her glasses. She opens her notebook. She rereads. Attentively.

> door to the apartment open
> loud music in the living room
> window open in living room
> chairs on the floor
> lamp overturned
> vase on the floor, broken
> water spilled
> figurine broken (porcelain cat)
> wine bottle
> two broken glasses
> lying on her back
> head to one side
> icy forehead, trickle of blood
> eyes open, puffy

She shakes her head. Turns the page.

Wearing a pretty dress
high heels

Eva Maria nods. She underlines.

Wearing a pretty dress

high heels

Clearly Lisandra had dressed to seduce. And such a desire to look good is rarely for oneself alone. So who was Lisandra out to charm that evening? A lover? Eva Maria gets undressed. She climbs into bed. Her little notebook by her side. Eva Maria tries to imagine the tribulations of an adulterous soul. What if Lisandra had invited her most recent lover home, determined to cheat on her husband in their own apartment, on their own dresser, on their own floor, in their own bathroom, in their own bed. That would explain the bottle of white wine, the two glasses, and the tango, so conducive to romantic couplings. And what if things went wrong with this man? That might explain the loud music, sound masking a deadly argument. And it's not that easy to find lovers who have Francisco's nobility of soul. He's a good guy, Francisco, Eva Maria knows that, everyone knows that. With Francisco, Lisandra did not go wrong. He had been the right person to do what she wanted, insofar as Eva Maria could understand what it was that Lisandra wanted to do with him. Eva Maria thinks of Francisco's hands as they folded a towel before him, as he was drying the glasses—maybe initially Lisandra had succumbed to the charm of his hands? Eva Maria could see why. Manly hands, but also light, agile, skillful hands. Eva Maria imagines them on her breasts, on her buttocks, his fingers sliding wherever she let them. Francisco is a good guy, but not all men are as gentle, as good; some volcanoes are dangerous and others are not dangerous at all. Perhaps his successor had been even more undisciplined than he was; there are those who stay in the room in hopes of impetuously declaring their love, and there are those who hurl things out of windows out of anger and spite; it can move from here to there, the cursor of passion. With another man Lisandra might have gone wrong, and if her choice had landed on a gray volcano, the most dangerous kind, a man who couldn't stand for Lisandra to be constantly calling the shots where his life was concerned, where his prick was concerned, well, such a man might have been capable of killing her. Those who are insane can take others down with them. Francisco was right. Was Lisandra a nymphomaniac? Eva Maria tries to imagine the tribulations of an adulterous soul. She never cheated on her own husband; she was never that hung up on sex, and besides, since Stella's disappearance, sex hasn't existed—a bed is only used to sleep in; a man is useless, or useless for that, in any case. There was her sexuality before the death of her child, then her sexuality after. A dead child returns to its parents' living bodies when they couple, and it inflicts the painful memory of their dead treasure's procreation, and that painful memory takes hold, plays over and over, and becomes abstinence. Or at least that was how it was for her. Eva Maria tosses in her bed. Turns. That posture, even more assertive from behind, skirt lifted, ass held out: what was the purpose of such posed embraces? Artificial embraces, on command: what was the purpose of such unvarying playacting? It was no ordinary adultery. Lisandra might have been a nymphomaniac, but it wasn't just that; there was something else going on. And what if the most important thing was not to find out *who* Lisandra was deceiving Vittorio with, but *why* she was deceiving him. Was it simply that Lisandra was cheating on Vittorio because there were things she could no longer do with him? That she no longer dared to do with him? Force of habit, the weight of everyday life had crushed the very

delicate temperament of eroticism. Her skirt pulled up over her
bare ass. That is not how you wait for your husband to come home.
"What are you doing in that getup?" he would have asked, one hand
on his satchel, the other holding a loaf of bread, and all that was left
for the bitch in heat to do was to pull down her skirt and roll up her
sleeves and make dinner. She would blush, not from the heat of the
oven, but from the slap given to her lustful appetite. Her husband's
appetites being located above his belt, below her own belt Lisandra
could sense her cunt weeping. *Take a lover. Take a lover.* All right. But
it wasn't as simple as that. And that business with the cologne? It
must mean something; it was no coincidence that Lisandra had
asked Francisco to wear the same cologne as Vittorio, no, it could
not be a coincidence. So what was it? A symbol for something that
must be terribly important to her. Something suddenly occurs to
Eva Maria. Could Vittorio have been impotent? She had never
talked about sex with him. She would have liked to, then she could
have recalled the advice he would have given her and tried to
approach the matter from that angle, to see whether any such impo-
tence or frustration surfaced anywhere in his words. And that might
be why he didn't tell her that Lisandra was cheating on him, not to
have to give himself away. And what if Vittorio knew that his wife
was cheating on him? Maybe they had even planned it together: the
hotels, the identity of the lovers, the limits beyond which they must
not go, perhaps the number of times per substitute lover, a number
they must not exceed, the gestures; and the cologne was intentional,
the better for her to imagine Vittorio, that was why she asked her
lovers to wear it. Eyes closed, too. No, it couldn't be; Vittorio would
have told her about it; he would immediately have suspected that
the crime might originate there. And he would have told her everything; but then, like all men, Vittorio cared more about his freedom
than his male pride. So he knew nothing about it. But then what?

How far back did the truth go? And what if the truth, instead of stopping with Vittorio, went beyond him, and what if Vittorio himself had been used by Lisandra? Maybe he already wore that cologne at her request. Maybe Lisandra had given it to him as a simple Christmas or birthday present, her gesture already concealing the desire for some lost paradise. And what if the key to the entire drama lay not in what came after Vittorio but in what came before him? The man she had come to weep about so helplessly in Vittorio's office, for example, the first time they met? What if he was the one behind all this? This so-called Ignacio. But how to find him? Eva Maria feels as if she has a tree in her head, and buds of suspicion are constantly sprouting, all of them valid, all of them pointless. But perhaps it's none of all that. Poetical, fantastical, Lisandra had come up with the dream-fuck plan, and she set it all out, everything she fancied, in the order she fancied. After all, it was an alluring idea. To give rhythm to the gestures of love, a kind of choreography. Lisandra was a dancer. And what if she found eroticism in extreme habit? But something suggests to Eva Maria that no one on earth enjoys habit to that degree. Eroticism also stems from surprise. With her hand on her cunt, Eva Maria feels a warmth she has not known in a long time. Tonight, in her bed, she feels like making love. An image springs to mind. Or perhaps she summoned it. Eva Maria pauses for a few seconds. Somewhat surprised. Somewhat bashful. She did not expect to be thinking about him. But she figures it is surely part of the game, and in the end it hardly matters, after all, whether it's him or someone else. With her hand on her cunt, Eva Maria blushes. She doesn't feel it. Her senses are elsewhere. Eva Maria had not had an orgasm in a very long time. She turns on her side. Eva Maria has not fallen asleep this quickly in a long time.

Eva Maria screams. She is suffocating. She cries out, frozen in her bed. Estéban comes into the bedroom. Eva Maria opens her eyes. She rushes to hold him.

"Stella, my dear, you are here; I was so afraid."

"It's me, Mama, it's me, Estéban."

Eva Maria pushes him away.

"Go away!"

Eva Maria hits him. In the chest.

"Go away! Go away!"

Estéban gets up. He leaves the room. Eva Maria goes on sitting there. Her hair is dripping. Another nightmare; she can't take it anymore, all these nightmares. Eva Maria tries to remember. Stella falls, there was a robin, and a radiator; what else? Eva Maria cannot recall. There was Francisco—yes, that's it, Francisco was there, too, or Vittorio; she can't remember. Eva Maria takes her head in her hands. She wonders what matters more with nightmares, the things you remember or the things you forget. Eva Maria rubs her mouth. She recalls the huge peacock in Vittorio's office. That, too, must have been in her nightmare. Francisco or Vittorio? In any case, there was a man, standing, from the back, wearing a jacket.

I couldn't sleep; I cursed myself for causing her to flee . . . I hunted for a clue in the few moments I had spent with her, a clue that might enable me to find her again . . . She was wearing slacks made of a light fabric, a sort of black cotton, and—how had I failed to notice at the time?—a fine pair of shoes, also black . . . high heels . . . and beneath her feet there were white spots on the carpet . . . While I hesitated to congratulate myself too soon, I did not hesitate to go around to all the tango places and milongas in the vicinity—she must have just come from one of them, and it couldn't be far, otherwise the talcum powder would have had time to disappear altogether . . . Now I had a lead, and I could find her again.

Eva Maria is following in Vittorio's footsteps. She decided to begin there. If she has to inform Vittorio that Lisandra was cheating on him, she would like to inform him at the same time that it was Lisandra's lover who killed her. To make him lose his pride but regain his freedom: this was the only way she could stand the thought of telling him that his wife had been unfaithful. Eva Maria's reasoning is simple. If Lisandra slept with Francisco, then surely she found her lovers in her immediate environment, picking them at random, so surely she would also have drawn from the very accessible breeding ground her tango classes offered. Eva Maria is following in Vittorio's footsteps. She has been going around and around the neighborhood since early morning.

"Did you know Lisandra Puig? Did Lisandra Puig come here to dance?"

Eva Maria thinks back to the moment when Vittorio finally found Lisandra. She wonders if it would not have been better if he had never found her. He didn't know then what was in store. How can you know that a terrible drama might arise from what initially seems like such a wonderful event?

I wondered what Lisandra would look like as a dancer, with her long brown hair pulled up into a chignon. Would I recognize her from behind? No, I wouldn't recognize her. I had not yet acquired the familiarity that enables one to recognize someone from behind.

Eva Maria thinks about the night of the murder. Vittorio would have acquired it by then, the familiarity that enables one to recognize someone from behind. When, from up in his window, he recognized Lisandra's body sprawled on the ground. Eva Maria is beginning to despair of ever finding the place. This is at least the tenth address she has tried. She is driven by a sense of urgency. She has only two days left until the next prison visit. A sense of urgency doesn't mean doing things quickly, but knowing that nothing can sway you from your path. She does not wonder whether it would be better never to find the place.

"Did you know Lisandra Puig? Did Lisandra Puig come here to dance?"

"Yes. Lisandra was my student."

Eva Maria looks at the man speaking. She smiles. Relieved. How can you know that a terrible drama might arise from what initially seems like such a wonderful event?

Eva Maria did not expect a man this age. Seventy, maybe more. The man holds out his hand, frank, lively.

"Pedro Pablo."

Eva Maria shakes his hand. She has the impression she has already seen this man somewhere.

"But people also call me 'Pepe.' What can I do for you?"

"I'd like to ask you a few questions about Lisandra."

Eva Maria does not tell him why. Nor does the old man ask.

"I'm listening; please, have a seat."

Eva Maria sits down.

"In the days that preceded her death—did you notice anything about her behavior? I mean, anything in particular."

The old man looks at Eva Maria.

"Lisandra hadn't come to dance for over a month, so if I noticed anything in particular, it was above all her absence."

Eva Maria can't think of anything else to say other than to repeat his words.

"Lisandra hadn't come for over a month."

The old man nods.

"For three years she never missed a class, three times a week, her silent, supple body always in the same place—look, over there."

The older man points to where Lisandra used to stand. Eva Maria turns around. She looks at the empty spot in the empty room. She feels a chill go through her. She thinks about Stella's room, empty like this. The old man goes on.

"One month without seeing her, you can imagine how worried I was, so I went by her place. I never do that as a rule, go by an absent student's place, but in this case I couldn't help it, no doubt because it was Lisandra. I liked her a lot."

Eva Maria shakes her head. She can't get herself out of Stella's empty bed, so many nights she slept there, hoping to feel her daughter next to her when she awoke, clinging with all her strength to the sheets not to scream at the terror of the solitary dawn. Eva Maria can no longer concentrate on the old man's words. She hears him from a distance.

"I liked Lisandra a lot; she was different, so gentle. She never showed up the way the others did, all full of their days, nervous and noisy. She would keep to herself, the way only children know how. She was reserved. Human beings lose this ability very quickly. They have to try and fit in. Solitude becomes impossible; they have to belong to a group, even when that group consists of only two people. But Lisandra was the kind of person who kept to herself; in any case, that was what I believed then. And she had another quality I found infinitely touching—because I am a dancer, above all—she was grace-ful; she had the grace of ten women put together. She had her own particular way of moving, smoothly, slowly; I don't mean sluggishly, no, slowly. No arrogant poses, although she had what might have been the most harmonious body I've ever seen. There was some-thing moderate about her entire person. When the others would burst out laughing, all she did was smile; that was one of the things I instantly noticed about Lisandra: she made no noise. One day, I pointed this out to her, and she blushed, astonished—oh, really? Is that what I thought about her? And then she added, somewhat dreamily, maybe she had left a part of herself somewhere, and that would explain it. 'I'll try to be more lively, I promise, Pepe.' She had taken my compliment for a reproach. She was like that, Lisandra: even a compliment would make her think. She had surprising reactions. 'Why do we dance?'—'To stop time.' Lisandra was the only one of my students who replied, 'To go back in time.' She believed that memory was written in the body and she danced to remember. 'Remember what?'—'To remember,' because by remembering she hoped she would feel better. She did not elaborate; she stopped short: she couldn't tell me, and anyway, it wasn't important. But I could tell that her reality was the opposite from what she said, and what she was trying to remember was, on the contrary, very important to her. Ever since that day, when I watched Lisandra dancing, I told myself that she was dancing the way you dance when you have a secret. Maybe that was why I went by her house. But above all, you know, when you see people disappear from one day to the next, your mind is not at rest, and the slightest absence can seem definitive, and that plants doubt in your mind, so you want to make sure. But I'm not telling you anything you don't already know."

Eva Maria straightens up. His last words bring her back to reality.

"Know about what?"

"That the slightest absence can seem definitive."

"Why do you say that?"

"Because you keep moving your arms . . ."

The old man leaves his words in midair. Eva Maria understands. He is waiting for her to reveal her inner self. Some of her identity.

"Eva Maria."

The old man smiles. He continues, quietly.

"Yes, Eva Maria, your arms move too much; your hands clutch at the slightest object—look, you've just picked up my pen, and before that it was your notebook you were turning every which way; your hands and arms are constantly fidgeting. As if they can't stand it anymore, not being able to hold someone who was dear to you."

Eva Maria feels increasingly nervous. The old man lowers his voice.

"Did you lose a child?"

"Why do you say that?"

"Because to stop your feverish gestures, you put your arms over your belly. Would you like something to drink?"

Eva Maria uncrosses her arms. She doesn't know what to do with them anymore. She doesn't like being read like an open book. She looks at Pedro Pablo's tall, slender body as he moves, a young man's body, not the slightest sagging, not the slightest stoop or limp, which would be the usual attributes of a body his age. His old face is deeply lined, but his body is as light as if it had been grafted upon him. Pedro Pablo vanishes from the room. Eva Maria is suddenly afraid he won't come back. But he does come back.

"I'm sorry: I asked you if you wanted something to drink and all I have is water; how idiotic our niceties are sometimes. Will water be all right?"

Eva Maria nods her head. She would have liked a drink. She feels her fingers squeezing the pencil ever harder. She puts her lips to the glass; she hates hearing herself swallow; she hates the taste of water. Eva Maria puts the glass down. The water didn't help. Her tone is hard.

"And how did Lisandra react to your visit?"

"She didn't react; she was there, and that was all I needed. When she opened the door, you cannot imagine how relieved I was. I wish my own brother would open the door to me one day like that, but I know it will never happen. Lisandra was there; I was reassured; it was a weight off my chest. I could have left, but something about her attitude kept me there—you know, that split second where when you find someone again, you can sense the tiny changes that have occurred, changes you forget about very quickly, because your eyes have adjusted to the new person standing there before you: a great weariness, a great weakness emanating from her body. She seemed not to want to let me leave. She motioned to me to make no noise, and while excusing herself for not being able to receive me in the living room, she led me into her bedroom, into their bedroom. She motioned to me to sit on the bed, on their bed. I was somewhat embarrassed, but I sat down.

"'Careful! Not on the jacket!'

"Lisandra sprang up from her chair to grab a gray jacket, a man's jacket that lay folded on the bed. She seemed to be torn between two irreconcilable things: to make the jacket disappear as quickly as possible and at the same time avoid spoiling or wrinkling it, which made her movements seem paradoxical. She really behaved in the oddest way: she opened a drawer in the dresser and stuffed the jacket into it, but not by rolling it up, as I might have expected, given her feverish behavior, but on the contrary by carefully laying it out flat. And then she turned back to face me as abruptly as if she had just concealed a corpse, I remember that, that was really the feeling I got. I asked her if she was all right. She told me she was. I asked her why she had stopped coming to class. She told me she didn't feel like dancing anymore. Coming from her, that surprised me and I asked her if she had changed teachers; sometimes people simply feel like a change.

"'Not at all, Pepe! How can you imagine such a thing!'

"I asked her if I had done anything wrong.

"'Not at all! You've done nothing wrong. Not you. It's not your fault.'

"'Not me. Who, then?'

"'No one. That's not what I meant. It's just life. A day comes when you no longer feel like doing something you wanted to do every day, before. It's nothing more than that.'

"But I could tell she wasn't in her usual state. I felt ill at ease, sitting there on the bed, on their bed, so I asked her if she wouldn't like to come with me for something to drink at the café downstairs. She looked like someone who hadn't left the house in a long time. I told her she shouldn't ever entrust everything to her mind, that she had to give what belonged to her body back to her body—movement, strolling, walking—our minds can bully our bodies and we mustn't let the mind get the upper hand, so to speak; it's not good for our health: a body is not meant to just lie there; that's the way obsessions are born. She ought to know that after all these years she's been dancing, how everything becomes illuminated when the body is moving.

"'I don't feel like going out. I don't feel like seeing anyone. I'm fine on my own.'

"That was when I heard a door open in the hall. Lisandra went 'hush' with her finger to her lips, like a child, and she got up. She went to peek out the half-open bedroom door. I could hear steps in the corridor, someone dragging their feet. Lisandra looked at her watch, then came back to me, somewhat embarrassed, and sat back down at her desk. A few minutes later, the doorbell rang and she went through the whole song and dance again: peer through the half-open door. Again I heard footsteps in the corridor, quicker this time, a woman's heels. She closed the door and came to sit back down. After that, she wanted to make small talk, as if she had not done what she had just done, or rather as if it didn't mean anything, didn't signify any unhappiness or distress. But I could tell she was unhappy: she was going around in circles. I realized during that second 'surveillance'—we may as well call things by their name—that her gestures had clearly been formed by repetition, that she had made them dozens of times. It was her new dance, without any music, without any pleasure: the dance of doubt. She had exchanged the tango for this new circle dance that she performed alone with a partner who surely did not even know he was dancing. Lisandra the sentry, Lisandra at her post, Lisandra the spy. I felt humiliated for her sake, my beautiful dancer reduced to these degrading gestures; when she could have had the world at her feet she was the one on the floor, schooled in the shame of spy mania, schooled in these odious gestures; when she was worth so much more, schooled in being suspicious, like those who took my brother away, like the people who took six years of peace in our country from us. I couldn't stand it. I got to my feet and I changed my tone, my voice.

"'We're going out; we're going to the dance studio.'

"'I don't want to see them.'

"'Who?'

"'The others.'

"'But what did they do to you, "the others"?'

"I asked her if someone in the class had made her feel uncomfortable, if something had happened that I was unaware of. She shook her head—no, that was not what she meant; nothing happened; it wasn't their fault, either; I mustn't worry. She put her hand on my cheek: 'It's so kind of you to stop by to see me.' With her touch, she felt familiar to me again. I knew I had to insist; she needed to speak to someone. I took her by the hand and pulled her to her feet.

"'There won't be anyone at the studio at this time of day. There will just be the two of us, and it will be easier to talk.'

"'I don't want to talk.'

"'Then we'll dance; that would be better than this miserable, sinister dance you just showed me.'

THE CASE OF LISANDRA P.

"Lisandra got up. And a teacher's authority is something you can regain very quickly over those who admire you and who once wanted to resemble or equal you. The link between teacher and student is more hypnotic than anything, even love, I think. The only authority that is greater is that of the torturer over his victim, because then fear is involved. Out in the corridor, Lisandra looked at one of the doors, the look of a lost dog. I told her to hurry and take her shoes. She grabbed a hat off the coatrack—it was the first time I ever saw her with a hat—and then she put on dark glasses and we went out. I hate the things weather uses to divide people. We walked all the way to the studio without saying a word; she had her head down, and yet again I thought of a lost dog, but this time I understood that she was hurt. Lisandra wasn't walking in her usual way, that confident, enchanting gait I knew so well. I took her arm. I was no longer a man: I was her cane. She did not so much walk as stagger. Once we got there, I put some music on, she put on her shoes, I took her by the waist, and we began to dance, silently. I didn't choose that tango by chance. The circle dance she had performed in her bedroom had made her transparent to me."

Has won your heart but, When the mu - sic starts,____
Cla - var tu da - ga, Tu des - den sin pie - dad____

My peace de - parts. From the mo - ment they play____ that lan - guor - ous
Por - que que - rer - te si a mi vi - da ____ traes so - lo llan-

ben cantando

strain, And we sur - ren - der to all ____ its charm once a - gain,
to Es que no pue - do a - rran - car - me tu en - can - to,

This jeal - ous - y That tor - tures me
Que me es fa - tal, y yo lo se,

"I felt her body beginning to relax, when Lisandra asked me a question that, in the end, convinced me I had not been mistaken.

"'Doesn't she get jealous, your wife, when you dance with other women? Jealous that you spend all day long going from one woman to another?'

"'What a strange question. It's my job, Lisandra.'

"'"It's my job"—that doesn't mean a thing, "it's my job." Our job is also who we are. Answer my question, Pepe.'

"'No, my wife doesn't get jealous. Or anyway she's never mentioned it.'

"'Maybe she just doesn't tell you. Do you think you know your wife well? Do you think she shares all her deepest thoughts with you? You know that's not possible, that it's never like that between two human beings. Be honest.'

"'Then I'll "be honest"—I've never wondered whether she gets jealous.'

"'You haven't? How selfish of you. Well then, I'm asking you. Does your wife have any reason to be jealous?'

"Lisandra would not let go of her question; I could feel it in her hand as it pressed against mine. I wanted to make light of it.

"'Have you seen how old I am? My wife has nothing more to fear.'

"But there was no getting through to Lisandra, no reasoning with her; even an attempt at humor did not work. Her thoughts came rushing out.

"'Age doesn't mean anything, either. And you've been giving classes for years, so there must have been a time when you could not have said that, an age where you couldn't say, "Have you seen how old I am?" So swear to me that you have never had wicked thoughts when dancing with another woman. Swear to me that it has never happened to you. I don't believe a man and a woman can be physically close without such thoughts pressing in on them. Even one floor in an elevator can be enough to initiate the thought. Go on, swear.'

"I thought about Mariana and I couldn't swear. But I went on dancing. I mustn't stop Lisandra. It would have been like slamming the lid down on a music box that was still playing, to force our bodies to bend just as they were spinning, gathering momentum. I had wanted to get her to speak; I had to hear her out. She went on, pressing her point.

"'So you see, even you, Pepe, even you have thought about it.'

"Lisandra's voice was flowing like poison into my ear. It was as if she were some monster blocking my path and forcing me to think about the worst things in my life, or the best, but which have ended: so the worst. Mariana came back to me, and I had almost managed to forget her, when once I had thought I could never forget her. Mariana had been my student, and the minute she moved I desired her, and the minute she stopped moving I desired her; I could no longer do without her, without her body. But we never left this place. It was always in the studio, yes, always in the studio. That way my betrayal would seem less terrible, as if it were beyond reality. Mariana was not competing with my wife, she was like my muse. That must be how I reasoned back then, although back then I didn't reason, I was simply fucking. I was fucking like a fifty-year-old man who is sheltered from remorse by his fear of regret. I deceived my wife with Mariana almost every day for close to a year. The last month Mariana took my hand and led me, unhesitating: she would stand with her back or her belly to the door of the studio and I took her there; that was the only place I was allowed to take her. I knew that was her way of asking me to take her somewhere else, anywhere else. The place of our lovemaking must have seemed too confined to her now. With one hand on me and the other on the door handle, it was her way of asking me to go out, or else she was hesitating between her freedom and me, or else it was just her way of saying good-bye; I never knew. I loved her all the more for it: for having known how to get away from me, to get away from this hateful system I had trapped her in, for having made the right choice.

"'Vittorio is being unfaithful to me.'

"And then, suddenly, Lisandra began to talk. To rattle on and on, even. Her soul laid bare. All of a sudden. Without me asking her a thing. As abruptly as if she had suddenly taken her clothes off, without a single gaze begging her to."

I'm sick.

It didn't start right away. But as soon as we met, I could tell that I was becoming unbalanced.

The first crisis was over three years ago. At the hotel. We had gone to spend a few days in Pinamar. It was around the middle of our stay. We had had dinner just the two of us. I don't remember what we talked about, but it was a good conversation. I've always been afraid I would bore him. And then we went up to the room. Vittorio switched on the television. I picked up a book. And I think I was still all right at that point. And then behind us, behind the head of the bed, there were sudden moans, faint at first. Then more precise, urgent cries, spontaneous. Cries of lovemaking. I no longer dared turn the page. For fear of making a ridiculous sound by touching the paper. It was terrible, horrible. The reflection of our own selves. Of our nothingness. Our absence from each other. To hear others getting their pleasure so nearby merely emphasized how lethargic we had become, sexually, by then. We didn't joke about it. Perhaps we should have. Well, if we had been able to. The silence became unbearable. Our silence. Because it wasn't silent around us at all. Their bed was creaking against our wall, banging against it. I could sense Vittorio's desire growing for that unknown woman. I was sure he would rather have been on the other side of the wall. With her rather than me. A useful night, a night he could remember. I looked at the sheets. I was sure he had a hard-on. I thought of going to draw a bath but I was afraid such an unusual idea might merely emphasize the noise even more, the moans, when all I wanted was to hide them. I told myself if I went out he'd masturbate. As if to a porn film without the picture. What sort of extraordinary woman would his imagination dream up? A brunette? A blonde, surely. Yes, a blonde, he, too, prefers blondes. That's his taste. The way you might prefer savory to sweet. The way you can't force your tongue to feel differently, such tastes are independent of our will, it's physical. So why did he choose me? A brunette. An accidental slip-up. What sort of woman would his imagination come up with? Would she be thin? Plump? She would have big breasts. Or maybe small breasts, but with pointed, twitchy nipples. But maybe she wouldn't even be an imaginary woman. Maybe she would be a flesh and blood woman. Quite simply. A woman he'd crossed paths with earlier that day. Recently. The latest one to kindle his desire. I thought about the girl at the reception desk and suddenly I couldn't get her out of my mind; I saw them, their terrible shapes, intertwined.

When Vittorio switched off the light all I could think of was how to get out of that room. I prayed it would stop. Darkness made the sounds even louder. You could hear something like words between their moans, but they weren't audible. An impression that the wall reduced. I told myself the wall would vanish and we would find ourselves there with our two beds back to back. The bed for fucking and the bed for boredom. She was moaning so much, moaning so magnificently. I figured that this woman surely made love better than I did, and I began to think about all the women who made love better than I did, and I felt guilty. Toward him. I, too, wanted to give him nothing else, nights he would remember; otherwise, what are nights for? But I couldn't. It was no longer possible. The weight of habit. Our skins touched. That calm skin of his. I wanted nothing to do with such motionless contact. But there was nothing else I wanted, either. I could not stand our dead, inert bodies, but I couldn't have stood it if our bodies were excited, either. The initiative came from him. Rage entered me at the same time he did. Who was he making love to? Who did he see behind his closed eyes? Maybe if he had looked at me, I might have calmed down; it was as if I was there but I no longer existed; I was sure that he wasn't making love to me but to her, the stranger behind the wall; I felt sure he was adjusting the rhythm of his thrusts to the sighs we could hear, not to my sighs, as if through me he was trying to go through the wall to penetrate the body of that Other Woman. I was the stimulant for lovemaking that did not exist, that would never exist; I was a means, an instrument, to enable him to take his pleasure through me but not with me, a lovemaking that was imagined and therefore more marvelous than reality. More marvelous than me. Because I was his reality. And I had always wanted to be his fantasy. Not his *reality*, I hate that word. *Reality*. My moans were not on par with the ones I could hear, they were not as genuine, not as voracious, not as expressive, inferior in every way. While I felt his cock moving about inside me, I remembered that during dinner he had recoiled when I took a bite from his plate. Before, he always used to let me taste his food. I think that jealousy really got to me that night because he didn't like it when I took a bite from his plate. That's when I became aware that there was a before. Because now we were in the after. That was when I knew he had grown tired of me. Without even knowing why, he was weary. Time had ridden over us, through us. When love begins, there is an hourglass somewhere that is turned and we head irrevocably toward the end. Before, we, too, would have made love, and perhaps we wouldn't even have heard them. Or we would have laughed about them. The hourglass of love had been turned. I told him I wanted to leave the hotel the very next morning.

"Why do you want to change hotels? This one is fine."

"I don't want to change hotels."

"Well, what do you want?"

"To go home."

It begins with a sort of paralysis. My throat tightens. My chest seems squeezed from within. And my heartbeat accelerates. At times like this, the heart is never on the side of the body, but in the middle. If there hadn't been this first time, there would have been another time. Vittorio had to induce me to feel jealous; it was part of our story. I knew that jealousy had just asserted its power over me, subjecting me to its madness. I couldn't breathe. I think that I have never gone back to breathing the way I used to. My heart was plugged in somewhere else. To the wrong rhythm. The wrong tempo. Except, perhaps, when I dance. Only then can my breathing relax.

Make them stop, make them stop. Oh, no, not louder. Be quiet.

"Are you asleep?"

He was asleep. The others went on fucking, but we had already finished. I told myself he wasn't sleeping, he wanted me to leave him alone, so he could listen to them in peace; I told myself I hadn't satisfied him, he would gladly have started all over. But next door. On the other side of the wall. Jealousy did not evaporate with his ejaculation. No, it settled in for good. It's a reflex now. Jealousy doesn't choose the person it will inhabit, it's more devious than that, more collective. Jealousy doesn't want to destroy just one person, it wants to destroy a couple. And everything that goes with it. And nocturnal jealousy became diurnal. He didn't want to have breakfast in the room.

"Let's go have it downstairs instead."

"Why?"

"Why not?"

"But why? We always have it in our room."

"And the coffee is always cold. At least downstairs we will have hot coffee."

A hot pussy, that's what he wanted. He wanted to see her. The girl from next door. He wanted to get her firmly printed upon his mind, that girl who was so good in bed. In the mental storeroom where he kept his fantasies, he wanted to see what she looked like, what kind of body she had.

"Let's sit here."

"But we're right in the middle."

"We're nearer the buffet like this."

You don't want to miss her, is that it? I got the impression he was looking at every woman who was busy at the buffet. Which one was she? The unknown woman with whom he had spent the night. One of them would be more beautiful than the others. I decided it was that one. My gaze went from him to the woman, constructing a couple that was more real than the one he made with me. I felt like hitting him.

"What are you looking at like that?" I asked.

"To see if they put any more salmon on the table."

Liar. Obsessed. You're looking at her. You'd love to go and give it to her, wouldn't you? Take her right away, there on the buffet: while she stuffs a slice of salmon down your throat, you'd stuff your cock up her cunt. Go on, then! Since that's all you can think about, go on!

"How many more times are you going to help yourself?"

"What's wrong with you this morning? Don't I have the right to eat?"

"You should have told me that we'd only come here to eat."

"Okay, okay, we'll go; let's go get some fresh air, it'll calm you down. I'm going back up to the room to get a sweater; you can wait for me here if you want."

"Why?"

"Why what?"

"Why do you want me to wait for you here?"

"I don't know . . . so you don't have to go back upstairs."

"Of course . . ."

"What, 'of course'?"

"I'm going up. I want to get a sweater, too."

"You want me to get it for you?"

"You really don't want me to come upstairs, do you?"

"No, that's not it at all . . . come up if you want, but stop attacking me."

If you think I don't know what you're up to. You want to run into her. Have a good slow look at her. They came out just as we were going into our room. The couple. Of course they hadn't had any breakfast, not those two, they'd been fucking.

"Did you see the way you were looking at her?"

"Who?"

"The girl leaving her room."

"But I wasn't looking at her."

"You wish you were in her room, right? You would rather be with her."

"What are you talking about?"

"Don't act all innocent."

It was the first time I slapped him. My hand shot out all by itself. My body flared with an intense heat. Hatred. After insulting him, screaming at him. Now the door was open.

Occasionally the jealousy left me alone, but it was only to seize hold of me all the better afterward, to crush me. Destructive. Definitively destructive. I knew I would lose Vittorio. Another woman would take my place. Would bring him the novelty that I could never bring him ever again. Like water spreading, implacably, the jealousy spread everywhere, to fill the tiniest cracks in my life, in my reasoning, in my emotions. In my identity.

Multiple fears, permanent fears.

A woman walking ahead of me, or toward me, a woman sitting down, a waitress, saleswoman, nurse, pharmacist, blonde, brunette, young, mature, wearing heels, wearing flats, a woman at a party, a primal scene where one evening I was sitting on his lap, his best friend nudged him on the knee when a beautiful woman walked in the room, except that he nudged the wrong knee and the knee he alerted was mine; how humiliating—how many codes do men have among themselves to signal a potential good lay to each other? A woman with long hair, a gamine, eyes of blue brown yellow black, a woman on a train, an air hostess, a virgin, the shopgirl where he goes to buy me flowers when he'd really rather give them to her, any woman, a woman on television, at the movies, a primal scene where I had my head on his shoulder and I felt his heart beating faster when a certain actress came on the screen—I can't even watch a movie with him anymore, I can't sit through a play at the theater, I imagine his fantasies about these actresses, I can't stand to see his gaze land on these women and follow them, undressing, assessing, even a woman in a book, the way he imagines her; what does she look like? What flesh and blood woman inspires him? Even a dead woman, a woman with freckles, the neighbor's daughter, any of them, they all convey a new perfume, a new charm, a new language, another culture, a Swede, an Italian, an Asian, the promise of new conversations, a girl in the next car at the traffic light, a girl he sees every morning at the bakery, the girl who brought a spare part to repair the fridge.

Another cunt to penetrate, simply, for a change.

These women are like wolves; I can't count them anymore. Like wolves, they place their paws in the prints of those who went before.

I would like to have the powers of a beautiful apparition yet remain the everyday woman in his life, his routine. I would like to transform myself to the rhythm of those who charm him. To have that power of metamorphosis. To become her when he is attracted to her, to become the other when he is attracted to the other. Not to always be me, inflicting myself on him. But to transform myself to the rhythm of his desires. To bring every single woman to him while remaining the Unique one. Life inflicts our uniqueness and individuality upon us, in a reduced and limited whole, and we have to endure it, put up with it all our lives. The same smile. The same laughter. The same eyes focusing into a gaze. The same hands in the same hair. The same shoulders, shrugging. The same legs, crossing. The same arms, stretching. The same yawns. The same voice. The same back. The same teeth. The same skin. The same breasts. How many times do we ourselves become weary in order not to weary others? How could he fail to find me repetitive? You can no longer light the fire when you are always there.

I am like a lookout. Absorbed by the coming disaster. A lookout who knows the storm will break, ineluctably. The warning signs fill my head. Danger reigns continuously.

I can enjoy dinner at a restaurant only if he sits facing the wall. The slightest footsteps in the street are torture; I lie in wait for his every gaze; wherever I go I am wary—which side will my enemy suddenly appear from? I freeze the images in my head. I scan them. I hunt for the detail, the proof that Vittorio has been attracted to another woman. A gleam in his eyes. I know that gleam, that quiver of hesitation in his eyes, which tells me desire has him in its grip. But then what thoughts arise? I am sure he uses those thoughts when he makes love to me, to lessen his boredom. I wish I could see into his head when he is making love to me; I wish I could invent a machine to see into another person's head when he is making love. Then no one could hide. No one could pretend. There would be plenty of surprises. Even when I go out for a walk on my own I cannot find serenity; I become his gaze and I look, I look all around me at the women he might fancy; I cannot remain detached, there are no more elegiac thoughts. I go hunting to find who might charm him. Even the sight of a little girl is cause for despair. So pretty. Her child's beauty, so promising. Could she be the one who, someday, ten years from now, fifteen years from now, will take Vittorio from me? Will bring him something new, when all he and I can do is repeat ourselves? When I wake up in the middle of the night, my brain immediately fills with thoughts of him. And when he sighs in the night, I hear his fantasies. And I imagine all the creatures haunting him. It is not their beauty that torments me, it is knowing that I am never there among them. You don't go searching in your dreams for what you have to put up with in your life.

I wonder who it was that began to take him away from me. Who it was that he looked at one day, when before, he had eyes only for me. He grew distant gradually. Falling out of love is progressive. Before you no longer love, you love less. And less again, then no more at all. But it's not something you are aware of. Falling out of love. A relationship gone lukewarm, humdrum, pragmatic, everyday, utilitarian and habit-worn, and you don't even think it through because you don't think about it at all. Some people can live without passion, but not me. I cannot live without passion. I will die because this man has stopped loving me. One day, when we were first together, he told me he didn't look at other women anymore. He never should have told me that. The unthinkable pleasure I got from hearing these few words was not worth the despair I felt one day when I saw him look at another woman. It would have been a smile that started it, creating the distance between us. Eyes. A gaze. A ponytail. A word. A pair of breasts. All of it dazzling in a panorama of all the women on earth. And he wouldn't even have noticed, not really.

I wanted to forestall the inevitable. I stopped using the same toothpaste, the same soap, the same shampoo as him, habits from a shared everyday life that cancel out the pH on your skin and tend to make them the same. Like the perfume you no longer smell on the other person's skin. I dyed my hair, gradually, week by week, so that I, too, could have that erectile blonde color, but it's too late now, it no longer has any effect on him, since I'm the one wearing it. If faithfulness were merely a matter of hair color it would be common knowledge. I have no more subterfuges. It's not just loud noises that accompany disasters, little sounds do, too, and even silence. There is no antechamber to unhappiness; unhappiness often just lands on you.

Vittorio has become distant. He says he hasn't but I know he has. I can feel it. He lies to me. He has a smell in the fold of his chin that disgusts me. The fold beneath his lips. No matter how much he washes, there is a place you cannot wash. That's the fold in the chin. And there I can smell it. I can describe her perfume, not an actual perfume but her female smell. The smell of this woman doesn't leave him. I tried to limit everything, to control and avoid and reduce. Our meetings with others. Our evenings out. Our trips. But I could not stop him doing his job. I am sure that is where he found her. I am sure it's one of his patients. The same patterns, over and over. Find a new woman the way he found me. In the same place. In the same circumstances. I took him from another woman; there's no reason why another woman shouldn't take him from me. It was bound to happen. How could it be otherwise? Shut away all day one-on-one. It's the law of close quarters. Of recurrent physical proximity. It's pernicious, the sexual tension is there, it's a fact, a reality with which two people in each other's presence must contend. Their stinking, simpering ways . . . I know very well what they're up to in there. And the laughter I hear—not all the women consult because they have problems, believe me. Before, between each appointment he would come to our room and give me a kiss. Say a few words. Now his trajectory is limited to the space between the office and the front door. No more detour to come and see me. I study his footsteps. The way he sees a patient to the door. If his steps are quick, I tell myself he's eager to see the next patient. If his steps are slow, I tell myself he's enjoying the company of this one. For months I've been cutting the telephone line in his office so he can't make any calls I cannot eavesdrop on. If I could, I'd install a camera in his office. To see everything. To know everything. I listen out for the inflections in his voice, for any slips. If only I could read his mind . . . that's all I can think of, reading his mind. Everything means something. I've become a lie detector. He's thinking about someone else, I know he is; the first chance he gets he lets go of my hand, finding something better to do than to let me leave it there. The dishes. Read the newspaper. Wipe his ass. I feel as if this mouth of mine where he used to drown himself—it stinks now, I feel as if it has taken on that fetid, bitter smell of a mouth that is too little kissed, too little loved. He goes to see her once a week, I know he does; he told me he goes to the cinema, to the theater—just because I don't feel like going out anymore doesn't mean he should deprive himself. I have been caught in my own trap. My jealousy gave him the best pretext to cheat on me with complete peace of mind. And now he even goes out two nights a week. Soon he'll want to go out every night. Every day without me. He'll want to leave. Never mind who with, I don't care who the girl is, I don't care how beautiful she is. Even subjugating beauty can't keep a man; only novelty has any appeal. Because what we really love about beauty when we encounter it is novelty. And even if beauty doesn't fade it does lose its intensity; a few months in its presence and even beauty makes us weary. There is no way to stop love's changing of the guard. This girl he sees every Thursday, I know, doesn't prove anything by herself. Other than the fact that he no longer loves me, or that he still loves me but I am no longer enough, which amounts to the same. It doesn't matter who she is, in a few months he'll turn away from her, too. She, too, will end up boring him, but I don't care about that; for me the harm has been done. He has moved on. And yet, we did love each other so much.

I am craving "us." An overwhelming desire to fuck. With him. I can think of nothing else. But only with him. And I wish I could think about it with everyone. Taking a first lover. And then another. Watch my desire diversify, multiply. And then I would understand why he, too, should have a mistress. Why he, too, should desire other women. Those first times we made love: I'd give anything for him to take me like that again, one last time, like in the beginning. Our lovemaking was so good before. Why do we do it so badly now? So rarely. So blandly. When we make love, I open my eyes and look into his closed eyes, and the only thing that will make me come are images of him with another woman. Because a man will go on fucking at home, even if he's fucking else-where, too. A man will fuck whenever he gets the chance. This is immediately obvious to a woman. When she's prepared to see it. So is everything doomed to collapse? In the old days practically all women fainted. Now almost none of them do. Where are the smelling salts? Where are the women? Everywhere they have become so strong, so powerful, so beautiful. Why not me? Those whose love will not die are dying from love. I am rotting. Fear makes a body heavy. I've put on weight, but I haven't gotten fatter. It's not fat. It's not water. It's fear. Fear makes a body heavier. I notice it when I dance. The lightness is gone. It's the fear of losing him. Jealousy has an influence on thoughts, but also on the body; my muscles, my nerves are completely focused on him. Filled with him. My bodily tissue is subjected to the orders of jealousy. I am suffocating.

How many times have I thought of his death? Not in a criminal way; simply to ensure my survival. I know I am in such great danger that I want to eliminate him. To recover some peace of mind, like when you switch off the music. Not because of the music, but to regain your tranquillity. But even the mere idea, the fantasy, of his death stimulates my jealousy. I can imagine him as all-powerful, infiltrating everywhere, able to see all the women, naked in their showers, in their bathtubs, in another's arms, Vittorio the Dead Man with a thousand lovers. But he's had his fill of me, he's saturated, disgusted; he won't even ever come to visit me.

The woman he knew before me. The woman with whom he is cheating on me. And the one he will leave me for. I can't find refuge anywhere. Not in the past, nor in the present, nor in the future. No refuge in time can shelter me. I have nothing left. I would like to meet my double to speak to her, and my opposite to distract me. I am suffocating. Jealousy is burning up my brain. The entire right-hand side of my head feels hot. Electricity from my neurons. Too many images, too much imagination, too many fantasies. I have cramps in my right eye. I would like to take photographs of my brain. Wherever it is that jealousy is located, so that I can have it surgically removed. I want a a knife, a flint, a pair of shears, that I could ram into my brain to cut it out. No more nerve endings. But you can't survive jealousy. It's an execution of the individual. A bullfight. One lance, then another and another; the picadors are busy. There, between the eyes, red, red, red everywhere. I am that enraged bull, meant to live in freedom, but let loose in an enclosure, in a bullring, before the excited gazes of those who will watch the bull die.

"Why do you shake your patient's hand when you say hello and when you say good-bye?"

"Why?"

"Yes. Why?"

"I don't know, I just got into the habit."

"All that, just so you can touch them, admit it, go on."

And I keep wondering which one he jerks off to. Maybe he doesn't wash his hands, so he can jerk off with the last one he touched.

I do everything I can to restrain myself. To act as if there's nothing wrong. I try to keep it all to myself. As much as I can. And often I deflect our arguments; I come up with any old excuse, everyday things, to vent my hatred, which in fact is stimulated by jealousy. But sometimes it breaks out. It boils over, it explodes; it's dreadful. Jealousy does not like discretion, jealousy drives its victims into a rage and then, only then, it exults. Jealousy starts in the head and ends up in the body, with blows. It's like a rush of air. Rising. In a second. A rush of air that radiates through my hands. That goes through me and settles into my palms. A cold rush of air, and that is when I want to hit him as hard as I can, to kill him. Shout scream hit him. So he will stop, so he will stop taking me for a ride so he will tell me so he will confess so he will talk so he will choose. *Go ahead, go ahead, since that's all you can think about, go on, get out, you don't owe me a thing, go away, get out.* Snap his penis in two, twist it, crush it. If Vittorio could read my thoughts, he would run for his life; he cannot imagine what is lying around in my brain, he simply cannot. Jealousy is a mental illness, the mother of all human failings, cruelty, hatred, misanthropy, the closing of your soul, selfishness, stinginess. And the worst of it is the horrible feeling that you are going mad. Because I can tell I'm going mad. And it serves no purpose, going mad.

Of course I tried to get over it. I've tried everything. But you cannot cure yourself of jealousy—you can dissect it, you can analyze it when you're aware of it, you can try to justify it, to explain it, but you cannot get over it. Because I read them all, all the books on jealousy, all the ones I could find in his office, every book, every chapter, every footnote, trying to find the needle in a haystack that might enable me to recover from this cancer of the soul and be cured. According to the books, jealous people have two alternatives: they can be either a "repressed unfaithful individual" or a "repressed homosexual." *Repressed.* That's all I am. But beyond these mediocre explanations, the texts about jealousy do not propose a treatment, they merely describe. "No solidity to narcissistic foundations." I know that when Vittorio entered me once and forever, the first time he kissed me I felt my body leave me behind and make room for a new body, his body in mine. This man has become my blood. Perhaps because of the child we never had. The child I never wanted to give him. Now I know it. It's not jealousy that makes a person unhappy, it's unhappiness that causes jealousy. The important thing is to know the source of the unhappiness that has caused the jealousy. And I know this *unhappiness*, I do, I know the wound. We always have every reason to be what we are. And I know why I am what I am.

That is why I am not angry with Vittorio. I cannot ask of him what no human being can give. I'm the one who is asking for too much. He is not the torturer. It is I who am the tyrant. But I will not be his prison. I will not become the woman he can no longer stand because he cannot leave her. I will let him go without a fight, because in love if you have to fight you have already lost. So I want to have the courage to leave. I've already tried packing my bags, several times. But then a furious hatred takes me in its grip and stops me. And a torrent of thoughts rushes over me. Where is he? And I can imagine him happy, laughing because he has forgotten me; I no longer exist in his thoughts, in his life I am no longer there, I have disappeared, he has regained the pleasure of thinking about someone else, of

HÉLÈNE GRÉMILLON

being with someone else and wishing for nothing else on earth but
to be filled to the brim by this other woman. So then I unpack my
bags, I stay there, and I cry. I dream of being able to leave, and I
dream of being able to stay with him all my life even if he is with
other women. To see without being seen. I get the impression that
this way, I will be happy at last. To see without being seen. Jealousy
is "repressed candaulism"; I didn't know the meaning of the word
"candaulism," so I looked it up in a book. And I found this list.

*Abasiophilia—Uncontrollable, repeated, and intense erotic
interest in choosing a partner who cannot move without the use
of a wheelchair or some other aid to walking.*

Acomoclitism—Sexual attraction to shaved pubic area.

*Allorgasmia—Sexual arousal brought on by fantasizing about
another person during sexual intercourse.*

*Anasyrma—Uncontrollable erotic urge on the part of a woman
to reveal her genital organs. According to Greek mythology,
Baubo lifted up her skirt to show her genitals to the goddess
Demeter. The gesture was meant to distract Demeter, who was
suffering from the loss of her daughter Persephone, abducted by
Hades, lord of the dead.*

*Apron fetishism—Attraction to women's aprons (and by
extension, to maids' outfits). Often coupled with an immoderate
passion for amorous adventures with servants.*

Axillism—Sexual attraction to armpits.

*Candaulism—Sexual arousal caused by the spectacle of sexual
intercourse between one's usual partner and a third person (or
several).*

Choreophilia—The condition of being sexually aroused when dancing.

Dendrophilia—Sexual arousal caused by trees.

Emetophilia—Sexual arousal caused by vomit.

Endytophilia—Sexual arousal caused by making love with a person who is fully clothed.

Erotophonophilia—Sexual arousal contingent on the death of another human being; common in serial sex killers.

Formicophilia—Uncontrollable sexual arousal caused by small animals (snakes, frogs) and insects (ants) crawling over the genital organs.

Godivism—Sexual urge to exhibit oneself naked on horseback. Exhibitionism on a bicycle may be considered a form of Godivism.

Hierophilia—Erotic arousal caused by sacred objects.

Lactophilia—Erotic arousal caused by breastfeeding women.

Maieusophilia—Sexual attraction to pregnant women.

Merinthophilia—Sexual arousal brought on by being tied up.

Pentheraphilia—A state of sexual arousal caused by one's mother-in-law.

Pygmalionism—Sexual arousal caused by statues.

Scatophilia—Sexual stimulation caused by excrement or acts of defecation.

Siderodromophilia—Sexual arousal from riding in trains. This fantasy may combine several factors: the intimacy of the compartment and its unavoidable promiscuity, the risk-free exhibitionism offered by a train going through residential districts, and the motion of the train itself.

Somnophilia—Repeated, intense, uncontrollable sexual interest in seeking erotic contact (caresses, oral-genital caresses, without forcing or exerting violence upon the person) with a person who is asleep.

Stigmatophilia—Repeated, intense, uncontrollable sexual interest in seeking out an erotic partner who has tattoos or scarifications or whose skin has been pierced in order to accommodate gold jewelry (rings or studs), particularly in the genital area.

Trichophilia—Sexual arousal caused by hair.

Undinism—Urinary eroticism; sexual arousal associated with urinating either on oneself or on the genitals of a partner of the same or opposite sex.

Zoophilia—Sexual attraction to animals. The act itself is not systematically illegal, depending on the country.

I almost forgot.

Pedophilia—Sexual attraction to children.

Lisandra was the one who closed the lid. Suddenly. The music box, slammed shut as her lips stilled, silent. Over this abominable litany she knew by heart. They were no longer dancing. The two of them stood motionless in the middle of the studio. Pepe was holding Lisandra in his arms and she had her head against his chest. She was nothing but a body locked inside a claustrophobic thought, a voiceless body, as if after an exorcism, a body that had been emptied out. She was beyond sorrow, and Pepe was stunned. He was holding his hand over Lisandra's eyes the way you hold your hand over the eyes of a dead person. He had heard enough. To be sure, he had managed to make her talk, but he could not understand her wandering; he would have had to go through this labyrinth of jealousy himself to have the slightest hope of understanding what torture it must represent. It was impossible to go on speaking; words seemed pointless to him compared to the sordid grace of the thoughts Lisandra had just shared with him. Even deep inside himself, he dared give voice to only a few words, which came to him in a rush: *You're imagining things. Maybe Vittorio isn't guilty. Maybe you're inflicting your own vision of the world on him—those are your fears you are projecting onto him; you have no proof he is cheating on you, and even if he were, he hasn't left you, that counts for something. This is a passing thing, I assure you, believe me, I ought to know, and even if he eventually left you, it wouldn't be the end of the world, you'll get over it, you'll meet someone else; you're young, you're beautiful, you're intelligent, don't reduce yourself to that love alone, Lisandra, don't reduce yourself to love; there are so many other beautiful things in life.* But in the end Pepe didn't say anything, because amid all this madness, he was struck by Lisandra's extreme lucidity, and he knew that she would have already made all these attempts to reason with herself on her own, and certainly more than once. Pepe's silence was a sign of helplessness, not disapproval, and yet that was what Lisandra took it for. Once it has been triggered, paranoia does not affect only one's love life, it spreads like a contagion to every layer of one's social nature.

"Do you think I am despicable?"

How could she think this? Pepe squeezed Lisandra tighter in his arms to indicate that she was not. You do not squeeze someone tight in your arms if you find them despicable. And eventually he began to speak, without quite realizing it, a simple statement that did nothing to alter Lisandra's pain but which, in his opinion, would rank it among the sorrows one knows will be forgotten someday. "You're so young." Lisandra arched her back, incensed: without Vittorio, her age hardly mattered to her, she could not go on living.

"I do wish I could help you."

"You can't help me. No one can help me."

"You can't let yourself be destroyed like this. You have to speak to Vittorio, tell him everything. He can help you, it's his profession, he'll understand."

"You don't go about having psychoanalysis with the love of your life. You don't open up the depths of your soul to someone when they are part of it. You cannot reveal your vision of the other person."

"Then go and see someone else, another shrink. It's not as if there aren't plenty of them around."

Lisandra had thought about it. But she was afraid they might know each other, they might meet, these individuals are above all conference-goers. *Lisandra Puig. Oh, she's your wife?* And they talk among themselves, and Lisandra could not bear to become the topic of the discussion, an intellectual quandary for Vittorio. You could fall in love with an intellectual quandary—it was even common to the point of vulgarity in their profession, to fall in love with a case— but that was before you'd slept with the "case" in question. Once you've slept with the "case," and slept with her again and again, the case loses its charm, becomes a deviancy like any other.

"Well then, go and see someone else, someone who is not a shrink. A doctor."

For him to knock her out with antidepressants, no, thank you, Lisandra wanted none of that. But one day she did go and see some-one all the same. It was her friend Miguel who had recommended him. He knew her well, Miguel. He had come by the house, he had noticed that she wasn't well, and he had left the address on the table in the living room, silent and modest the way he always was. In the waiting room the radio was playing Mozart's Piano Concerto No. 23. Lisandra smiled. Miguel is a great musician; Lisandra thought this must be a sign, she really believed this doctor would be able to help her. She told him she was jealous. She asked him if he could help her. He answered that it wasn't as simple as all that. She replied that she knew perfectly well that "it wasn't as simple as all that"; she just wanted to know whether he could help her. The man opened an enormous red book and while he was running his finger hurriedly through the pages, he embarked on a thorough interrogation: "Can you stand tight clothes? Turtleneck sweaters? Do you bruise easily? Do you prefer red or white wine? Do you have trouble waking up in the morning? Do you have hot flashes? Why do you keep turning around? Does the sound of the light bother you? Do little noises in general bother you? Are you subject to tinnitus? To repeated sore throats? Do you have a tendency to keep your sorrow to yourself? When you cry, do you have spasms, or do you sob, calmly? Do you get cold easily? Do you suffer from neuralgia? Headaches? Muscle contractions? Menstrual pain? Irregular periods? Accompanied by cramps?" Lisandra concentrated hard on her replies. Answered so thoughtfully. Reading more into them than what they signified. She would have liked for the litany never to stop. She could have spent her entire life answering these questions. She suddenly had the impression that this man could do anything, that he was going to save her. *The result.*

"Are you claustrophobic?"

"No."

"Are you subject to vertigo?"

"No."

"Are you—"

"Actually I am. I do get vertigo. In the staircase. When I go down."

"And when you go up?"

"No. Only when I go down."

The man went on for a while with his questions and then he closed his book. He got up and went to open a small cupboard behind him, full of numerous transparent tubes filled with tiny white granules. He took one of them and poured the equivalent of a small handful into an envelope, which he handed to Lisandra. "Take this tomorrow morning, under your tongue, before you eat." Lisandra spent all evening and all night convinced that her salvation lay in the envelope. She placed it under her pillow, telling herself that by next morning the tooth fairy would have come and gone. As she replayed the entire session in her head, repeating the questions and answers as best she could remember, she finally came to a realization, and knew it had all started there.

With the *staircase*.

She couldn't go on pretending nothing had happened. If she really wanted to find a solution, she would have to begin to face the truth. It was with these very words that Lisandra turned suddenly to face Pepe. Abruptly. All at once she'd been disconnected from her jealous delirium.

"Do you want to help me, Pepe? But of course you want to help me. You're even the only one who can help me. With you I can go there. I can do it if you go with me."

Pepe nodded without even knowing what he had agreed to, and Lisandra's face suddenly lit up and won him over to her cause, without any further questions. Lisandra then withdrew from his arms.

"You are right, Pepe, let's stop there, let's stop all this moaning. I have the solution. I've had it for a long time. And now I have to apply it; the time has come. I know what will fix everything. I know what I have to do. I simply have to find the courage to confront him."

Pepe had loved her tone, suddenly so categorical, so positive, but he had never told her to "stop her moaning." He would never have allowed himself to brush off her distress in that way. It was she herself who used those words, the words she had actually wanted to hear, the only words that could compel her to act and force her to leave behind her world of contemplative, destructive observation. Jealousy as mystical ecstasy. Lisandra left the dressing room wearing makeup and perfume, her hair done, her ponytail high on her scalp, freeing her face, and Pepe thought that here was the woman he knew, at last. Still wearing her sunglasses, but stable and focused now. She hadn't exactly perked up—for that she would have had to experience a joy she didn't feel—but strong, yes; the strength now came from the strength of her body. If Pepe had not been her confidant, he would never have imagined that Lisandra's soul was so full of dark thoughts. They took the bus, hardly speaking. Pepe could not help but wonder what *solution* Lisandra had been referring to. But he no longer had the nerve to ask her anything. He was being extremely cautious—cowardly, perhaps—he didn't want to start anything, set anything off. He was still in shock after her terrible monologue. And besides, Lisandra was so focused, she kept biting her lips and sighing deeply, staring straight ahead. Pepe felt embarrassed. He wondered if she was thinking back over everything she had confessed to him; he thought perhaps he ought to tell her that he would never speak of it ever again, unless she wanted to. Suddenly Lisandra turned and looked at him. She wanted to stop off in the neighborhood of San Telmo.

"I have a present to buy."

Pepe watched her go into the shop, not understanding what she could possibly want there. What impulse purchase had she suddenly gotten into her head? He gazed at the shop sign swinging in the wind.

A toy store, a strange place for a jealous soul to find comfort. Lisandra did not stay there very long. A little while, all the same, enough for Pepe to grow worried and hesitate to go and find her. But Lisandra had made him promise to wait outside and not come into the store. Pepe looked at the little green shop, a sweet place, the way neighborhood shops often are. At last Lisandra came out. She went up to Pepe, her gaze vacant, her hands behind her back.

"Pick a hand."

"I don't know . . . the right hand."

Lisandra opened her right hand and gave him a little porcelain cat and then she opened her left hand, which held another one exactly the same.

"I took two of the same, one for you, one for me . . . *because a porcelain cat doesn't meow over love.** The truth sometimes lies dormant in songs."

Lisandra thanked Pepe for having been so kind to her. For listening to her. It had done her good to talk. She gave Pepe a hug and a kiss, then withdrew very quickly. Clearly, she did not want to prolong the moment.

---

* Lyrics to the tango "A media luz" (Edgardo Donato and Carlos Lenzi, 1924).

"I'll get going now."

"You don't want me to come with you anymore?"

"No, thank you, I'll be all right, Pepe. Now I can go home. Now I'm not afraid anymore."

"Afraid of what?"

"Nothing."

Lisandra shrugged. She was still a bit pale, but it was no longer with fatigue or weariness. It was excitement, Pepe would have staked his life on it: excitement. But what Pepe remembered very well above all, was that at that very moment he had an intuition that something definitive had been set in motion—and he wasn't just saying that now in light of what had happened; no, he really had felt a shiver, like a sort of unease. But perhaps his body was simply reacting to the sound of the sign creaking in the wind—"Lucas Juegos"—the kind of creepy noise that horror films are full of. "Lucas." There was nothing frightening about the name. Lisandra waved to him one last time. Pepe didn't even have the presence of mind to wave back. He watched as her blonde head moved away, that beautiful hair of hers, but now Pepe knew why it did not seem to match her complexion. It was common knowledge that students often gave lessons to their teachers. That evening when he went home, Pepe asked his wife whether she was jealous, whether she had ever been jealous. His wife didn't turn around, but he knew she was crying: she lifted her shoulders, one after the other, to dry the corners of her cheeks where her tears must have been flowing. "If you're asking me, it must mean I no longer have any reason to be." That night Pepe gave his wife a long kiss, too long for a kiss that wasn't asking for forgiveness. When he switched off the light, he thought about Lisandra, hoping she was all right, hoping she, too, was finding reconciliation with her husband, that at last she had "confronted him," the way she had said she would. Her husband was going to help her: that was his job.

And now it looked like he, Pepe, had been a long way from the truth. He felt so guilty, he could not help but think that if he had let Lisandra go on doing her sinister dance from the door of her room to the chair at her desk, from the chair to the door, a round that was completely harmless in the end, nothing would have happened to her. Pepe had committed the sin of pride. If he had not gone looking for her that day, trying to remove her from her cocoon, which may well have been unhappy but was, in the end, a sort of chloroform, if he had not driven her to confess her tragic story to a witness, then none of this would have happened. Seeking liberation through words, is that really a positive thing? Pepe doesn't think so. Words set free are sometimes more dangerous than words that are silenced. He felt so guilty. But that's normal. It's troubling to see a living person on the day they are going to die; you always feel guilty afterward. You tell yourself that you could have, should have, stopped something from happening.

"Because all of this happened the day she died?"

"Yes. That afternoon."

"So you are the last person who saw her alive. Other than her husband."

"I don't know . . . perhaps."

"And do you think that Vittorio killed her?"

"How should I know . . . Everything seems to point that way. A crime of passion, perhaps."

"I'm not asking you if 'everything seems to point that way,' I'm asking you if you, personally, think he killed her."

"How I am supposed to know that? I don't know him. All I know about him is what Lisandra chose to tell me. I simply saw him waiting for her a few times, on the sidewalk, when he came to get her. I remember how he put his arms around her and they'd go off down the street, the two of them, but that was already a few years ago, at the beginning of their relationship."

"And of course you told the police that he no longer came to get her after class, that the good old days of marital harmony were long past."

"The police? What police? No one came to question me. You're the only person who has come to see me to talk about Lisandra's death."

Eva Maria stuffs her hands into the pockets of her coat. She is sure she has seen Pepe somewhere before. But where? This feeling of déjà vu is getting to her. Eva Maria looks all around her in the bus. He is gifted, the old man who can read body language. But others, these passengers, like her, have their hands in their pockets, and surely not all of them have lost a child. Eva Maria is satisfied that the way she carries herself means nothing. Pepe could not have concluded anything from it other than that she felt cold. Which is true. "Crime of passion." So he, too, thinks Vittorio may have killed Lisandra. Pepe didn't know whether Lisandra was telling the truth, whether Vittorio really had a mistress, and since the only modus operandi of jealousy is suspicion, one can never know whether the words of a jealous woman are the truth or wild imaginings. But Pepe also knows that Lisandra might have been right. He knows that it was perfectly possible Vittorio had a mistress. Eva Maria is sure that he didn't—if Vittorio had had a mistress, the police would have found out. Pepe had said that the police didn't always find out everything. Which was true. But if Vittorio had a mistress, he would have told her, Eva Maria. Pepe had replied that it wasn't always the easiest thing to confess. Eva Maria gets off the bus. He is gifted, the old man who can read body language, but there is one thing he missed. Eva

Maria is almost smiling. With petty triumph. Never for a moment did Pepe imagine that Lisandra herself might cheat on Vittorio.

A woman who has a lover doesn't act the guard dog at her husband's door while he's working. A woman who has a lover uses the time her husband is at work to go and be with her lover.

He may be good, the old man who can read body language, but he's fallible. Lisandra was cheating on Vittorio—in any case, she did cheat on him, at least once, at least four times. Eva Maria remains convinced of that. Francisco wasn't lying about their brief affair at the hotel; everything he told her, you don't go making that up. Lisandra really was "unfaithful," even if Pepe believes the opposite. Eva Maria did not set him straight. She didn't tell him about Francisco; there was no point inflicting a new image of Lisandra on him when he thought he knew her so well, might as well let him keep the image he wanted to keep. Eva Maria is pensive. One question keeps nagging her. Why, if Lisandra was so obviously in love with Vittorio, did she cheat on him? Such behavior doesn't correspond to a jealous soul. Eva Maria shakes her head. After all, what does she know about jealousy? It's a feeling that is completely foreign to her. Maybe these two states of jealousy and infidelity are not so incompatible in the end. Maybe Lisandra wanted to try it with other men so she could forget Vittorio, so she could lessen his hold on her, regain a bit of autonomy and independence, which were so vital and so sorely lacking in her life. Or maybe it was to find out whether it would help her problem, the way the books seemed to suggest. "A repressed unfaithful individual." And the choreography—that was what she liked to do with Vittorio. And the cologne was to remind her of Vittorio, to make it seem as if it were him, to motivate her for the task. Eva Maria thinks about the black vultures who inhabit the craters of volcanoes, who are loyal the way few men are. One solitary partner, the same one, their whole life long. Eva Maria tells herself that Lisandra should have been born a black vulture. Eva Maria slows down. She looks at her house, a few dozen yards from here, and suddenly she thinks of her husband and wonders if she ever truly loved. Can one love if one is not jealous?

A woman who has a lover doesn't act the guard dog at her husband's door while he's working. A woman who has a lover uses the time her husband is at work to go and be with her lover.

He's gifted, the old man who reads body language, and what if he wasn't fallible? Simply ingenious and clever. Machiavellian. And what if Pepe was perfectly acquainted with Lisandra's penchant for lovers? He was in a good position to know.

One month without seeing her, you can imagine how worried I was, so I went by her place. I never do that as a rule, go by an absent student's place, but in this case I couldn't help it, no doubt because it was Lisandra. I liked her a lot.

And what if he loved her, period. Quite simply.

But Lisandra . . . kept to herself; in any case, that was what I believed then.

And what if one day she went and stood in front of him, like she'd done with Francisco, to invite him to sleep with her. How could he resist?

She was graceful; she had the grace of ten women put together . . . She had what might have been the most harmonious body I've ever seen.

And then she was young, so young. Could Pepe have been Lisandra's lover? His tall, slim body still had the strength, more than enough. And what if this Mariana whom Pepe had spoken about was none other than Lisandra herself? That, too, was possible. And what if that crazy adventure had occurred only recently? And that, like with Francisco, Lisandra had grown weary of him? What if she had broken it off? And what if Pepe had disrespected the contract, the way Francisco had? That would explain why Lisandra hadn't been to class for a month. And what of Lisandra's jealous laments? His own, Pepe's own demons, his own madness expressed through Lisandra's words. And the reconciliation with his wife, a sentimental enough story, the better to throw her off the track. Eva Maria removes her coat. She hangs her bag on the coatrack. Her gestures are hurried. She opens the door to the bathroom. And what if she'd been misled by that man? It's not the case that because his insight was virtually divination he was necessarily a good person. On the contrary, his extreme acuity about people made him formidable. He could control, bewitch, skew things. Perhaps he had manipulated her all through their conversation. He didn't seem the least bit surprised when she showed up at his place to question him about Lisandra, and he engaged with her endeavor with astonishing understanding and zeal, like an arsonist helping firefighters to extinguish a fire he himself ignited. And that feeling of déjà vu? Her sixth sense? Her sixth sense that was trying to get her to focus on Pepe: *Watch out, girl, there is something going on here, pay attention, don't let this guy just slip by.* What if he were the lover Eva Maria had been looking for all this time? Supposing on the evening of the murder Pepe went to Lisandra's place to try to get her back, a desperate, last-ditch attempt. He knocked on her door. Lisandra opened, a glass of white wine in her hand. *What are you doing here?* Pepe gave her no time to react, he pushed his way past her through the open door. Lisandra was alone. Pepe went into the living room where the tango music was coming from, and he saw this as a good sign: maybe if she was listening to tango it meant she was thinking about him. And he opened his heart, naïve as he was. *Lisandra, I can't live without you. I told my wife everything. That I love you. That I want to live with you. Lisandra. Look at me. And don't tell me you don't love me. Not after what we have had together. Don't take yourself away from me. You are my reason for living. It is only when you are near me that I don't hear the seconds ticking by. Come back to me, Lisandra.* And what if Lisandra had told him to leave? Coldly, the way she had ended her relationship with Francisco. *But I don't want you to leave your wife. I never asked you to. Don't act all surprised. Don't act as if we have some big love story together. Don't let your imagination play tricks on you. We were fucking, that's all. And you know it very well, it was just a way to kill the boredom, to follow through on the principle that underlies any attraction between a man and a woman who spend too much time in each other's presence. To remove the tension. That's all that happened. It went further than expected. The context was favorable. But Pepe, a favorable context, an opportunity, that's not what life is made of. And at your age . . . I can't be teaching you anything new.* "Don't bring my age into it." *And yet that's the root of the problem. If you want my opinion, you've chosen the wrong sorrow. It's not me you want to hang on to; you want to hang on to an equivocation, not love—what you want is to go on not thinking about death. It's true that I was attracted to you, but that's over. I'm sorry. I never force attraction, just as I never compel it. You and I fucked just as I fucked others, and it was no more important with you than it was with the others.* And the more Lisandra spoke, the louder Pepe put the volume on the record player, to drown her out. She shouted, *Stop, stop that at once!* Her gaze fell on one of the little porcelain cats in her collection on a shelf in the library—maybe it had been a present from Pepe—and she picked it up and threw it to the floor. Thus triggering the irreversible. And what if Pepe was Lisandra's murderer? He still had the physical strength, more than enough. An old volcano is sometimes more dangerous than a young one. Go after another body. Catch it. Shake it. Push it out the window. "A crime of passion." What if it was his crime? "It's not every day that casual fucking of this caliber comes knocking on your door." Francisco's right, an insane person can drive you insane, but so can a young one. Francisco was too young to know it, but young people can drive their elders crazy. Particularly where their bodies are concerned. Above all when youth flaunts its sexuality in front of old age. Their skin is too smooth, their thighs are too firm, and their breasts are too haughty for old age ever to agree to let them go without pride taking a severe beating. And wounded pride can turn criminal. Eva Maria flushes the toilet. When will the range of possibilities ever stop expanding? It's all just supposition and guesswork. No tangible proof. No material proof. Hearsay, from this person, from that person. Eva Maria's head is splitting from all the words. And she feels sick. She can't think anymore. But what about that feeling of déjà vu? Was it Pepe's voice that reminded her of someone? Was Pepe one of Vittorio's patients? Had he been using this subterfuge in an attempt to see Lisandra one last time, or worse, to reveal everything to Vittorio—the fact that he loved Vittorio's wife, was crazy about her, crazier about her than about any other woman he had ever loved, because he knew she would be the last one? Had Pepe's voice been on one of the cassettes? Pepe's secrets? Had there been a man telling Vittorio the story of his passion for a married woman, hoping to get him thinking, already planning to tell him in the last session that this married woman was none other than Vittorio's own wife? No, that wasn't the case.

Eva Maria picks up the telephone. After all, it was the last place Lisandra went, it might be important; she mustn't leave anything up to chance.

"Good morning, señora, I'd like the number for a toy store in San Telmo: Lucas Juegos."

"One moment, please, I'll check that for you . . . 361-7516."

"Thank you. Have a good day."

Eva Maria hangs up. Dials again. It rings for a long time. Finally a man's voice replies.

"Lucas speaking!"

"Good morning. I'm sorry to bother you. I'm calling because some time ago now, already a few weeks ago, a young woman stopped by your shop. She bought two little porcelain cats. And I would like to know—forgive me, I know this is a rather strange call—but I would like to know whether you noticed anything odd about her behavior, I don't know, if she said anything in particular to you."

Only silence on the line.

"Or maybe you weren't there?"

"Yes, yes, I'm the only one here . . . Two little porcelain cats, you said?"

"Yes."

"No, to be honest, I don't remember; I'm sorry, but I can't keep track of all my customers."

"Of course, I see. I'm the one who's sorry; forgive me for disturbing you."

The wrong track again. Simply an idea of Lisandra's to thank Pepe for listening to her, give him a little present. Eva Maria stifles a cry. Of course! That's it, of course, that's where she saw Pepe.

Eva Maria tears into the bedroom in a rage. She opens her desk drawer. She recognizes him at once. Pepe. There. On the photograph before her eyes. The old man at the funeral, of course; that's where she's seen him. Eva Maria reaches for her glasses. She leafs through the photographs. It's him all right, crushed with sorrow; he looked much older than the man she has just left but it was him all right. Eva Maria thinks back. He and his wife had stood for a long time by the coffin; she had assumed they were Vittorio's parents. This is not how you come to mourn the passing of a mistress. With your wife's hand held tight in your own. The old woman looked as upset as Pepe did. To have wanted to slip a mistress between this touching couple seems sacrilegious now. Eva Maria is sorry she even thought of it. She was wrong. Pepe had never been Lisandra's lover. Eva Maria wonders whether the old woman can also read body language, if it's a thing that "runs in couples" the way you say "it runs in families." Eva Maria looks closer. She picks up her magnifying glass. A face as smooth as her hair is white. A candid gaze. The same wisdom. But suddenly it's another face that draws Eva Maria's attention. She holds the glass closer to the photograph. What was she doing there? At the back. This lovely young woman, too calm. Eva Maria leafs through the photographs.

Feverishly. There she is, there. And there. Her face too impassive to be attending a funeral, almost detached. Something about her physique, about her attitude, intrigues Eva Maria. It's not the fact that she's beautiful, no, that's not it. It's that she *made herself beautiful*. The young woman had done herself up. Her eyes more made up than mourning, her lips more colorful than distressed, she'd made herself beautiful, the way you do to go to meet your lover, not to go to a funeral. Her outfit reflected more of a desire to be stylish than to show traditional restraint; only the black coat was in keeping with the occasion, but in other circumstances that black would have been sexy. Eva Maria goes from one print to the next. The young woman's gaze is veiled, it's true, but with a strange sort of veil. A veil of absence, when you're hoping to see someone who is not there, but not a veil of death, when you've lost all hope of seeing someone who won't come ever again. And on this photo, her gaze is riveted on the police car: who was she staring at so intently, with what Eva Maria sees as desire? Did she think Vittorio was in the police car? Behind the tinted glass windows? Eva Maria is worried by the presence of this too-beautiful woman. She looks every bit the mistress who has come to signal to her lover, *I'm here, I'm still here*. Of course she would still be there. She couldn't go see Vittorio in prison without running the risk of betraying them; if there is proof that a man has a mistress then he seems even more likely to have killed his wife. Of course she would be there, that made-up doll, hoping to see Vittorio at the funeral, from a distance, hoping to exchange a gaze with him that would keep them going for days, weeks, a smile, a handshake. Had she prepared a few words, a love note, a letter, a photograph of herself naked, something, some lover's idea? This too-beautiful woman worries her. Eva Maria had not noticed her in the photographs until now. To notice her, she would have had to suspect, for even just a second, that Vittorio had a mistress. Now at last Eva Maria is forced to consider what she should have thought of right from the start: what if Vittorio really did have a mistress? What if Lisandra had been right? Eva Maria can't think straight anymore. Because she knows what she has to think next. Eva Maria gets up. She heads to the bathroom. She opens all the cupboards. She slams them shut. She opens the dresser where she keeps her underwear. She rummages among her bras, tosses them on the floor, opens the drawer below, rummages, gives a kick to the open drawer. The wood splits. Eva Maria leaves her room. In a rage.

"Estéban! Estéban!"

Eva Maria goes into the living room. Estéban is sprawled on the sofa. His bandoneon between his feet. Eva Maria stands in front of him.

"I forbade you from going through the things in my room: where are they?"

"What are you talking about?"

"Stop this right now—where are my bottles? Answer me. I can't stand it when you lie."

Estéban runs his fingers through his hair.

"Oh, okay . . . you mean, 'Where are *my* bottles?' Since I'm the one who always finds you dead drunk . . . they're sort of my bottles, too . . . well, as it happens . . . I drank them . . . to see, Mama . . . to see what it is that gives you greater comfort than I do . . ."

Estéban gets to his feet and staggers. Eva Maria slaps him. Estéban lifts his hand to his cheek.

"My mother has just touched me . . . for the first time in all these years . . . this slap is like a caress on my cheek . . . Here . . ."

Estéban takes a banknote out of his pocket. He flings it in Eva Maria's face.

"Go get yourself something to drink . . . it's true, it helps . . .

you can celebrate good riddance to me . . . I'm leaving . . . you happy now? . . . For five years you've made it clear I have no more mother . . . so tonight, lemme tell you, you have no more son . . . I won't come back . . . I tell you . . . solemnly . . ."

Estéban stands up straight.

"'Cause if I don't tell you . . . you won't even notice . . . I come back later and later every night but what good does it do . . . Not once did I find you worrying yourself sick on the sofa . . . the way any mother on the planet would do . . . you hear me, Mama? I know you don't see me anymore but you spend all your time listening to my tape recorder . . . that means you can hear, right? . . . You think they're inhuman, those people who killed Stella, but look at your-self . . . you managed to kill us, as surely as whoever killed Stella."

Eva Maria slaps Estéban again. With full force. On both cheeks. Estéban lifts his chin.

"I talk about my sister if I want to talk about my sister . . . You're sorry it wasn't me who died . . . instead of Stella . . . you would rather I had died in Stella's place . . . isn't that what you told your shrink? Well, sorry, Mama . . . forgive me for being alive . . . but I'm out of here . . . there . . . Mama, I'm gonna do like you . . . I'm gonna go and mourn my sister and try and forget I even have a mother . . ."

Estéban picks up his bandoneon. He walks unsteadily out of the room. A few false notes escape from the instrument. Eva Maria doesn't move. She hears the door slam. She looks at the banknote in her hands. Eva Maria doesn't move.

Eva Maria leans over her handbag. Her hands are trembling. She takes out the photo. The early morning has made her lose her composure from the night before. And finding herself across from Vittorio again, too. Eva Maria puts the photograph on the table between them. She murmurs, "Who is this woman?" And yet Eva Maria had prepared something very different. Mentally.

I know this woman is your mistress, Vittorio. And that is why you argued with your wife that night. Because you had a mistress. Your wife had asked you, for the umpteenth time, to stay with her, and not to go out that evening; she had put on a new dress to try to boost her chances, but you didn't notice, because you had her there all day long before you, your wife, and because you already possessed her you didn't see her anymore, you were too full of thoughts of another woman, you didn't give in, you were annoyed and eager to leave, like any husband who thinks that nothing sublime can ever occur anymore between those four walls of home. That is why neither the usher nor the box office attendant remembers seeing you that night, for the simple reason that you weren't at the movies. Because you were with another woman, somewhere, at her house or at the hotel. And when you'd finished, because any mistress worthy of the name is someone you leave during the night, you went home; and you say that the door to the apartment was unlocked, and you immediately noticed a terrible draft, there was loud music coming from the living room, and everything was in a mess as if there had been a struggle; you instantly knew something had happened, you closed the window and looked for Lisandra everywhere, you ran into the kitchen, the bedroom, the bathroom, and it was only then that the fear of understanding came over you. You stepped over the broken vase on the floor, with the puddle of water all around it, you heard a shrill cry in the street, and you opened the window in the living room again, and Lisandra's body was lying downstairs. I believe all that, Vittorio—I want to believe you—but admit that this woman is your mistress, tell me the truth; I have to be able to trust you if I'm to go on helping you; rest assured, I won't jump to any hasty conclusions, I won't judge you.

But the early morning has made her lose her composure from the night before. Eva Maria murmurs.

"Who is this woman, Vittorio?"

"I don't know her."

"You don't know her?"

"No, what is this photograph about?"

Eva Maria leans over her handbag. Her hands are trembling. She puts the photograph away. And her hopes. Of frankness. Sincerity. Eva Maria knows that Vittorio is lying. If Pepe had been there, he would have confirmed it; the old man who reads body language would have proved it to her, and the proof would have been implacable: a raised eyebrow, a movement of his head, tension in the jaw, Vittorio would have betrayed himself. Eva Maria puts the photograph in her handbag. She thinks of Estéban; he didn't come home all night, he didn't come back. Eva Maria has lost heart. She is ready to give in; her body is suddenly too heavy to carry. Just shifting it to sit down across from Vittorio is overwhelming. Eva Maria begins to cry. Vittorio draws closer.

"What is going on? Where did you find that photograph?"

"I took it at Lisandra's funeral."

"Why are you crying? Calm down."

Eva Maria does not calm down. She looks at Vittorio, and behind him, at the dirty beige walls of the visitors' room. She articulates.

"That huge peacock in your study, that huge painting, it was a present from Lisandra, wasn't it?"

"How did you know?"

So she was right. At least partially. Eva Maria composes herself. She will start over again from there.

"You don't know the legend?"

"What legend?"

"The legend of Argos?"

"No."

Eva Maria feels her resolve grow stronger.

"Hera, the wife of Zeus, had him watched by Argos, the spy with a hundred eyes. That was the best she could do, given his rich love life. Argos had a hundred eyes spread all over his head: fifty that were asleep and fifty that were constantly on the lookout, so there was no way to get around his vigilance. Zeus was in love with the priestess Io, and this aroused Hera's jealousy. To reassure his wife, Zeus turned Io into a white heifer, but their affair continued in secret. So Hera decided to hand Io over to Argos to get her away from Zeus, but Zeus sent Hermes to kill Argos and free Io. Despite the failure of her plan, Hera rewarded the dead giant's loyalty by transferring his eyes to the feathers of a peacock, her favorite animal. So you see, that painting in your office is the ultimate symbol for Lisandra. And I am sure that was the point, in a way: the peacock was keeping an eye on you. Did you know how jealous your wife was?"

Vittorio would never have come up with such an interpretation. He takes his time to reply.

"Lisandra was jealous, that's true . . . but the way women often are."

"No, that's just it; not 'the way women often are'—she was pathologically jealous, or didn't you know that? But I understand, when you stop seeing someone, you hardly pay much attention to how they are feeling."

Eva Maria no longer displays any tact or discretion. She has decided to lay her cards on the table. Eva Maria tells Vittorio that Lisandra was cheating on him. Vittorio doesn't believe a word: he would have known. Eva Maria quotes him: "The very principle of a lover is that the husband doesn't know he exists." Vittorio is adamant: Lisandra was not that type of woman. Eva Maria replies that his classification doesn't mean much. Vittorio asserts that Lisandra loved him. Eva Maria retorts, "Are the two so incompatible? It is precisely because she loved you that she was unfaithful to you." And Eva Maria now describes the scenes of love, the unequivocal words that Francisco had used to describe the affair.

"Doesn't that resonate with you? Or do you recognize your wife? Lisandra was in such pain that she had only one thing in mind. To find in another man's arms the best of what you had given her. But which you no longer gave her. The very things you no longer noticed—that was what she was prepared to give someone else. And she died because of it. I have two theories regarding what might have happened on the evening of the murder."

Vittorio sits up straight. Eva Maria continues.

"Say your wife received her lover at home: was that the first time or was it something she did regularly? I haven't a clue. She had put on a new dress, high heels, to try and exert her power over you; she knows she won't be able to hold you back, she knows where you stand, she's no fool, she knows you've fallen out of love, you're having an affair with someone else, and she knows that even the newest dress cannot compete with a new woman, no matter what she's wearing, but she hopes at least your gaze might linger on her, and even if she is prepared to go with another man, she cannot help but reproach you for not noticing her new dress, because that Other Man is nothing more than an accessible You—available, different, but he is you, all the same. Whence the argument. Your quarrel. The neighbor's deposition. None of which stops you from going out. So she goes and gets two glasses and a bottle of white wine, thinking how vulgar it is, a woman who has to pour the wine for herself. And then she switches on the radio and she waits. The doorbell rings. She asks twice over, *Who's there?* because she's fearful; she hears the right answer and she opens the door. And the lover waits for the few seconds required by the script while she goes back into the living room and pulls up her dress to give him that first image she always gives him. Her ritual. But to undo his trousers, the lover has to put his flower bouquet on the table ... what kind ... let's say a bouquet of red roses ... and Lisandra sees them out of the corner of her eye. She stands back up, very straight, and smoothes down her dress; she tries to control herself, she tries to deflect her anger through movement, so she picks up the vase, goes to fill it with water, then comes back into the living room; but it wasn't enough, the sight of the bouquet of red roses is still unbearable to her, so she opens the window, she tries to deflect her anger with some fresh air, and she leans out to breathe deeply; but that's not enough, so she turns around, takes the bouquet of red roses, and throws them in her lover's face. *Get out. Who do you think you are? I hate roses.* The truth is not that she hates roses, the truth is that you, Vittorio, you would have given her lilies, her favorite flowers, isn't that what you told me? The hapless lover then picks up the bouquet and goes off with his flowers under his arm, leaving behind the water that was waiting for them in the vase, orphaned—yes, orphaned, because it's not enough merely to note that the water from the vase was spreading across the floor, without wondering where the flowers went. How to explain the fact that nowhere in the crime scene did anyone find a trace of these flowers? And unless your wife had the strange mania of filling up all the vases in the house with water, with or without flowers, the only explanation would be that her lover went away again with his bouquet under his arm. But not before taking the time to shove Lisandra out the window next to which she might still have been standing, maybe to banish the effluvia from the roses. If Lisandra hadn't leaned out a few seconds earlier to take a breath of air, maybe he would never have thought of doing such a thing, but therein lies the mystery of how another person's gesture can drive someone to commit a murder. But naturally Lisandra would have resisted, so the chairs got knocked over, and the lamp, too, the little porcelain cat got broken, and the vase, naturally, but the hapless lover won in the end. Out the window for the woman who didn't like roses. The woman who liked only lilies. Who loved only you. Who had just driven her lover mad. The murderer-lover hurried to leave the premises. And then you arrived. That's it."

Eva Maria stops talking. She thinks it's easier to admit to having a mistress when you know your wife has a lover. So she tries again.

"Who is that woman in the photograph, Vittorio?"

"I told you, I don't know her. What are you trying to make me say, in the end? That she's my mistress? You're completely off your rocker."

"Right. I'm completely off my rocker, forgive me. So then my second theory must be the right one."

"Which is?"

"Can't you guess?"

"No."

"When you got back from the movies, you found your wife with her lover. And you're the one who threw out the flowers. And you're the one who pushed your wife out the window."

Vittorio shakes his head.

"I think you'd better leave now."

"I think so, too."

Eva Maria stands up. She wishes Vittorio would say, "Stay. Yes, that woman is my mistress, it's true, but I didn't kill Lisandra and I still need you; you have to go on helping me to find the true murderer." But Vittorio says nothing. Vittorio doesn't try to hold her back. Vittorio lets Eva Maria go. But not quite yet. One last question.

"This lover. Who was it?"

Eva Maria turns back toward Vittorio.

"Who was with her on the night of the murder? I don't know. It would seem she had several lovers."

"No, the one who told you everything they did together."

"You don't know him."

Vittorio shook his head.

"You have forgotten my profession. To say that I 'don't know' this man proves, on the contrary, that I *do* know him. If I didn't know him, you would simply have given me his name. So tell me. Who is it?"

Eva Maria thinks. Since Francisco had decided to tell the police, then she could tell Vittorio.

"Francisco."

"Francisco . . . from the Pichuco?"

"Yes."

Vittorio doesn't move. Eva Maria takes a few steps toward the door. She turns around. Her hand on the handle.

"On second thought. What about you? When you say you 'don't know' that woman in the photograph, what am I supposed to conclude? That you *do* know her?"

Eva Maria does not wait for his answer. Eva Maria leaves the room.

Eva Maria is exhausted. She is about to fall sleep. She hears the sound of the bandoneon coming from Estéban's room. Estéban is one of those souls who are too courageous to leave; Estéban has come home. Eva Maria is relieved. For the first time in all these years, she fixes dinner. For the first time in all these years, she knocks on the door to Estéban's room. Estéban doesn't hear it at first. Or rather, he can't believe his ears. Eva Maria doesn't open the door. She speaks through the door. They are not ready to look at each other yet. There are hardly any words.

"I made some sandwiches if you want; they're in the kitchen."

Silence. Eva Maria has three fears. That Estéban won't answer her. That Estéban will say no. That Estéban will open the door. Eva Maria hears Estéban's voice. Relief. It's still from the same distance.

"All right."

Eva Maria leans closer to the door again.

"See you tomorrow."

"See you tomorrow."

Eva Maria is about to fall asleep. She has given up on the truth. She's stopping everything. Vittorio will have to manage without her. She will have to manage without him; Estéban is here, that's all that matters. Eva Maria is exhausted. She wishes this night would last for two weeks, like on the moon. As a child she thought those hollow spaces on the moon were craters, but there are no volcanoes on the moon. Eva Maria thinks about Olympus Mons on Mars, a volcano that is fourteen miles high. For the first time since Stella disappeared she is thinking about height without thinking about falling. She is thinking about a distance: fourteen miles—that would be the same as from where to where? Eva Maria is about to fall asleep. She wishes this night would last for two weeks, with neither dreams nor nightmares. Is that someone ringing at the door? Or is it a note from the bandoneon? She doesn't know. All she knows is that Estéban has come back. Eva Maria smiles.

"Mama?"

Estéban opens the door to Eva Maria's room.

"There are two men here to see you."

Eva Maria slips out from between the sheets.

"Two men here to see me?"

Eva Maria puts back on the clothes she only just took off. In the living room, two men stand waiting for her.

"Eva Maria Darienzo?"

"Yes."

"Good evening, señora. Commissioner Perez. Lieutenant Sanchez."

The two men put their badges away. Eva Maria walks across the living room. Lieutenant Sanchez goes out of the room. Estéban stands next to Eva Maria. Commissioner Perez hunts for something in his pocket.

"I'm sorry to disturb you so late."

Commissioner Perez hands a piece of paper to Eva Maria.

"We have a search warrant."

Lieutenant Sanchez comes back into the living room. He is holding Eva Maria's bag underneath his arm. In his fingertips, three keys hanging from a key ring in the shape of a key.

"These keys do not fit the lock on your door."

Eva Maria looks at the four keys, one of which is a fake.

"They're not mine."

"Whose are they, then?"

"A friend's."

"The name of that friend wouldn't happen to be Vittorio Puig, by any chance?"

"It is."

"How did you happen to find yourself in possession of his keys?"

"They were given to me."

"They were given to you?"

"Yes. A young man who was there on the night of the murder."

"The night of the murder? Interesting."

"It's not what you think; Vittorio misplaced his keys by Lisandra's body—they must have fallen out of his pocket—the young man was in the street, he found them, and came to return them."

"'Lisandra'—it would seem that you were well acquainted with the victim."

"No, not at all. It's just that, with all this—"

"All this what?"

"All this thinking about the murder. She has become familiar to me."

"I see, but how do you explain that the keys are now in your possession?"

"I read about what happened in the newspaper, the murder, Vittorio's arrest, so I went to his place, to see, to make sure, I couldn't believe it, it was a real shock to me—you know that Vittorio has been my psychoanalyst for five years."

"We know."

"I rang the bell at Vittorio's, and that's where I met the young man who had come to return the keys. I told him I knew Vittorio and that I could pass them on."

"I thought you had noticed the young man wandering a bit suspiciously around the square, just where the victim's body was found, and that then he came up the stairs to Dr. Puig's apartment, that you followed him and that is how—by pretending to be a neighbor—you suggested he give the keys to you."

"That's right. But who told you all that?"

"It's our job to know, Señora Darienzo."

Eva Maria remembers Vittorio's neighbor. Lieutenant Sanchez puts the keys down on the table. He goes out of the living room. Commissioner Perez continues.

"If 'that's right,' Señora Darienzo, why did you just give us another version of the events?"

"To save time, because it amounts to the same thing; the young man gave me the keys, and that's it."

"Don't try to 'save time,' Señora Darienzo, take all the time you need to tell us the truth, and spare no detail. Could you describe this young man? What did he look like?"

"I don't remember, fifteen, sixteen years old. Short, chestnut hair, his eyes . . . I don't know . . . it was too dark in the stairs."

Commissioner Perez turns to Estéban. Then back to Eva Maria.

"Was he sort of like your son?"

Estéban goes to stand between Commissioner Perez and Eva Maria.

"What is the purpose of all these questions? Be quiet, Mama; let them carry out their search, but stop answering their questions."

Commissioner Perez takes a few steps into the living room.

"Ah! The enthusiasm of youth! Don't get so carried away, young man. If we find the keys to a murdered woman's apartment in your mother's possession, it's only fitting that we should try to determine why."

Estéban runs his fingers through his hair. Commissioner Perez turns to Eva Maria.

"And so you went to see Dr. Puig in prison in order to give him back his keys."

"Yes. To help him."

"The way he helped you, with your sessions."

"No doubt."

"But to help him do what, Señora Darienzo?"

"To find Lisandra's murderer."

"So you do not believe he is the actual murderer."

Eva Maria hesitates. Slightly. A split second.

"No."

"I see. Apparently you are also in possession of some photographs of the victim's funeral. May we see them?"

Eva Maria leaves the room. Goes down the corridor. Opens the door to her bedroom. Lieutenant Sanchez is in there. All her books are on the floor. Her Neapolitan gouaches have been removed from the wall. She opens the desk drawer. Takes out the photos. She returns to the living room. She hands the photos to Commissioner Perez. He places them in a large transparent envelope.

"How did you get these photographs?"

"I took them on the day of the funeral. Just in case. To show them to Vittorio. I figured the murderer might be there."

"We should hire you!"

Commissioner Perez takes a bundle of photographs from the pocket of his raincoat. He hands them to Eva Maria.

Eva Maria looks at one photograph after the other. She sees herself. In the church. In the middle of the gathering. Behind the tree, captured as she herself is taking pictures. Commissioner Perez holds out his hand to retrieve the photographs. He smiles.

"Great minds think alike. But these photographs, Señora Darienzo—let's just stop for a moment—why have you never shown them to Dr. Puig?"

Eva Maria remembers. She had them in her bag the last time she visited, but Vittorio had interrupted her, asking her to reread the session with Felipe, their conversation had degenerated, they had argued, and in her anger she had forgotten about the photographs.

"Argued? With Dr. Puig? But you get along so well . . . What did you argue about?"

Eva Maria doesn't answer. Commissioner Perez continues.

"It would seem, Señora Darienzo, that you have been going through a difficult period since the death of your daughter. First you split up with your husband, but above all . . . it would seem that you have had, shall we say, a few problems with alcohol. Which have earned you, moreover, a reprimand from your place of work."

Estéban looks at Eva Maria.

"What's he talking about?"

Eva Maria lowers her head. Estéban goes pale.

"But why didn't you tell me?"

"Señora Darienzo, you know that Dr. Puig was thinking of terminating your sessions."

Eva Maria sits up straight.

"What do you mean? There was never talk of any such thing."

"He was thinking of referring you to a psychiatrist who specializes in this type of . . . how to put it . . . addiction. He no longer felt competent to help you, and, above all, it was getting too complicated."

"Too complicated? What do you mean?"

"He said you were transferring your feelings onto him."

"Transferring? What feelings?"

"Feelings of love."

"That's not true; what on earth is this all about? Vittorio would never have told you anything of the sort. You're trying to trick me."

"Don't get carried away, Señora Darienzo."

"But do you realize what you just said?"

"Weren't you a little bit in love with Vittorio Puig? Apparently it happens rather often, patients falling in love with their shrink."

"No. I swear I wasn't. I swear on my son's life."

"Given your relationship with your son, that unfortunately doesn't carry much weight."

"I forbid you to speak like this. My son is the dearest thing left to me on earth."

"Just because he is the dearest thing left to you doesn't mean that he is dear to you."

"How dare you."

"You had a session with Dr. Puig on the day of the murder. You could have stolen the keys from him."

"Never."

"And that way you could have gotten into his house that evening, no problem. Were you jealous of Lisandra Puig?"

"Not at all, I didn't even know her."

"You don't have to know someone to be jealous of them. Señora Darienzo, it would seem that you are convinced your daughter died under torture at the hands of the army or, to be more precise, she was thrown from an airplane into the Rio de la Plata. If such things had been going on, we would all know about it."

"But we do know about it. What have you done with all the testimonies? All those disappeared?"

"Wild imaginings. Señora Darienzo, don't you find there is a certain similarity between the way in which you have been fantasizing about your daughter's death and the death of Lisandra Puig, thrown out the window from the sixth floor? In both cases you can say the victims fell through space. Maybe you wanted to reenact the scene?"

Eva Maria freezes.

"What on earth are you talking about? I didn't want to reenact any sort of scene."

Eva Maria gets to her feet.

"This has gone on long enough. Leave my house."

Estéban moves closer to Commissioner Perez. His fists clenched. The commissioner shakes his head.

"I wouldn't do that if I were you, young man. Don't even think about it."

Commissioner Perez turns back to Eva Maria.

"Señora Darienzo, did you know that you are the only one of Dr. Puig's patients who has been to see him in prison?"

"So? Just because someone is the only one, does that make them guilty?"

"I'm not suggesting that at the moment. I just wanted to tell you that Dr. Puig paid close attention while you were conducting your investigation. And so did we. You don't actually think we would let just anyone speak to him without surveillance? The case that Dr. Puig has drawn up against you is damning. You will read it for yourself; the logic behind it is edifying. Everything fits."

Eva Maria paces back and forth in the living room. Her thoughts are confused. She is trying to understand. So Vittorio is accusing her. Vittorio would want to find another potential murderer, anyone, so that he could manipulate the truth to fit his needs. The way he did with Felipe. Find another culprit, whatever the cost. Get him—or her—locked up in his place. And anyway, to lock up a woman who spends all her time weeping over her daughter's death is a lesser evil. Weeping over her daughter in prison or at home—what difference does it make? Whereas he still has thousands of things to do in life, hundreds of patients to help, dozens of women to fuck. So he steered the police onto her track. He had to find someone to serve as culprit if he were to be let off. Eva Maria stops. Abruptly. She walks out of the living room. She comes back with her battered brown backpack. She opens it and spills all the cassettes at Commissioner Perez's feet.

"And all this? Did he tell you, the excellent Dr. Puig, that he was recording his patients during their sessions, did he tell you that?"

"Of course he told us. But you're getting ahead of me; I was just about to ask you to give us these cassettes. Because they're important. They are precisely what first alerted Dr. Puig; in particular, the sessions that you insisted upon, the ones that might reveal your own potential motives: Alicia, to start with, that woman who was jealous of youth, then Felipe, who you wanted to see as the reincarnation of your daughter's torturer, when in fact he's just a poor guy who's having problems with his wife."

"And his stolen child—what do you have to say about his stolen child?"

Commissioner Perez bursts out laughing.

"What are you talking about? There's no stolen child. Anywhere."

"Ask Vittorio's lawyer; he'll tell you."

"We don't like associating with lawyers, those people who just go about inventing problems so they'll have plenty of work to do . . ."

"And Miguel's testimony—what do you make of that?"

"Miguel? Which Miguel? Dr. Puig didn't mention him."

"Then listen to his cassette, and you'll see, you'll see whether or not such things existed."

"Señora Darienzo, we will listen to what we have to listen to. It's not up to you to go telling us how to do our job. Your little role as investigator is over. And what's more, you have forgotten one essential thing about this entire period: a shrink is always a shrink. Even behind bars."

And suddenly Eva Maria fears the worst. What if Vittorio really was guilty? She closes her eyes. What if he really did kill his wife? And what if he wanted to make her, Eva Maria, take the blame—his most fragile patient, he'd bet on her right from the start, with a Machiavellian plan, with masterful orchestration right down to the smallest part. He knew her so well, knew she wouldn't be able to stand seeing him locked up without trying to do something; she was both too fragile and too broken by injustice to subject herself to that injustice yet again; she was incapable of fighting for the memory of her daughter; she would fight for him, she would transfer everything onto him, she would effect the transference, she would go see him in prison and try to help him—he had prepared it all, every step, every performance, and anyway, that business with the cassettes, that so-called personal technique, maybe he'd even made all that up, too, the better to trap her: he was the one who'd told her about the funeral, he knew her better than anyone did; had he used her so he could kill his wife and clear his own name? Eva Maria feels dizzy. She opens her eyes. But he had underestimated her. He didn't think she'd find out he had a mistress. And now his perfect plan is about to collapse.

"Vittorio is deceiving you. He told you all that because I just found out he had a mistress and he was afraid I might denounce him. Give me the photographs, I'll show her to you—it's obvious, when you know; you see no one but her—maybe I've been mistaken right from the start. Maybe he really did kill his wife."

Commissioner Perez holds Eva Maria's plastic bag to one side. "There's no point."

"What do you mean there's no point?"

"Dr. Puig already told us about it. And that, indeed, was the last straw that drove him to share his suspicions about you with us. Just because a woman is wearing makeup, from there to assume she's a man's mistress: that is the fruit of an overactive imagination, Señora Darienzo."

"But wait, just because he says she's not his mistress doesn't mean you have to believe him."

"True. But rest assured, it is our job to leave nothing to chance, and we have just come from her house. She is indeed a fine-looking girl, but she is simply one of Lisandra's childhood friends, you see, hardly the stuff of novels."

"'One of Lisandra's childhood friends,' how convenient, Lisandra isn't around to say otherwise. And anyway, does one exclude the other? Even if she was *one of Lisandra's childhood friends*, how do you know she wasn't also Vittorio's mistress?"

"It's natural for you to project the role of a mistress onto this woman, to fantasize about another woman's status that you would like for yourself: you're jealous."

"That's absurd! And the water from the vase? What is that supposed to mean? Don't you wonder why no flowers were found at the crime scene?"

"That is indeed the only gray area in this affair, and we have been wondering about it, but perhaps you will help us get to the bottom of it."

"I tell you: Lisandra had a lover there that evening. Lisandra had her lovers, too."

"We know."

"Vittorio showed up, he surprised them, and he threw the lover and his flowers out the door; an argument broke out—you go and see your mistress, I have the right to receive my lovers, and so on ... It degenerated; maybe it was just an accident. But I'm convinced of it now, Vittorio really did kill his wife."

"Interesting. But Dr. Puig has another theory. The water in the vase might be the symbol of the one element that was missing from your imagery that night: the water from the Rio de la Plata. You absolutely insist your daughter died there. It's an incoherent gesture, the poetic license of a drunken woman."

Commissioner Perez and Lieutenant Sanchez are standing in front of Eva Maria. Suddenly, she sees them differently. What if these two used to be involved with the junta, and now they'd gone over to the police? There must be a lot of them. And what if they had planned all of this with Vittorio, of a common accord—have her locked up, because she would not leave it alone, she was ready to testify against the former regime at any time. Lock up an innocent woman who had bad ideas and release a murderer who had good ones. The contract with Vittorio. Exchange the repositories of guilt, and in the place of murderers, lock up any remaining subversives. Same old story. But now that they couldn't do it quite so openly, they had to find a stratagem. And maybe they even planned murders—what if some crimes were orchestrated to make innocent people take the blame? That way they could cover up the bad memories once and for all and stifle any gossips. Eva Maria steps closer to Commissioner Perez. She spits in his face. Lieutenant Sanchez hurries over to stop her; Commissioner Perez motions to him to stay where he is.

"Señora Darienzo, where were you on the night of August 18?"
Eva Maria doesn't reply. Commissioner Perez tries again.

"Señora Darienzo, where were you on the night of August 18?"

"Here."

"Is there anyone who can confirm this?"

"No. I was alone."

Estéban interrupts.

"When I came back at around three o'clock in the morning my mother was here; I checked."

"How do you know you checked on that particular evening? I must say, only young people can claim to have such a good memory."

"I check every evening when I come in . . . to make sure everything is all right."

"I see. But forgive me, just because your mother was here at three o'clock in the morning doesn't mean she was here earlier that evening, at ten o'clock. The approximate time of the crime. Señora Darienzo, we must ask you to come with us. We are taking you into custody."

Eva Maria collapses on the sofa.

"But I haven't done anything."

The commissioner steps closer.

"Perhaps you simply don't remember. If it can help, that is Dr. Puig's theory. He thinks you were under the influence of alcohol that night. You will be able to plead attenuating circumstances."

Suddenly Eva Maria is afraid. Afraid they might be right. Because when she drinks, she can't remember, and that is why she drinks, for the black holes that feel so good. And what if Vittorio really is convinced she is guilty? Then the keys, those keys, how would she have ended up with them in her possession? She never makes up false memories; she remembers that young man—she may be an alcoholic but she isn't crazy, no way, not crazy. But suddenly Eva Maria is no longer sure of anything. She looks at Estéban; what if she had made it all up, and the young man in the stairs was no more than a projection of Estéban, and the "crime of passion" was her own? But that can't be; she's not in love with Vittorio, of that she is sure—she would know, after all. Eva Maria's gaze lands on the pile of cassettes, which Lieutenant Sanchez is putting into the big plastic bag. Eva Maria grabs the bag from him, pounces on it.

"I'll show you I wasn't in love with Vittorio. You're going to listen to my cassette, and you'll understand right away."

Eva Maria is on her knees on the floor. Estéban goes out of the living room. Eva Maria rummages through the cassettes. Like a crazy woman.

"I don't understand . . . it was here; I saw it several times . . . I know it was here . . ."

Estéban comes back into the living room. He goes over to Eva Maria. Helps her to her feet.

"I have it. I'm sorry, Mama, I couldn't help it. I listened to it."

Estéban has the cassette in his hands. Broken. The tape dangling, crumpled, illegible, unusable. On the side, a label: "Eva Maria." Commissioner Perez reaches out for it.

"You destroyed it to protect your mother."

Estéban runs his fingers through his hair.

"I would say, rather, to protect myself."

"What do you mean?"

"Let's just say there's nothing nice about me on this cassette. It made me angry."

Estéban runs his fingers through his hair.

"But I can confirm, gentlemen . . . after listening to it . . . that my mother has no ambiguous feelings toward Dr. Puig. We cannot say that much about everybody."

"What do you mean by that, young man?"

"What do I mean?"

Estéban runs his fingers through his hair.

"What do you think is going through the mind of a 'young man' like myself, as you put it, when he sees his mother slowly wasting away . . . and the more she saw of this guy, the more distant she was with me . . . and the worst of it was that I was the one who had advised her to go and see him; I would have done better to have kept my mouth shut, but I'd heard so many good things about him . . . My mother was not at Vittorio Puig's place that night."

"It's natural for you to think like that. A child can never believe in a mother's guilt. But you keep out of this, young man."

"Stop calling me 'young man'; I'll say it again, my mother was not at Vittorio Puig's place that night . . . it's true she often went there, too often, given the little good it did her, but she never went there in the evening, that would be the last straw . . . But I was there."

"What did you say?"

"I killed Lisandra Puig."

Eva Maria lets out a cry.

"I killed that woman to show the bastard what it means to lose the person who is dearest to you on earth . . . and after what I heard on the cassette, I'm not the least bit sorry. He let my mother say that she wished I had died instead of my sister, and he didn't even object— I don't feel an ounce of remorse . . . that guy deserved to be taught a lesson; it was about time someone stopped him from causing any more harm."

The lieutenant moves closer to Estéban.

"Señor Darienzo, we'll be taking you into custody."

Eva Maria turns to the policemen.

"Don't believe him, please, you mustn't believe him, you can see he's just making things up, he's just saying that to protect me—my son would never do such a thing, he would never kill anyone."

Eva Maria turns to Estéban. She moves closer to him. Takes his hands.

"Go get your bandoneon, Estéban, play for them, then they'll see what a beautiful soul you have. My child has fingers of gold, and a heart of gold; he could never have killed that girl, he's just saying that to protect me, don't you see? He didn't even know her! And she didn't know him. She wouldn't have opened the door."

Commissioner Perez shakes his head.

"I'm not at all sure about that."

Estéban holds out his wrists to Lieutenant Sanchez.

"A woman always opens the door to a florist ... It was just bad luck that my mother decided to defend that man ... bad luck or her unconscious, because she didn't want me around anymore, so she led you to me without even realizing. This way she won't have to see me around anymore, since I constantly remind her of my dead sister."

Eva Maria throws her arms around Estéban.

"Don't say that, Estéban, hush!"

Lieutenant Sanchez slips the handcuffs over Estéban's wrists. Eva Maria steps between Estéban and Commissioner Perez. She is shouting.

"Stop it! Vittorio was right. I stole the keys from him during our last session, I killed Lisandra, it was me, I did it; Vittorio has been right all along, about everything he told you, I'm fragile, I'm an alcoholic, I can't get over my daughter's death, I'm in love with him, I was jealous—there, I confess, I confess to everything, what else do you want me to confess to? It was me, it was me, I killed that girl; tell me where I have to sign my confession, I'll sign it right away but don't take my son, please, please, leave me my son, leave my son out of this, take me, I'm ready, I'll come with you."

Commissioner Perez and Lieutenant Sanchez stand on either side of Eva Maria.

"You'll sort it out at the station. In the meantime, we're taking both of you in. We have an innocent man to set free."

Vittorio Puig has been set free.

Eva Maria Darienzo has not retracted her confession. Eva Maria Darienzo says she killed Lisandra Puig. An investigation into the murder has been ordered. Eva Maria Darienzo could get life imprisonment.

Estéban Darienzo has not retracted his confession. Estéban Darienzo says he killed Lisandra Puig. An investigation into the murder has been ordered. Estéban Darienzo could get life imprisonment.

The investigation lasts twenty-one weeks. The trial, nine days.

The jurors leave the courtroom.

The deliberation is lengthy. Complicated. The jurors are hampered by the double self-accusations. They are unsettled in their convictions. As a last resort, the jurors decide to go along with the findings of the psychiatric expert.

Eva Maria Darienzo could have killed Lisandra Puig. Estéban Darienzo could have killed Lisandra Puig. Either of them, for different motives. But in all likelihood, Eva Maria Darienzo is merely covering for her son's guilt. Estéban Darienzo is the true murderer.

The jurors file back into the courtroom.

Estéban Darienzo is sentenced to fifteen years' imprisonment for the murder of Lisandra Puig.

Eva Maria Darienzo is acquitted.

Eva Maria rushes over to her son. The police officers stop her. Eva Maria calls out to her son. She shouts to him that she loves him. Estéban turns his head toward his mother. Eva Maria is in tears. She shouts to him that she loves him. He smiles at her. Gently. Sadly. Estéban is handsome. Awkward. He runs his upper arm over his hair. With his wrists confined in handcuffs now, he can't run his hand through his hair, he can no longer respond to the tic he developed after Stella's death.

Vittorio is sitting in the gallery. He holds his head between his hands. Relieved. Satisfied. He pulls his gray jacket tight. The jacket he found hanging on the coatrack in the entrance to his apartment the day he got out of prison. It wasn't his jacket. It must have belonged to one of the many cops, journalists, and photographers who had set up their headquarters in his apartment while he was rotting in jail. Gang of primates. He had slipped on the jacket. It fit. Tough luck for whoever forgot it. Finders keepers, it was his now. For a split second the thought that it might belong to Lisandra's murderer crossed his mind, but he immediately shrugged it off. If the cops had found the jacket at the crime scene, they would surely have reserved a different fate for it than to hang it on the coatrack. It was time to stop seeing evil wherever he turned. His wife's murderer has just been sentenced. His heart sinks. Lisandra always used to buy his clothes: without her, he will end up wearing the same thing all the time. And this jacket? A sign from Lisandra. Signs, signs . . . He was beginning to think the way she used to. He hadn't checked the pockets in the jacket. His curiosity was always limited to human beings, never objects, let alone clothing. And if he'd been the curious sort, or simply a creature of habit, someone who was forever putting his hand in his pocket, what would have happened? In the right-hand pocket of the jacket he would have found a business card. "Lucas Juegos." And then what would he have thought? Nothing, in all likelihood. What are you supposed to think about a business card from a toy store? So he would have thrown it out. Which is what he did, a few days later, but without realizing, along with other parking and restaurant receipts that he'd been stuffing in the jacket pockets since he'd started wearing it. Quite a few people had come to the hearing for his sake. His family, of course. And patients. Including Alicia. Including Felipe. Friends, too. Including Miguel, who had returned from Paris specially for the trial. Everyone has been congratulating him, telling him how relieved they are.

Only Pepe, off in a corner, isn't applauding. He sees Vittorio's smile, sees him turn briefly to look at a woman in the back of the room. *The woman in the photo.* Eva Maria doesn't see her. Because she has eyes only for Estéban. And in any case Eva Maria wouldn't have recognized her. Because the woman is wearing dark glasses. Pepe hates those objects that the weather places between people. Vittorio gives her a scarcely perceptible nod. The woman smiles back. She is among the first to leave the courtroom. Discreetly. Only Pepe notices people's gazes. Their smiles. Vittorio's smile. But he won't denounce him. It wasn't the smile of a murderer who has just had someone else put away in his place. It was the smile of relief of an innocent man. The smile of a man in love.

People file out, using their designated doors. The door for the court and the jurors. The door for the public. The door for the condemned.

I am standing invisible in the room. Screaming. But no one can hear me. Screaming. So will no one ever know what really happened? Even though Lisandra planned everything so that the perpetrator would be punished. I am screaming. I am the daughter of Time, I am the mother of Justice and Virtue. Why has Life not given me the power to prevail? I am Truth. And I am screaming, from the memory.

LUCAS JUEGOS

Sale and Repair of Antique Toys

Defensa 1092, San Telmo
Buenos Aires
(011) 361.7516

Monday–Friday
9:00–12:00/15:00–19:00
Saturday 9:00–13:00

Lisandra slips the business card into her pocket. She leaves the shop. She goes over to where Pepe sits waiting on a bench. "Pick a hand." "I don't know... the right one." Lisandra opens her right hand and holds out a little porcelain cat, then she opens her left hand, which contains a similar cat. "I took two of the same, one for you, one for me." Pepe thanks her, puzzled. "Because a porcelain cat doesn't meow over love," hums Lisandra, quietly. "The truth sometimes lies dormant in songs." She thanks Pepe for waiting for her. She thanks him for being so kind to her. For listening to her. It has done her good, to talk. Lisandra puts her arms around Pepe and hugs him. She pulls away again very quickly; she doesn't want to prolong the moment. She can go home now; she feels better; he doesn't need to come with her. Lisandra gives Pepe a little wave. She walks away. She feels her heart sink. She doesn't turn around. Don't turn around, anything but that; he'll understand. Pepe is someone she loves infinitely. If only all men could be as kind as he is. Lisandra is agitated. She wants to walk home. Even if it's a long way. She wants to walk. She slips her hand in her pocket, feels the business card beneath her fingers. She can't get over it. She did it! Like with the others. And it wasn't any harder. Just act as if it's not him, just act as if it's not him, he won't recognize you. And he took the bait. She had really hoped it would go like this. She can't get over it. So she hadn't been mistaken. When she first went into the shop, she didn't look at him. She walked around among the shelves. That smooth, emphatic walk of hers. She leaned closer to see the toys on the lower shelves. She bent down without crouching. To arch her back. To give him something to fantasize about. Lucas is looking at her. She knows he is. Out of the corner of his eye. She keeps telling herself that Pepe is outside. That there's no risk. So she acts as if she is trying to reach a toy that is too high up for her. On tiptoe. Her arm stretched out toward the inaccessible toy. Her sweater pulling up on the side, she can feel the air. A patch of bare skin. What better promise. Lucas is looking at her. She knows he is. She's on the right track. He doesn't think she's so ugly anymore. He comes over.

"Can I help you? Which one would you like?"

In her mind she answers, You.

"The little cat, up there."

"The stuffed one?"

"Yes, and the porcelain one, too, next to it. 'Because a porcelain cat doesn't meow over love.'"

"For sure, those cats don't make much noise."

Lisandra pretends to compare the two little toys. She doesn't look at Lucas.

"Do you have a cat?"

"No."

Lisandra turns to face him. Her expression as blank, as neutral as possible, so that he can project anything he desires onto it. And also because she cannot smile.

"I am sure you have a dog," she says.

"You're a bit of a magician, aren't you."

"A bit."

Lisandra turns back to the two little toys. Goes on pretending to compare them.

"I'm allergic to dogs."

"That's a pity."

"I agree. A real pity."

Lisandra hands him the little porcelain cat.

"I'll take two of these."

"Very good."

Lisandra heads toward the cash register with him. She can feel his gaze behind her. On her body. She closes her eyes. She represses a tremor. Clenches her jaw. She feels him brush past her to go behind the cash register. Lisandra takes out two bills. She puts them down on the counter. He takes the bills with his right hand. He leaves his left hand under the counter. That's a good sign. She's on the right track. She notices the shop's business card.

"May I?"

"Go right ahead. Do you live in the neighborhood?"

Here we go, he's fishing for information. Lisandra doesn't answer. She takes the business card. She acts surprised.

"You also repair toys?"

"Of course."

"Dolls as well?"

"Of course."

"I have a broken doll at home. A big doll."

Lisandra's words are full of innuendos. Nothing is more exciting than coyness. When it comes from an exciting body, of course.

"Could you come by and see whether you can repair it? It's a childhood memory; I'm very fond of it."

"Of course, I can make house calls."

"Like a doctor?"

Another coy remark. Lucas smiles.

"So to speak."

Lisandra stakes everything on her next question.

"This evening?"

"Why not."

Almost there.

"Oh, no, not this evening, how silly of me, tonight I'm working. And I won't be home before half past nine. That surely won't be possible for you. What a pity. It would have been a good opportunity."

Lisandra goes heavy with the innuendos. Lucas hears them.

"Half past nine, no, that's okay, I can come by."

Bingo.

"I can use the time in between to do my inventory. I've been postponing it far too long."

"Oh, really, are you sure, it's not an inconvenience?"

"Not at all."

Lisandra gives him her address. Just once. She is sure she doesn't need to repeat it. A man's powers of concentration are phenomenal when he senses the possibility of a fuck in the air. Lisandra picks up her change. She knows she ought to let him touch her skin. But she can't. It's too hard. She doesn't hold out her hand. She waits for him to put the change down on the counter.

"Would you like this gift-wrapped?"

"No, it's for me, for my collection."

"Oh? You have a collection?"

"Yes."

And besides, you'd need both hands to gift-wrap it, so go on hiding your wedding ring; you know very well what is going to happen this evening, in the staircase, when you come to my place—you'll take it off, if you haven't already, but tonight you will for sure, the way all the others did. Lisandra takes the two little cats from the counter. She looks Lucas straight in the eye.

"So, I'll see you this evening. It would be wonderful if you could repair it."

Lucas looks down before she does. That would be a first. Lisandra never thought she'd be able to look Lucas straight in the eye. She'd been too afraid he'd recognize her, but he's not in a mood for analyzing, he's in a mood for fantasizing. He doesn't even see her standing there before him, he's already seeing her naked, moaning as he feels her up, his cock in place. Now Lisandra has to get out of there. It's getting too difficult for her. A woman in love can't look a man in the eye, she's too upset. Love leads to tenderness, and to really look a man straight in the eye the way they like it there must not be any tenderness. That is what is lacking in married men. Lisandra slips the business card into her pocket. Lisandra takes one step. And another. She did it. She did it because there was nothing else she could do. Now she knows; now she is certain. She is no longer afraid. She can go through with it. There's no going back. Everything has been said. She has planned for everything. She has tried everything. She has exhausted every line of thought. Imagined every possible outcome. When you have reached the end of your line of thought, afterward, you go back over things, and going back over things is a form of death. Lisandra knows that. Going back over things makes for a dull life. Above all, Vittorio has reached the end of their love story. Lucas was going to pay. It was all his fault. It had taken her a long time to admit it. First of all she'd had to take stock of the damage. And only life going by allows you to take stock of the damage. She'd had to grow up. She'd had to get older. The pattern had to become obvious, repetitive. And then she'd had to relent, and confront the truth. She was her own worst enemy. Of course. But only because she'd been taught that she was. Because Lucas had taught her that she was. Initially she had thought it was no big deal. She'd live with it. It was in the past;

she had to move on, turn the page. The past can be forgotten. But she hadn't been able to turn the page because she had become the page. She hadn't been able to forget the past. So she had wanted to know everything. For her stability, for her mental well-being, she could not go on living like that. She had to know. For Vittorio's sake. To understand. No, in fact, not to understand, because there was nothing to understand. Things like that cannot be understood. She just wanted to know. How it had all begun. How long it had lasted. Once you know, you figure out how to live with it. To remember everything, in the end, would enable her to forget everything, in the end. She had summoned the past. She'd conjured it, by force of will. She had applied all her concentration to it. She had analyzed so many of her dreams. She had tried everything. Hypnosis. Automatic writing. Even dance, she'd turned to dance, inhabited by that desire. The remembrance of the past. But memory is versatile. Impenetrable. Nothing had come back. The mysterious life of memories consists in yielding and in holding back. Memories are free. They play with us. They get fainter, they expand, they retract, they avoid us or strike like lightning. Once life gives birth to them, they become the masters of life. They are time's foot soldiers, driving us mad. Without memories we would be free. Memory is time's bad fairy. No memory brings true joy, serenity. Regret, remorse—memories are like so many dissonant little bells clanging inside us. And the more life goes on, the more the little music of memories rings false. You think you are your own self, but you're nothing but your memories. Lisandra fought against amnesia. Against the electricity in her brain that tossed a black cloth over memories, memories that ought only to be veiled in the gentle white glow of childhood. Amnesia had encoded her brain, had subjugated it. Lisandra had to face facts. Four pictures. Four moments. Four images that had been shifting since the day she had remembered. Her memories always begin with the same moment and always end with the same moment. Never an additional detail. Perhaps we only ever remember the things we know we can bear? Since then, Lisandra has been locked in her present, her hand shading her eyes; she's asking herself where else does injustice plan to enter and assail her yet again? Others would surely have reacted differently. She withdrew into the cruel workings of jealousy. Others would have taken refuge in anger. Others in a hyperactive joy, a pretend joy, a joy that is exhausting because it is mandatory. Others in aid work, altruism at any cost to forget oneself. Why jealousy? Now we're getting at the mystery of individual tragedy. Of personality. Lucas had taught her how to be. Four pictures. Four moments. Four images shifting since the day she had remembered. Her memories always begin with the same moment and always stop with the same moment. Never an additional detail. But she wanted to remember everything, every single time. How it had all begun. How long it had lasted. So she had hoped he would be able to tell her everything that she could no longer remember. They could pool their memories to reconstruct the story. Lucas owed her that much, that nobility of soul. She had taken a long time to make up her mind, but once she had, it hadn't been very hard to find him. She'd always kept the memory of his first name. She'd always kept the memory of his last name. They often ran through her head. Find him. She had to. For her stability, for her mental well-being, she couldn't go on living like that. Maybe Vittorio wouldn't come back to her. But if she was better, she could accept his departure. She figured that maybe when she saw Lucas it would all come back. She would look at him from a distance and it would all come back with a bang; okay, it might not be very pleasant but it would all come back. So then she'd take her little bundle of memories, all her memories at last reunited, and she'd set off down the path of life, she'd move on to other things. She would be stronger. More solid. She couldn't stand feeling fragile like this anymore. Remembering everything would, at last, enable her to forget everything, at last. So she found his address. How many months did she stay like that? She had his first name. His last name. She had his address. Vittorio was deserting her. She'd made up her mind. So she walked past Lucas's place. The way you walk past anything, when you're out and about. She didn't slow down any more than if the place had nothing to do with her. Far from it. But she had hastened her step. Which wasn't good. You can't be perfect. But she would have liked to be perfect. Vittorio would have stayed with her. He wouldn't have gone looking elsewhere. But it wouldn't have changed anything. Lisandra knows this. Time destroys perfection. You can be perfect for a few days. A few weeks. A few months at best. Imperfect for the rest of her days. Because love is a principle that is in constant motion. You always end up knowing your partner inside out. The principle of dissatisfaction. Dissatisfaction with yourself, which drove you to your partner in the first place. Then dissatisfaction with your partner, which drives you to someone else again. And again. All in an attempt not to see that it's not you or anyone else who is so unsatisfying, but life itself. Because it makes you die. That was one day. And then another day she walked past Lucas's place again. The way you walk past anything when you're out and about. But she had slowed down. That was one day. And then another day she stopped. As if the place did have something to do with her. She stationed herself outside his house. And she saw him come out of his place. Lucas had changed, but she recognized him. And would he recognize her? He hadn't changed much. She'd changed drastically. With the gap in their ages it was inevitable. There he was before her eyes but nothing came back to her. That was the worst thing she could have imagined. And she realized that she wouldn't go and talk to him. She couldn't go and ask him. His memories, too, would be deficient. Because of the time that had gone by. And above all because of the shame. Not only would Lucas not tell her anything more, he would deny it. He would never confess. He would claim she was insane. And if he was brave enough, and scared enough by the threat she represented, Lucas would kill her. She had let a few weeks go by. But the more her love story with Vittorio lost its potency, the more courage she found to go on with "her little investigation." That was what she called it. And then another day, not only did she see Lucas leave his house, she even followed him. To his work. She had imagined a hundred different professions for him. What might he have chosen to do for a living? She had no job. Other than that of loving. Other than that of being jealous. He takes the bus, she takes the bus. She stays as far away as possible. He gets off. She gets off. He walks. She walks. He stops, he takes out his keys, and he opens a little green shop. Lisandra looks up. She looks at the sign. "Lucas Juegos." The shock leaves her rooted to the sidewalk. He raises the green iron shutter. Children's toys invade the display window. Disgust rises to her lips. But he'd gotten control of her, without knowing it he held sway over her, and she began to follow him. Day after day. It was the fascination of evil. The fascination of the past. She followed him from a distance. To the restaurant where he had lunch every day. She would sit down behind him and observe him. His movements. His body. His hair. It began with a knife. She stole objects he had touched. A napkin. A fork. A newspaper he tossed into the garbage. The empty packs of cigarettes he tossed into the garbage. She put all the objects away at home. In a little suitcase. From time to time she would open it and look at them one by one. Without any thoughts. That was one day. And then another day, she had seen him in his doorway kissing his wife. So Lucas had a wife; she should have suspected as much. What she could never have imagined was that tiny hand, that tiny arm she had seen coming out the door at the last minute, and running, running with all her little body, running up to him to give him one last kiss. A kiss for a good day. Lucas had smiled. So Lucas had a child. A little girl. She didn't. Lisandra had never been able to imagine having a child. Children scare her. She thinks of them as little vermin, often lovely, but little vermin all the same. She cannot stay alone with a child. She is afraid of herself. As if it weren't already enough to have experienced it one day, you also have to live with the idea that you'll be the cause for others to experience it one day, too—isn't that what everyone says, after all? Lisandra would so have liked to know what it meant to want a child, maybe everything would have been different with Vittorio. A child doesn't stop you from falling out of love, but perhaps with a child she wouldn't care about the loss of love. Lucas smiled. That day, because of his smile, because of that little girl, Lisandra knew she would have her revenge. Her desire to gain access to the past would be transformed into a hatred of the past. When she understood that he was happy and she wasn't, that he had obtained everything life makes it possible to obtain, and she hadn't. Lucas was going to pay. Everything was his fault. Lisandra didn't know what she was waiting for. She was waiting. For something. She had no precise idea. She knew that life, at some point, would give her the opportunity. A situation where the Idea would be born. It's always like that. She was waiting. She was in no hurry, not really. You're never in a hurry with this sort of thing. And Vittorio was still making love to her. Not as well. Not as often. But still. There, she had it. This morning Lucas left the house with a shopping bag. He took the bus. He got out at the usual stop. He walked past his green shop without opening it. He

went further on. And he went through the door to the dry cleaners'. She got her Idea. Lisandra knew what she was going to do,
even though she'd never thought about it. What she had to do. She
went through the door after he did. Right away. Behind him, without waiting. She looked at him from behind, standing in front of
her. This, she was used to. But she had never been this close to him,
well, not this close in all these years. Lucas opened the shopping
bag and left a gray jacket on the counter. She listened to his voice.
It was the first time she'd heard his voice. She didn't recognize it.
Which was perfectly normal—he didn't have that voice yet, back
then. He took his receipt. "Good-bye." Lisandra looked away. She
heard the door open. She heard him going out. Quick, her turn
now, quick, find a way to grab the jacket—don't leave them the
time to take it. Think later on. Analyze later on. Now was not the
time. She turned to the man behind the cash register. "Hello, I
don't know what to do; a few days ago my husband dropped off a
skirt for me and he's lost the receipt." Lisandra stared at the gray
jacket, there, right in front of her, a few inches away. She could
reach out and touch it. "It's a red skirt. Woolen." "Red, did you say?
Let me take a look. Long?" "No, short." *Don't take the jacket. Don't
take the jacket.* Completely absorbed by his new mission, the man
left the gray jacket on the counter by the cash register. He disappeared into the hanging rows of clothing wrapped in plastic.
Lisandra grabbed the gray jacket from the counter, spun around,
and hurried out of the dry cleaners'. She ran. She ran down the
street. As fast as she could. The gray jacket hanging from her hand.
She ran. Now she knew what to do. Now she had everything she
needed. She knew. She knew without even having planned it. She
was determined. She had it all worked out. All she had to do now
was wait for the right moment. And life would bring it to her, the
right moment. It was always like that. She wouldn't see Lucas

again until the great day. She'd been hoping there wouldn't be a great day, she'd been hoping that Vittorio would come back to her. But Vittorio hasn't come back to her. And now the great day has come. What's the point of going on? She can't, without him. All that is left is for her to make him pay. Vittorio is going out more and more frequently in the evening; Vittorio will be wanting to leave her soon. She will not be a prison for him. The conversation with Pepe has opened her eyes. Pepe is right. She has to find a solution. And she has the solution. She's had it for a long time. And now she has to implement it. Lisandra gets home at last. As she goes through the door to the apartment, she falters. Briefly. Barely. So will it be tonight? She takes her shower. Usually running water relaxes her. Not this time. That's normal. She's human. She puts on a new dress. High heels. She's always known how to do this, at least, she keeps telling herself. A chance. One last chance. Make yourself beautiful. Very beautiful. He has to see you. He has to. Only Vittorio can make her stop. This is their only chance. He has to remember how they used to love each other. He has to stay. He can't have completely forgotten the way we used to be. What we were. How beautiful it was. Vittorio hardly looks at her. He is elsewhere. Lisandra can't help herself, force of habit. "You haven't even noticed my new dress." The rest, the vulgar stuff, she keeps to herself—*Go and be with your mistress, did you think I wouldn't realize?* Lisandra asks him, to see if this evening, like all the other evenings, he is going to lie to her.

"Where are you going?"

"To the movies."

"Again?"

"Just because you don't want to go anymore doesn't mean I shouldn't go, either."

Lisandra can't help herself, force of habit.

"You didn't use to go so often."

"That's how it is, depends on the period. It clears my mind. I need that."

"Of course, you need it."

But Lisandra immediately regains her composure. She doesn't want this to turn into their usual argument. Not tonight. There are other things at stake tonight. She asks again. To protect him. To make sure he won't have any problems.

"Are you sure?"

But Vittorio stiffens and it ends like all their arguments have ended, for weeks.

"You're suffocating me, Lisandra, I can't take any more; I told you I'm going to the movies, just come with me if you don't believe me."

She knows he's lying. Vittorio knows very well she won't go with him. Just because you lose all hope, it doesn't mean you lose all pride. He would deserve to have it all land on him. Suddenly she thinks that if she didn't put the gray jacket out, Vittorio could get into trouble. But she will put out the gray jacket. She has other aims, far beyond punishing an unfaithful husband. Lisandra even manages to see him to the door. Lisandra even manages to smile.

"Have a good evening."

Lisandra closes the door behind him. And that's when her determination falters again. But only briefly. Barely. She goes over to the radio. Puts on some music, loud. She hums. "I took my first steps here; now I'm back again with my cards worn down."* She mustn't think too much. She may be courageous but she mustn't think too much. She looks at the clock. He will be here soon. Lisandra can't believe it. Lucas will be here in less than one hour. He will ring the

---

* Lyrics to the tango "Las cuarenta" (Francisco Gorrindo and Roberto Grela, 1937).

bell. To her door. She goes into her bedroom. She opens the dresser drawer. She takes out the jacket. Unfolds it. A man's jacket. The gray jacket from the dry cleaners'. She puts it on. She looks at her reflection in the mirror of her vanity table. He's right, she's not beautiful. She looks at the business card between her fingers. "Lucas Juegos." It disgusts her. She slips the card into the right-hand pocket of the gray jacket. Lucas is right-handed, she knows that. Thanks to memories. Thanks to images. When you're right-handed, you stay right-handed. What if he doesn't come? She puts the jacket on the back of the armchair. He won't see it. But the policemen will, they'll see it. She laughs like a child who's come up with a good prank. A surprise. She laughs. With fear, too, a little bit. Pepe is no longer there to protect her. She double-checks. The door is bolted. Lucas can't come in without her knowing. He will ring. And Lisandra goes back into the living room. She takes out a bottle of white wine. A glass. Two glasses. She pours a glass for herself. She drinks it down in one go. Don't drink too much. She throws the glass onto the floor. The other glass, too. She dances, dances, dances. How will Lucas react when he realizes? She whirls around the armchair. She whirls around the lamp. She whirls around the vase, and then her determination falters. No, not her determination. Her heart. Lisandra thinks of Vittorio. Of all the beautiful flowers that were in this vase one day. Flowers of love. She takes it in her arms. Fill it up. Fill it up. Fill it up. She squeezes the vase to her chest. She heads toward the bathroom. She puts the vase down in the bathtub and runs the water into it. She looks at the clothes on the floor. Near the bathtub, her clothes. Near the shower, Vittorio's. Before, their clothes formed a single pile. She begins to cry. Her tears mingle with the water in the vase. Her knees are bent, on the floor, and they are hurting. But she doesn't feel it. She stands up. She goes back into the living room. She puts the heavy vase onto the little table. She puts the music on even louder. She looks at the clock. She looks at the vase. She stifles a sob. She lifts both hands to her mouth. She bites herself. There. There where it's easy to get to the flesh, between the thumb and index finger. This vase will never hold another woman's flowers. She shoves the vase with her two outstretched arms. Her hand is purplish where she bit it. But she doesn't feel it. The vase shatters. The water spreads across the floor. Are those tears on the floor? She turns around, knocks over the lamp, flings a chair to the floor. Then the other one, the one holding the jacket. She makes sure it can't be seen. All that matters is that the policemen see it when they pick up the chair. She can't help double-checking that the business card is still in the pocket. When the policemen find it they will go straight to the address of the shop and they will arrest Lucas, who won't be able to defend himself. Unless he tells them the whole truth and admits to his real crime. Lisandra dances, dances. And she waits. If she only knew. When Commissioner Perez picks up the chair he'll shrug his shoulders. "This jacket must belong to the victim's husband. Is there a murderer on the planet who would forget his jacket at the crime scene? In the middle of winter on top of it?" Commissioner Perez will hang the jacket from the coatrack in the entrance, but he'll check the size, all the same: 52. And because it's his job to leave no stone unturned, he will ask Vittorio to state his jacket size. "Fifty-two." Just as he thought; yet again, he was right: this jacket belongs to Dr. Puig. Lisandra waits and she dances, she dances. What is he doing? She heads over to the window to open it. She almost forgot to open it. What an idiot. She feels the cold air rush in and over her. Instantaneously. Sometimes she watches herself dancing. Now she can't. The doorbell rings. That's it, he's here. She looks all around her. Everything is ready. She goes over to the door. She looks through the spyhole. Lucas is there. She looks at his face that doesn't know she is looking at him. "Just a second. I'm coming." She slides the bolt. It's all over; she won't be afraid anymore.

"Come in, I'll show you my broken doll. Her name is Lisandra."

Lisandra walks back into the living room. She hears him mumble to himself, behind her, "Lisandra." She walks quickly; she walks straight ahead. The pieces of glass crunch beneath her shoes, but she doesn't feel it. She leans against the window. She looks at Lucas. She smiles at him. At that very moment, he recognizes her. She knows. She can tell. And she stamps her foot, short and sharp. She doesn't jump. No, she doesn't jump. Anything but that. Just a short sharp stamp of the foot, as if she'd been pushed. As if Lucas had pushed her, and she feels her body fall. She could have done it without him there, but then he'd have had an alibi. And he mustn't have an alibi. Lucas had to pay. Lisandra's mind goes spinning. Images rush by. At full speed. The way life goes in its final fleeting moments.

6TH FLOOR

Lucas is my nanny Nati's son she's nice Nati but she's still Lucas's mommy daddy drops me off there every morning before work and mommy picks me up every night after work you have to find someone to watch your kids when you work and you have to work to provide for your kids the house is next to the road I go in through a big iron gate I cross the patio I jump from one white stone to another white stone to avoid the crocodiles that are watching me on the yellow stones I get to the front door I go in and there's Negrito who gives me a nice bark to say hello and the kitchen is on the right and the living room is on the left to watch TV and straight ahead there's a corridor which goes on and on and on with the door that goes down to the basement by the stairway that is like a comma actually this house looks a lot like my house like a lot of houses actually too bad for me I see this house a little wherever I go I lived there on Monday on Tuesday on Wednesday on Thursday on Friday from the time I was almost four months old to the time I was nearly five years old I don't want to brush my teeth in the morning anymore like lots of kids it's true I'm not hungry in the morning anymore like lots of kids it's true or in the evening either I feel sick in the car in the morning like lots of kids you couldn't guess why it's true but I wish someone had guessed because what I went through there it's true too I sit on the floor on the carpet my back against the sofa I'm watching TV and Nati says "I'm going shopping you keep an eye on her I won't be long" Lucas is lying on the other part of the sofa he answers "yes" when the front door closes he sits up and he says "come with me" and I get up I know the way I open the door in the corridor I go down the stairs that are like a comma my head is spinning the way it does when I'm on the swing too long I stop on every step but Lucas shoves me in the back so that I'll keep going downstairs there's a room with a washing machine and an ironing board with a bed there too and I sit on the bed Lucas takes off all my clothes I don't know how to get undressed by myself yet after that he takes off his trousers he is standing up he is tall and he forces me I look over to the door because I want someone to come faithful Negrito comes but a dog can't do anything I listen to the sound of the washing machine

5TH FLOOR

"stop following me everywhere like this!"

"when is mommy coming? when is mommy coming?"

"later"

"when is mommy coming?"

"stop asking that question"

"when is mommy coming?"

"never"

I start crying I am so afraid so afraid

"no it's not true that was just a joke she'll be here soon your mommy"

and Nati takes me on her lap

"you won't go shopping will you huh you won't go shopping?"

"no I don't have any shopping to do today"

"Lisandra didn't stop asking for you today"

mommy: "is that right?"

me: "yes"

mommy: "but you mustn't darling you know I won't ever forget you"

I look down and I wish I was a boy if I was a boy Lucas wouldn't do that to me I'm under the table in the dining room I always have my blanket with me Lucas pulls me out from under the table he knows I'm not playing hide-and-seek but he wants to pretend to play it with me but I don't want to and this time Nati is here she's doing the dishes she didn't go shopping I feel strong and protected so I bite him he pulls back his hand I'm happy but at the same time I'm a little scared "come here!" it's Nati calling "why did you do that? say you're sorry" I don't say sorry "you don't want to say sorry? you want me to show you what that feels like? you want me to show you?" and Nati bites me hard on top of my hand there there where it's easy to get to the flesh between the thumb and index finger and she says "you see how it hurts now say you're sorry" I say sorry "you're a very bad little girl and I'm going to tell your mommy tonight" and she doesn't speak to me all day long "I don't speak to

4TH FLOOR

naughty little girls I sure don't" she says and that night in the car mommy kisses me where the bite mark is and it makes it feel better I think she understands but then she says it's not nice to bite other people only naughty little girls bite so everyone agrees with him I'm naughty so I'll go on hurting when he's inside my bottom with his weenie next to the bed there's the washing machine and in the washing machine there's me not to be scared anymore I listen to the noise going round and round and it makes me feel better because I know that a washing machine it has to stop and so that means that he's going to stop too I have my face up against the windowpane I look at that house across the street where I could wait for mommy it would be the same but it wouldn't be the same it would be better Lucas walks behind me and he pulls my hair hard just like that for no reason and I don't say anything I can't say anything anymore even though Nati is here I could go tattle like any little girl "Lucas pulled my hair" but I can't tattle anything anymore all the big bad things like all the little bad things they're all stuck in my throat I can't tattle anymore I'm not a little girl anymore I'm an ugly liar who deserves it and her parents are going to die the front door slams the keys turn in the lock Nati has left to go shopping Lucas gets up he walks by me he doesn't touch me I don't know if he's looking at me I've got my eyes on the floor my thumb in my mouth and I'm trying to drown in the smell of the blue blanket I use to rub my nose when I have my thumb in my mouth keep my thumb in my mouth keep my thumb right in my mouth so he can't put anything else in there he goes out of the room the door slams silence I don't dare move which door will open first the one that will give me back my freedom with Nati back from shopping or the terrible door the other one the one that will bring Lucas back in it's the terrible one I grab the doll on the floor and I start playing with it I make her talk dollie talk and I shake my head as if I were playing even harder and I mustn't be disturbed Lucas goes over to the other part of the sofa with a magazine in his hands I go on talking dollie talk

3RD FLOOR

but not too loud not to disturb him if he wants to read or if he wants to watch TV don't disturb him let him forget about me I don't dare leave the room I have the feeling he'll forget me better if I stay curled up in front of him than if I leave if my body moves it will make him think about my body whereas my motionless body I hope it won't Lucas is absorbed in his magazine I don't know what comes over me I drop my dollie I'm so scared that I don't have the strength to make believe anymore "come and see" what was I thinking to let go of my doll I pick her up again I concentrate on her and I don't answer him if I don't speak to him maybe Lucas will go do something else maybe he won't come for me I can feel him leaning toward me "come and see I said" I get up but I stay there maybe he's going to show me from a distance and afterward I can sit back down and it'll be over his legs are on the living room table like an A with the magazine on his thighs I know the letter A it's the one you get in mAmA and in pApA Lucas isn't looking at me he's looking at his magazine "look she's my favorite but come and see" Lucas strikes his hand on the page that's on his thigh I go closer I stand there and I lean my head over toward the magazine a blonde woman with very big breasts her legs spread is looking at me sticking her tongue out she's wearing tons of makeup she's naked "come on" and once again the door to the corridor that goes down and the stairs like a comma and my head spinning and Lucas behind me pushing me at every step a little brown-haired girl with no breasts no makeup legs spread all naked sticking her tongue out "open your eyes and look at me I said you're really hopeless not like that are you an idiot or what? do like her look at me!" he asks me to act as if I'm his *favorite* and it all starts again his tongue his weenie it all starts again like every time but I'm not his *favorite* he keeps saying I'm ugly so ugly that he's doing it to me because I'm not pretty so ugly "I don't know how your parents manage to love you on top of it you're naughty" and I don't know why I'm

2ND FLOOR

not pretty and I don't know why I'm naughty he could do this to me and make me believe I'm his *favorite* if he'd been older at least he would have given me candy before or afterward maybe before or afterward he would have said I was a princess his princess so pretty with my pretty hair my pretty eyes my pretty smile but Lucas is only fifteen and he hasn't yet reached the age where you try and hide your vice under candy under caresses under being nice he's only fifteen that's an age when you're still pulling wings off flies and if anyone says that at fifteen you can't hurt a fly well I know what they are going through those flies and it's not nice being a fly in Lucas's hands Lucas does this to me because I deserve it he does it and if I tell anyone for sure no one will believe me for sure everyone will call me a liar and worst thing of all my parents will die if I tell my parents they will die there on the spot and afterward I'll be alone all alone all alone once again these memories these images come back to me the door to the corridor the stairs the room

GROUND

That is her final image. Lisandra's body hits the ground. She dies instantly. Lisandra does not feel her high heels piercing her ankles. Her thighbones splintering. Her hips breaking. She doesn't feel her body bounce. The back of her skull hitting the ground. Shattering. She doesn't feel her blood spreading all through her. Outside her veins. Lisandra doesn't feel her body bounce one last time. She doesn't feel her hair fanning all around her head. Her blonde hair that doesn't seem to match her complexion. Lisandra doesn't know that Lucas will never be convicted. That the morning after Eva Maria's phone call he moved away and from now on he'll be living a low-profile sort of life, fearful of another call about *the woman with the two porcelain cats*. Lisandra doesn't know that an innocent man will be imprisoned. For the love of his mother. Who will be his again at last. As the weeks go by, Eva Maria will not miss a single visit to Estéban in prison. Lisandra doesn't know that Vittorio will have a child. With another woman. That it will be a little girl. And that he will call her Lisandra. And that little girl—one can only hope that no one will ever touch her.

ACKNOWLEDGMENTS

The American version of this novel owes everything to Patrick Nolan, who not only reads and defends my work but also trusts me as an author. I am deeply grateful for this. I would like to express my gratitude to Lindsey Schwoeri, who went through great pains to take care of both the form and content of my work for even the smallest details. It goes without saying but still deserves to be mentioned: a translation would never exist without the translator, so thank you, Alison Anderson. Last but not least: thank you to Chrissie McDonald, who made working with this wonderful team possible, without ever having to worry about a language barrier.

This book would never have existed without the vital contribution of Charlotte Liébert-Hellman; without Teresa Cremisi, who placed her trust in me from the start; without Alicia d'Andigné, who followed its development with great sensitivity; or without her ally Anavril Wollman.

My thanks to Bertrand de Labbey for taking me under his wing.

Thanks to my Love who has accompanied me with such intelligence along the chaotic path that is writing. Thanks to Léonard, because his intrusions into my study will be the most beautiful images I retain of my time at work. Thanks to my parents and my brother, steadfast pillars of support. Thanks to my lovely stepchildren who have learned how to fill such a significant place in my life. Thanks to Marine Autexier and to my friends who know so well how to be present, now and always. Thanks to Brigitte Rouillon, precious assistant. Thanks to Ludy and Elsie, everyday angels.

The "Miguel" session owes a great deal to the testimony of Miguel Ángel Estrella, and I thank him for his willingness to add his voice to those who chose to speak (*Gueule d'ange*, by Tristan Mendès France, Éditions Favre, 2003, and *D'encre et d'exil 5: Buenos Aires–Paris, allers-retours*, Éditions de la Bibliothèque publique d'information, Centre Pompidou, 2006).

Thanks to Lucía V., my Argentinian *eye*. To Stéphane Durand-Souffland, my legal *eye*.

Because death so sadly is part of life, I also dedicate this book to the memory of Françoise Cachin and Isabelle de Roux Revay, who disappeared too soon.